# Claiming Her Inheritance

OTHER CROSSRIVER BOOKS
BY DEBRA L. BUTTERFIELD

FICTION

*Mystery on Maple Hill,* a short story
*Discovering Her Inheritance*, releasing August 2023

NONFICTION

*Self-editing & Publishing Tips for Indie Authors*
*7 Cheat Sheets to Cut Editing Costs*
*Unshakable Faith*, a Bible study
*Unshakable Faith Leaders Guide*
*Carried by Grace: a guide for mothers of victims of sexual abuse*

COMPILED AND EDITED

*Abba's Promise: 33 Stories of God's Pledge to Provide*
*Abba's Answers: 30 Stories of God's Answers to Prayer*

# Claiming Her Inheritance

## Debra L. Butterfield

ST. JOSEPH, MISSOURI USA

# Chapter 1

## Chase

My child, listen to what I say, and treasure
my commands. Proverbs 2:1

This is outrageous! Who in all creation is Sally Clark?" said my eldest child, Leslie, as she pounded a fist on the long oak table in the conference room of our lawyer's office. "Daddy, I don't understand. A complete stranger gets one-third ownership in the ranch and 10 percent of the magazine? That 10 percent should have been mine."

The room echoed with "Sally Clark?" as my six children looked at one another for some recognition of who knew her.

"Leslie's worked at the magazine since she was sixteen and has been managing editor for three years now. She's right. It doesn't make sense to give each of us other kids 10 percent but to cut Leslie out," Emily, my youngest, said. "For me the magazine is a job. It's not my heart's desire. But it's Leslie's dream."

We all had just come from Pop's funeral reception at my ranch outside Great Falls, Montana. Emotions ran high as the hot July sun that beat down on us for the hour the reverend had preached at the graveside. I allowed the general outrage among my progeny to continue for a moment, then put up a hand to silence them.

"Enough!" I turned to Karl Kandell, the family lawyer. Karl and his father and his father before him had served the many generations of Chase Reynolds for nearly as long as our family had been in Montana. "There must be some mistake, Karl. No one here even knows who this woman is."

"There's no mistake, Chase. That's why I've gathered you all here. Better to explain it once and have done," Karl said. "And he didn't cut Leslie out. She gets $200,000."

"That's nothing—a pittance!—compared to a share in the magazine. Why did Poppie do this to me?" Leslie griped.

"It's far from a pittance, young lady," I reprimanded her. I turned to Karl. "Pop told me several months ago he was thinking about making changes in his will, but this? It's not what I'd call a few changes. This is major. Pop never indicated to me the magazine would go to anyone other than Abby, and he *never* mentioned a three-way split of the ranch."

"Your father had me make all these changes six months ago along with adding Ms. Clark."

"What!" Leslie screamed, bolting out of her chair. "Didn't you advise him against it? What kind of lawyer are you, anyway?"

"Sit down. It's not like Poppie was senile," said Emily, the peacemaker of the family. She tugged at her sister's arm, but Leslie shook her off.

"Leslie, sit down, calm down, and stop interrupting," I told her, directing a stern gaze at her until she sat down. "Karl, he didn't say a word to me about all this, and I'm his executor." Why did Pop do this? I ran my fingers through my hair as though it would bring sense to Pop's actions. "Abby, did he say anything to you?"

"No, he didn't. Karl, why don't you start with what you can tell us about Sally Clark?" said my sister, Abby. She reached over and gave my forearm a squeeze of encouragement.

"Your father met her back in 1985 when he and your mother were vacationing in Paris."

"That's all we need, some senile old foreign broad!"

"Leslie!" I rose from my chair, hoping the bulk of my broad shoulders and chest would convey my parental authority. "Control that tongue of yours or leave the room, now!"

She matched my gaze, anger flashing from her eyes. She turned away, and for a moment I thought she was going to leave. Instead, she let out a humph and stomped to the window, her back straight and stiff. I sat back down. Her behavior reminded me of the temper tantrums she threw as a child. I thought she'd outgrown those, but it would seem not.

"Ms. Clark is fifty-eight, far from being old or senile. And she's from Nebraska, not France. She is currently living in Kansas City." Karl took a long drink from his glass of iced tea. A bead of sweat trickled from his forehead down his pudgy cheek despite the coolness of the air-conditioned room.

"She's my age," Abby said excitedly. "Single? Married? Employed?"

"Single, works as an editor in a small publishing firm. She saved your parents from being mugged while they were in Paris."

"Terrific," Leslie groaned.

I ignored her. "Go on, Karl. How did she save them?"

"A case of right place, right time. Ms. Clark was a Marine Corps MP serving at the American Embassy at the time. She spotted the mugging in progress one evening and intervened."

"And so Poppie decides she deserves to own my magazine," Leslie spouted from her perch by the window.

"Leslie, Ms. Clark has been given only a 10 percent share in the profits. She won't own the magazine," Karl said. "Rest assured, the inheritance has conditions."

"Conditions?" Leslie spun away from the window to face the group again. I noted her wrinkled brow and clenched jaw. A favorite expression of hers that never bode well for anyone but her. I watched as a degree of relief washed over her face. "What are they?"

"She has to spend four weeks at the ranch."

"So what?" Leslie said.

"She has to complete the full four weeks or no inheritance," Karl explained.

"I don't see that as particularly reassuring. Anyone can stick it out for four weeks when the reward is big enough." Leslie grunted, moved to the table, and glared at me. "Poppie gives his own grandchild $200K and a perfect stranger gets 10 percent of *Cattle and Cowboy* magazine and a third of the ranch. Daddy, it's just not right. Do something." The whine in her voice grated my nerves, and at that moment I saw her for the spoiled woman she had become.

"I will *not* do something. This is what Pop decided and we won't stand in the way of that. Now sit down, and, Leslie, one more outburst and you will leave this room." I held her gaze as she took her seat, then I glanced over at her husband, Jake. His silence at her behavior surprised me. Why wasn't he doing anything to calm her down?

"Mr. Kandell, you said conditions, plural. That's only one," Leslie said. "What are the other conditions?"

"Not really a condition, but Ms. Clark must actively participate in the daily ranch activities," Karl clarified.

That seemed to mollify Leslie, for the moment. She grinned.

"Why four weeks?" my sister, Abby, asked.

"As your father explained it to me, he didn't want it to be 'here you go, it's all yours, goodbye.' He wanted her to get acquainted with all of you and for you to get to know her."

"I'm sorry, but none of that explains why Poppie singled me out," Leslie said.

"No, it doesn't. He did leave this envelope for you." Karl leaned forward, reaching his arm across the table, a business-size white envelope in his hand.

I and my children and their spouses all watched as Leslie took the envelope from Karl, stared at it for a long moment, then shoved it into her purse.

"I'm sure all this will make more sense as you get acquainted with Ms. Clark," Karl said.

"All that aside," Leslie interjected, "she'll never last four weeks, especially if she spends any time in the saddle with Four and Michael."

"What's being a rancher got to do with the magazine?" Chase IV asked.

"Identifying with the heart of the rancher and the realities of the job," Karl said.

"Duh, Four," Gabe said, a big smile erupting.

Karl sat back in his chair, his red eyebrows raised, arms crossed and resting on his rotund belly. The prolonged silence became uncomfortable.

Everyone trained their eyes on Leslie.

"Stop staring at me," she said as she stomped her foot like a bratty teenage pop star. "I still don't like it."

"I know this has been a shock, but if Ms. Clark doesn't stay the full four weeks at the ranch, her share of the ranch is split between Chase and Abby, and her 10 percent of *Cattle and Cowboy* goes to Leslie. Which means, Leslie, that the $200,000 stipulated in the will for you cannot be distributed until after Ms. Clark has completed her four weeks. And when she dies, it all comes back to the family."

"Holy buffalo chips, Karl, why didn't you say that twenty minutes ago?" I said.

"Because I kept getting interrupted."

I could see the frustration on Karl's face. For him, reading Pop's will must have seemed like dumping a truck load of cow manure on Central Avenue in downtown Great Falls.

"Right now I have a more difficult issue to deal with. Ms. Clark hasn't responded to any of the letters I've sent her. We can move forward with distributing the bulk of your father's estate, Chase, but as for Ms. Clark, the law requires me to do several things in attempting to locate an heir and a waiting period after all efforts have been exhausted."

"How is that going to effect the daily workings of *Cowboy*? We can't just stop everything we're doing," Leslie protested.

"None of this affects the daily routine for anyone, Leslie. All can continue as is. We're talking about the distribution of profits, not management of the magazine, or the ranch, for that matter." Karl scanned the grieving faces of my children and their spouses. "There are a lot of scenarios to this situation. While you are all deep in grief at this unexpected passing of your grandfather is not the time to discuss them. Let's get through the weekend first. Bottom line: Ms. Clark inherits 33 percent of the ranch and 10 percent of *Cowboy* magazine and all the profits that come with them."

"Can we contest this?" Leslie said.

"We will not contest this, Leslie. I told you that already," I said.

"Legally, anyone in the family can contest the will, but let's cross that bridge if we get to it," Karl said.

That seemed to settle Leslie's dissatisfaction for now. I gazed at each of my six children, attempting to read their emotions. Four, Michael, Peter, and Gabriel seemed calm, and why not? They had never been involved in the magazine and had now gained 10 percent of it. In addition, they knew that once I was gone, the ranch would be theirs. Emily appeared overwhelmed with grief. Of all the kids, she was most like my father and had had a special connection with him. I made a mental note to keep an eye on how well she was processing her grief, then I turned to observe Leslie.

She sat directly across from me, head down, her face in her hands. Her silky brunette locks fell forward, brushing the table. I could see the slow rise and fall of her shoulders and hear the deep breaths she took in, held, and then released. I recognized the body language; she was working to calm herself. Unlike my other children, she acted as though her world had fallen apart. But was her grief for Pop or about 10 percent of magazine going to a total stranger? At the cemetery, she hadn't shed a tear. Her reaction to all this alarmed me.

"Well, kids, your grandfather's will dealt us a big surprise, but I, for one, am looking forward to meeting Sally Clark. Let's go home. We have a ranch to run." I stood and watched them all file out the office, conversing softly among themselves. Karl stopped Abby and me as we reached the door.

"We need to talk more about this. There are details about Ms. Clark I can tell only you and Abby."

# Chapter 2

## Sally

O LORD, hear me as I pray; pay attention to my groaning.
Psalms 5:1

Here's today's mail, Miss Clark."

Startled by the voice, I jerked in my chair. "Joey, one of these days I'm going to end up with coffee in my lap." I turned from the computer and reached for the letters. "Do you sneak in here on purpose?"

"No, ma'am, I'd never intentionally try to scare you."

Seeing the concern on the teen's face, I tried to calm him. "Relax. I'm just teasing. I'm an editor here, not your boss." I flicked my right hand at him. "Be off with you, fair knave, and let me get back to this stuff my boss calls Gothic fiction."

He smiled—would a teenager even know what knave meant?—and continued with his office rounds. I tossed the mail onto my desk without looking at it and turned back to my computer. Rainbow-colored bubbles floated and bumped across the screen. If only those bubbles could wash away the filth in that manuscript I was editing. I wiggled the mouse and stared at the flashing cursor that appeared. My fingers hovered over the ctrl, A, and delete keys, urging me to do a select-all delete. Gothic erotica. How much more of this stuff could

I stomach? I headed down the hall to my best friend and coworker's office.

"Jen, you free for lunch?"

"Hi, Sally. I didn't hear you come in. Sure, I can do lunch. You buyin'?"

"As long as you're up for Wendy's. No time for anything fancier." A fancy restaurant would have been nice. But I needed a diversion from that manuscript, and any restaurant would do.

Jen pulled her purse from her desk drawer, and we dashed out the door before our boss could spot us leaving. We drove to the nearest Wendy's, ordered, and found the most deserted corner available.

"Okay, spit it out," Jen said just as I'd begun eating.

I stopped mid-chew, eyebrows raised.

"Not your food, your problem."

Jen knew me so well. I finished chewing. "I can't deal with these stories anymore."

"I thought you loved editing."

"I do." I leaned forward so I could whisper. "Jen, after reading erotica all day, I go home feeling like I was raped."

"I know what you mean. Makes me feel grimy, too."

"Mr. Snyder's been there for three months. I think that's time enough to know the direction he plans to take Pendrake Publishing. Besides the fact, I can't even walk down the hall to the restroom without him asking me where I'm going."

"And?" Jen leaned back against the cushion of the booth seat and looked at me as if I had a fly caught in the corner of my mouth. I wiped my lips.

"I have an idea I want to run by you. It came to me the moment Snyder started accepting sub-par manuscripts. And I've—"

"Hey, that's my job you're talking about."

"Sorry. I didn't mean—"

"I know you didn't. I'm only one of a committee of five, remember?"

"Yeah, and the only female. I know those choices all boil down to the bottom line. And there's big dollars in erotica." I shook my head as I spoke, grieved that people catered to their flesh in this way. "I thought about finding another job, but let's be real. Who's going to hire a fifty-eight-year-old? I know the realities of today's economy. Companies want young blood. The hiring manager can't ask your age, but you can't hide your age like you can ignorance and immaturity. The big six-O is right around the corner."

"I know what you mean. I'll hit fifty this year."

In her fifteen years with me at Pendrake Publishing, Jennifer Maxwell had become the sister I wished I'd had growing up.

"Oh my goodness!" I dropped back against the seat. "I just realized, next month I'll have been at Pendrake for twenty years! Mr. Pendrake and I had discussed the possibility of me becoming editorial director. I was so excited about that, but then he had that heart attack and died. Now…well, I'm rather miserable." I shook my head as the realization hit me. "But I really think you'll go for this idea I've got!"

"You're still grieving Mr. Pendrake's death. It's only been four months. Right now, you're probably just overworked and lonely."

"No, being lonely isn't the problem. I reconciled myself to oneness decades ago while I was in the Marine Corps." I took a bite of my burger and tried to swallow my anger along with the burger.

"I can see the hurt in your eyes, so don't tell me you're not lonely."

"Okay, I'm lonely. I've had one date in the past eighteen years."

Jen reached her arm across the table and squeezed my hand, french fry and all. "Sally, I'm sure it's just grief talking. Maybe you should see a counselor." She released my hand and I gave her a napkin to wipe the honey mustard dipping sauce from my french fry off her palm. I flashed her a smile.

"Thanks, Jen. I'm fine. You and John are the siblings I never had. Maybe some of this discontent is grief. You know how important Mr. P. was in my life." James Pendrake, founder and owner of Pendrake Publishing—Mr. P., as I affectionately called him—was probably rolling in his grave over what the new CEO was doing to the company. But I'd dare not dwell on sweet ol' Mr. P. or I would be in tears.

"Mostly, I think it's the erotica Snyder keeps sending my way." Berkley Snyder was Pendrake Publishing's new CEO. Not only was he rude and arrogant, he micromanaged everything. "What was the board thinking when they hired that man? This erotica he insists on… Seriously, Jen, have you guys in acquisitions lost your collective mind? Pornographic nature aside, it's hard for me to find the story arc because the stuff is riddled with typos and terrible grammar."

"I know. But, hey, it's job security for you. So, tell me. What's this idea you have?"

"I want to start my own publishing company. And I want you to be my partner."

Jen dropped the french fry she held and leaned back, stunned. She blinked several times, trying to take in what I'd just said.

"Do I need to repeat myself?"

"No," Jen said. "Wow, totally took me by surprise. How much have you thought this through? It takes money to start a business."

"Sort of. If we work from home, we'll cut way down on overhead. Once we're bringing in decent profits, we can decide if we need a dedicated office. We both know publishing. We can do traditional publishing, but offer self-pub options as a side gig."

"You have thought this through. How are you going to pay your bills before we start turning a profit?"

"I've got six months of monthly expenses saved in an emergency fund. We can start slow. Keep our jobs at Pendrake while we set up the details and get things going."

Jen leaned forward, excitement shining in her eyes. She grabbed the fry she had dropped and tossed it into her mouth. "Six months' worth of savings? How do you do it?"

"Discipline, I guess. Besides I don't have the extra expenses that come with being married with kids." I sat up straight. My gray cells shifted into sixth gear as excitement replaced my grief. I looked at my watch. We had just enough time for the drive back to work. "Let's get together tonight and discuss it. And I think John should be in on it. Do you want to meet at my place or yours?"

"My place, at 7:00," Jen told me as we dropped our trash into the waste bin and left the restaurant.

That night over pizza and pop, Jen, her lawyer husband John, and I hashed out the pros and cons of starting a publishing business. John shocked me with his encouragement of the idea. I thought he'd be less inclined to financial risks, but he saw how excited Jen was. My cell phone read midnight when I crawled into bed, still wide awake from the adrenaline pumping through me. As I lay there, I attacked every pro and con again from several angles. I couldn't shut my mind off. Finally, at O dark thirty I dropped off to sleep.

When I entered the office the next morning, excitement coursed through my body. I tried to keep from smiling, but it stole its way across my lips all the same.

"Good morning, Mr. Snyder," I chirped as I entered the conference room for our usual Friday morning editorial meeting. I rarely ever greeted him, and a strange look darkened his face.

"You're certainly cheery this morning. Big plans for the weekend?" he asked.

"Nope, just work."

"Oh. Well, it's not my fault you work too slow to meet the deadlines without working weekends." Every Friday Mr. Snyder held our feet to a thirty-minute accounting of our progress. As if the problems we editors encountered mattered. He never budged on a deadline, even if the author failed to get us their revisions on time, and because editors are salaried, he never worried about paying overtime.

I would have liked to slap him with some snappy comebacks, including one about his poor grammar, but I decided to not let him spoil my good mood. It was our monthly casual Friday, and my favorite Wrangler straight-leg denims, an emerald green polo shirt, and Birkenstock's contributed to my good mood. Heaven had kissed my day.

When I got back to my desk, I discovered yesterday's unopened mail. Three of the four letters went straight into file thirteen. The fourth came from the Kandell Law Office in Montana. I'd had one letter from them already, at my home address. I furrowed my brows. Hey, if I could have raised one eyebrow like Dr. McCoy always did in *Star Trek*, I would have. Kandell's first letter said something about an inheritance. I had chocked it up to a scam or a case of misidentification and tossed it. I ripped open the newest letter and read.

"Dear Ms. Clark: It is imperative you contact my office as soon as possible concerning an inheritance you have received from Chase Reynolds, Jr. I sent my first attempt at notification to the home address we have on record. Having not heard back, I am sending this letter to your work address. Please call my office any time between 8 a.m. and 5 p.m. Mountain time, Monday through Friday. Respectfully, Karl Kandell, Esq."

The letter didn't say what I had inherited. That in and of itself made me skeptical. Why keep it secret?

I examined the classy linen stationery with accompanying embossed letterhead. Pretty elaborate for a scam. Leaning back in my chair, the letter in my lap, I searched my memory for Chase Reynolds, Jr. Nothing. A few minutes on the Internet should yield some answers. I searched "Kandell Law Office, Great Falls, Montana." Legit. I moved on to Chase Reynolds, Jr. That search yielded more pages than I had time to sort through. Many of them were for a running back who played for the St. Louis Rams. I ruled him out; he wasn't dead. The obits might be easier. I did a search on Montana newspapers obits and struck gold. "Multi-Millionaire Cattle Baron Chase Reynolds, Jr. Dies at 80." Good thing I was sitting down.

I read through the obituary and learned his millions had been earned in cattle ranching but that he also owned a successful magazine. I skimmed through a few more articles. For a brief moment I allowed myself to dream. A chunk of money from a millionaire could provide just the start-up capital Jen and I needed.

"Sally, quit dreaming and get real. Your own parents didn't want you. Why would a perfect stranger give you anything? It's all some elaborate scam." I tossed the letter in the trash and turned back to my computer.

All Friday night that letter from Kandell Law Offices plagued me. As I lay awake at two a.m. I decided to dig the letter out of the trash and make the call. Only then was I able to drift off to sleep.

I slept till eight o'clock, much later than my usual and later than I intended. Oversleeping always left me feeling out of sorts because I missed my favorite part of the day, sunrise. One mile into my three-mile run, a horrible thought jolted me to a stop. The office cleaners come on Friday night. I might have thrown away a blessing God intended me to have. Then again, maybe this was God's way of protecting me from a trap. I hate those kinds of dilemmas, not knowing whether God is opening a door or closing it. I finished my run, showered, swilled down some coffee, and dashed to the office.

The moment I opened my office door I could see the wastebasket had been emptied. My stomach flip-flopped. I trudged over and looked in. Yup. Empty. I plopped down into my chair, punched the power button of my computer, and leaned back in my chair to watch the computer boot up. What would it have hurt to make that phone call? After all, Kandell Law Offices was legitimate. I guess my years as an MP in the Marine Corps made me second-guess acts of kindness that came my way.

Wait a minute. I sat forward in my chair. Just because I didn't have the letter didn't mean I couldn't call. I Googled Kandell Law Office in Montana. Three results gave me phone numbers for offices in Billings, Helena, and Great Falls. I searched my memory for which city and then jotted down the number for Great Falls. If I had it wrong, maybe they would tell me which office I needed.

That done, the rock in the pit of my stomach disappeared and a semblance of peace settled over me. First thing Monday, I'd be making a phone call.

# Chapter 3

## Sally

*Only ask, and I will give you the nations as your inheritance,*
*the whole earth as your possession. Psalms 2:8*

My nerves jittered all Monday morning in anticipation of calling Mr. Kandell. Since he was on Mountain Time and I was Central, I waited until break time to call. I closed my office door to ensure privacy and dialed the number on my cell phone rather than the office phone.

His secretary put me right through.

"Ms. Clark, I'm so glad to finally connect with you."

"When I read your first letter, Mr. Kandell, I figured it was a scam. I threw it away. But after getting one at work, I thought it was worth the phone call."

"A scam? No, I assure you, this is quite the opposite," he said.

"If it isn't a scam, then why the secrecy about what I've inherited?"

"It's a substantial sum and I felt it preferable to at least discuss by phone if not in person."

"That's a decent reason, but it doesn't make me any more confident about its legitimacy." I nearly hung up the phone there and then.

"Miss Clark, please. How much more would you think it a scam if the letter said you're looking at a six-figure yearly income?"

"Six figures! Holy cow."

"This is not a scam, and I truly am talking about six-figure annual business profits. Perhaps you'd feel more comfortable if we met face to face and discussed this. There is one condition to receiving the inheritance."

"A condition?"

"Yes. Mr. Reynolds conditioned the inheritance on you spending four weeks at his ranch in Montana."

Four weeks! Six figures? I rocked my office chair like a frantic mother with a colicky baby. I still couldn't remember any Chase Reynolds. "I... why me? I don't remember any Chase Reynolds."

"You met him and his wife in Paris back in 1985. You saved them from being mugged."

"No wonder I can't remember him." My mind flashed back to my time in the Marine Corps. "I was stationed at the American Embassy in '85. I saw more strangers in a day than a New York City taxi driver. But that doesn't answer the question of why me?"

"Like I said, you stopped an armed mugger from robbing and possibly injuring them. Mr. Reynolds tried to reward you then, but you refused everything he offered."

As a Marine MP for fifteen years, I had intervened in my share of trouble in Paris and in many not-so-friendly places. "Is this Mr. Reynolds' wild idea of a reward with thirty-odd years of interest?" I chuckled nervously. "How do his wife and family feel about this?"

"His wife passed away ten years ago." Mr. Kandell paused. "Miss Clark, I understand your hesitancy. Mr. Reynolds gave this decision considerable thought. The family owns a private jet. I can fly to Kansas City sometime this week. We can meet for supper and discuss all this."

A private jet! This was big. "If you insist. I can meet you at the airport if you like."

"No, that won't be necessary. I'll call you in the morning to arrange a time and place to meet."

"How will I recognize you?"

"You needn't worry about that. I'll know you. Mr. Reynolds provided a picture."

"Okay." I gave him my cell number and with that we hung up.

He has a picture of me? This situation grew more bizarre by the moment. The word stalker came to mind.

I sensed sincerity in Mr. Kandell's voice, yet there was something more. He wasn't telling me all of the story. Maybe the rest of the family wasn't so happy about what they surely deemed their rightful inheritance. Did I face years in court with the family contesting the will? Excitement and doubt about this inheritance jerked me up and down like a yo-yo.

Deep within I felt an excitement I hadn't felt for years. A six-figure income annually. That would provide the capital Jen and I needed to start our own business and some cushion until the business pulled in a decent profit. I took a deep breath and held it for a moment. What a game changer to my discontented, dull existence. No more kowtowing to my overbearing, micro-manager boss or editing the tasteless manuscripts he insisted on publishing.

I breezed through my work that day barely aware of what I did. I left the office at eight, a spark of hope flickering in my spirit.

# Chapter 4

## Chase

The godly are directed by honesty; the wicked fall
beneath their load of sin. Proverbs 11:5

Today, my sister, Abby, and I were to meet with Karl. Four days
had passed since Pop's funeral and the surprises in his will. Over
the weekend, many a discussion had ensued at the ranch about
Sally Clark. Once the family had time to think about Pop's will, most of
the kids seemed positive. I sensed they looked forward to meeting Ms.
Clark. Leslie, however, complained almost incessantly.

Why didn't Pop talk to me about making such a major change in his
will? His only comment had been an offhand one that left me with the
impression that his changes were minor. But a total stranger? Who was
Sally Clark, and what transpired in Paris to make such an impression
on Pop? What power did this woman hold over Pop? Blackmail? The
very thought staggered me. No! Pop's integrity was incontrovertible. If
anyone exemplified Christ, it was Pop.

During my quiet time with God each morning, He kept bringing
me back to Proverbs 2:1, "My child, listen to what I say, and treasure
my commands." I knew God was trying to tell me something, but I just
wasn't discerning it. Maybe my grief and shock were interfering with
my ability to hear God. I prayed Karl would be able to provide some
answers during our meeting with him.

I had plenty of questions but no answers when Abby and I entered Karl's office. We each shook hands, and then Karl closed the door. "How are you and the family doing?" he said as he took a seat behind the ornate mahogany desk his grandfather built seventy-some years ago.

"Let's see...grieving. A bit shocked. Leslie's angry. What other adjectives can I find?" I took a seat in the brown leather chair that stood in front of Karl's desk.

"That bad, huh? If you don't mind me saying, you seem rattled. That's not like you."

"No, not rattled. I guess I'm disappointed and hurt that Pop didn't trust me enough to tell me about this change to his will."

"He trusted you implicitly; you know that. Perhaps he just never found the right time. There are deeper issues at hand as well." Karl drummed his chubby fingers across a bulging file folder that lay in the center of his desk. He opened the file and fished out a green thumb drive. "He made a video for you. It's only about five minutes long, but why don't you two grab a cup of coffee and get comfortable while I plug in this flash drive and retrieve what I need."

Karl pushed the thumb drive into his computer and turned the monitor around for Abby and me to view. I fixed coffee for myself and Abby and then took a seat next to her.

"Can you see the screen well enough?" Karl asked.

"Yeah, we're good," I said as Abby nodded.

Karl nodded, clicked his mouse, and then leaned back in his chair.

"Chase, Abby, I made this video in the off chance that I never found the right moment—more likely never found the courage—to speak to you about Sally Clark. Abby, this impacts you more than any other member of the family."

Abby glanced over at me, her face covered in questions.

"This was a decision your mother and I made together, believing it was for your best. Guess I'd better stop pussyfooting around. Abby, you're adopted."

Abby sputtered a mouthful of coffee all across the corner of Karl's desk. A fit of coughing ensued. I jumped out of my chair. "Adopted?"

Karl pulled a handkerchief from his suit coat breast pocket and handed it to Abby. He stopped the video while she wiped her mouth and sopped up the splatters of coffee from his desk.

I took several deep breaths as I watched Abby dab at the coffee seeping into her pale pink suit coat and pants. Then I turned and stared at Karl with what I hoped was a questioning-please-continue look in my eyes, but Karl just sat there like a dog refusing to fetch. He took a deep breath, clearly concerned and struggling for words. "Maybe the coffee wasn't such a good idea. I'll pay to have your suit cleaned, Abby. Let me rewind the video a bit—you missed some—and we'll start again." Karl fidgeted with things and started the video again.

"Are adopted. Your mother and I chose not to tell you all those years ago because you were an orphan. We didn't want you to constantly wonder about your biological parents, and knowing they were dead, there would never be an opportunity for you to meet them. Hindsight is 20/20, as they say. Your mother and I were both very sorry we never told you.

"But after meeting Sally, we felt we should. We had many a discussion after returning from our trip to Paris. We had decided to make things right, and then your mother got sick…"

At this point, Pop paused, and I knew he was trying to compose himself. Pop had loved Mother deeply, fiercely. Her illness and death ripped him apart. He continued.

"Sally Clark is the spitting image of you, Abby. Your mother and I were both convinced she is your twin. Every time Sally spoke, we heard you. Her walk and many of her mannerisms are just like you! Once we got back from Paris, we had Karl do some research, but he was unable to find anything to connect the two of you. I know you will forgive us, but I ask it all the same.

"We never forgot Miss Clark or her bravery in stopping that mugger. We had Karl do what he could to keep tabs on her. Then, several months ago, the Lord began working on my heart to bring her into the family. The Lord and I had a lot of conversations, and I took it all to Karl for his spiritual discernment. He too believed the word I had received was from God, and he set to work to make it happen.

25

"Forgive me, Chase, for not coming to you to discuss this, but the Lord said no, I was to take it to Karl.

"Well, I guess that covers everything. I know you will all come to love Sally and she you. That is my heart's desire.

"My final words to you come from Proverbs 2:1, receive my words and treasure my commands. I love you."

The video ended. Karl, in his wisdom, gave me and Abby several moments to absorb it all. He putzed around ejecting the drive and putting it back into his file, then finally looked at me.

"Do you have a picture?" I asked.

"Yes." Karl pulled it from the file and handed it to me.

Abby and I examined it. My parents and Miss Clark—in her Marine Corps uniform—together in front of the American Embassy.

"Wow," was all Abby and I could say.

I handed the picture back to Karl and walked back to the sideboard for another cup of coffee. I refilled Abby's as well and poured a tall glass of iced tea for Karl.

"Thanks," Karl said as I handed him the glass. "Sit down. You're making me nervous."

"I prefer to stand." I combed my fingers through my hair. "Sally Clark and Abby, twins?"

"I did an exhaustive investigation, but adoption records from the 1960s aren't what they are today." Karl turned to Abby. "I can only find records for your adoption, Abby, but nothing on Sally. A DNA test may be the only way to determine if you two are truly twins and not just dopplegangers."

"I…I…don't know whether to be confused or excited," Abby said.

"My father handled the adoption. You were two months old when they adopted you, and at the time, Chase, you were too young to know any different."

"Pop, what were you thinking?" I said, looking up to heaven.

*My child, listen to what I say, and treasure my commands.*

Now the pieces fell into place and I understood what God had been trying to tell me earlier. God was applying that verse to Pop's will. Pop had ended his message with that same verse.

"Chase, you look like a light bulb just went on," Karl said.

"It did. Something God told me. What else can you tell us about Miss Clark?"

Karl shook his head, concern written across his brow. "What records I could find state that Sally's mother died when Sally was ten. I don't know if this woman was Sally's biological mother or an adoptive mother. The father was an alcoholic, in and out of trouble after her mother's death. Sally joined the Marines right out of high school, served fifteen years."

I drank the last of my coffee and set the mug on the corner of Karl's desk. God, give me wisdom and strength. "Karl, why didn't you show this during the reading of the will?"

"Your father instructed me to show you two first. Given the potential impact on Abby, I thought it was a wise choice."

My sister looked at me, then at Karl. She stood and began to pace the room. "Should we ask for DNA testing? But that wouldn't change the will. Might change everybody's attitude. It'd be nice to have a sister. I—"

"Abby," I said to interrupt her out-loud thinking. She smiled at me and sat back down. "You're right. A DNA test won't change the will. I think the kids need to see the video. Except for Leslie, none of them are upset, but I think they are probably very confused. This will answer any questions or doubts they might be harboring."

"I did ask him to reconsider this change," Karl said, "but he was as certain of God's leading as he was that Miss Clark is Abby's twin."

"I'm excited about having a sister, and it doesn't matter that I'm adopted. Pop was my father in every way that counts."

"I heard from Miss Clark yesterday. I'd like to use your jet to make a trip to Kansas City to meet with her. She's rather skittish about it all. Thinks it's a scam."

"You can be sure I'll be on that plane as well!" Abby said.

"Now, wait a minute, Sis. We don't want to give the woman a heart attack," I said.

"Don't be silly. She was a Marine. She's not faint-hearted," Abby retorted.

"I agree with Chase," Karl said. "Not that she'd have a heart attack, but learning about the inheritance and the potential of a twin sister is a lot to take in all at once. How would you have felt if you'd learned it all last week, Abby?"

"I see your point."

"I'd like to go to Kansas City as soon as possible. My schedule is empty for Wednesday and Thursday. Can you notify your pilot to make the necessary arrangements for a flight down there on Wednesday and then back on Thursday?" Karl asked.

I pulled out my phone and checked my own schedule. Nothing that couldn't be rearranged. "I can make that work."

"Chase, she's skeptical enough already. I don't want to overwhelm her," Karl protested.

"I'm going. And that's that."

"I feel rather cheated," Abby said, "but I have to head to Michigan for that press trip on Wednesday. I already had Steve put it on his schedule."

"That's easily changed. He can fly us all to KC, then take you to Michigan. And he can fly back from Michigan to KC on Thursday to pick up me and Karl and take us home. How long is your press trip?"

"A week," Abby said.

"Okay. I think the next step is to tell the kids as soon as we're done here."

# Chapter 5

## Chase

Charm is deceptive, and beauty does not last; but a woman
who fears the LORD will be greatly praised. Proverbs 31:30

The flight to Kansas City had been smooth. But the moment I
stepped outside the jet I thought I'd stepped into a steam room.
The temperature and humidity produced instant perspiration,
like stepping fully clothed into a hot tub. Karl's face turned redder than
usual, and droplets of sweat dripped down his temples.

"Chase, I really think you should have stayed in Montana," Karl
protested as our taxi pulled out of the airport and headed to the restaurant.

"Your argument is lost on me. Be thankful Abby isn't here too. What
time did you tell Ms. Clark to meet us?" I asked, glancing at my watch.

"Six-thirty. She's been working all day and bound to be hungry. She
won't be late."

"Let's hope so. I missed breakfast and lunch. I'm starving."

"I guess that explains the burr under your saddle. It's not like you
to be so agitated. Have you been like this since I saw you last at my
office?" Karl said as I watched the cab driver manuever through what
was surely rush hour traffic.

"No. Actually, I've been tumultuously up and down. Just grief, I
think. I'm not sure."

"Understandable. Take a deep breath and say a quick prayer. This meeting will go fine."

We rode the rest of the way in silence, both of us thankful for the cab's air conditioning. The cabby deposited us at the door, Karl paid him, and I stood long enough to take a few deep breaths and say a prayer as Karl advised. I needn't have worried Ms. Clark would be late. She stood waiting in the foyer as we entered. Despite knowing she looked like Abby, the resemblance was striking and a wave of shock washed over me. For a moment I stopped my forward motion.

"Miss Clark," Karl said, extending his hand as he strode toward her at the hostess's post. "I'm Karl Kandell, and this is Chase Reynolds, the third."

She shook Karl's hand and then mine. A firm grip, if a bit sweaty. She must be nervous.

"My condolences on the loss of your father, Mr. Reynolds."

"Thank you, Ms. Clark." If I'd had my eyes closed, I would have sworn I was talking to Abby.

The hostess checked the seating layout, then led us to a table. We took our seats as she pronounced the specials for the day and took our drink orders.

Ms. Clark sat straight and rigid in her chair, her teeth clenched. No red lipstick adorned her lips. No rouge reddened her cheeks. No makeup of any kind called attention to her Montana-sky-blue eyes. She wore her field mouse-brown hair in a style cut almost as short as a man's crew cut. The name Jane would have suited her better. Abby was a beautiful woman; so was Ms. Clark, but she seemed to downplay that beauty. Of the three of us at the table, only Karl appeared calm. After we placed our order, Karl got down to business.

"Miss Clark, let me be up front with you—"

"Definitely, Mr. Kandell. I'm still not convinced this isn't some elaborate scam. I have friends at the FBI I won't hesitate to call."

A look of surprise crossed Karl's freckled face, and he fell back in his chair as if she had punched him. He smoothed back a wayward strand of red hair. "As I tried to explain on the phone on Monday, the inheritance is quite legitimate. But as I told you, Mr. Reynolds placed a condition on receiving it."

A waiter brought our drinks, allowing time for Karl's statement to sink in. Karl and I both watched and waited for her reaction.

"Nothing in life comes without strings." She crossed her arms and leaned back in her chair. "Just what is it Mr. Reynolds has conditionally willed me?"

In addition to her defensive posture, I detected a tone of bitterness in her voice. I wondered what struggles life had dealt her.

"Thirty-three percent ownership of his cattle ranch and 10 percent ownership of *Cattle and Cowboy* magazine."

Sally's jaw dropped open and her arms flew forward, her hands grabbing the table as if to catch herself. "What?"

"Owner—"

"No, I heard you. I just…don't believe you."

"Miss Clark, maybe it's your military police background that causes your skepticism, but believe it," Karl said.

Her cheeks grew brick red and her mouth still hung open. We sat silent for several minutes while she scrutinized first Karl, then me. Her unplucked blonde eyebrows furrowed. Finally, she spoke.

"Gentlemen, I…what I did…doesn't warrant such a gift. I…" She shook her head as she spoke. No doubt as shocked as I had been when I first heard the news. As she continued to shake her head, I began to think she might decline the inheritance right there and then. I immediately felt a check in my spirit. Pop wanted this. He had his reasons, and I had to remind myself regularly of God's message from Proverbs to treasure His commands—and Pop's.

"Let me remind you of the one condition you must meet, Miss Clark. Four weeks at the ranch, working alongside the family."

She leaned forward in her chair, her arms resting on the edge of the table, fingers intertwined. I noticed short nails and no polish. "And the purpose of this requirement?"

"So you have an understanding of my father's hard work in building our ranch and the men who work those ranches," I explained. "After all, we are talking about ownership of a cattle ranch and *Cattle and Cowboy* magazine, designed to help ranchers be successful in the cattle business."

She nodded her head in agreement, having recovered from her initial shock. "Why didn't Mr. Reynolds simply will me a sum of money?" She turned to me with a look of ice in her eyes. "I can see you're none to happy about this, are you, Mr. Reynolds?"

"Quite the contrary, Ms. Clark. However, this bequest surprised my family as much as it has you. I have no idea why Pop didn't give you a lump sum. Karl, do you have any insight into that?"

"He saw a potential in you that he wanted to encourage. He felt a sum of money wouldn't serve that end."

Sally's eyebrows shot up. I watched concern and doubt flit through those entrancing blue eyes. Then her face became one big question mark.

"Did you expect the full inheritance, Mr. Reynolds?"

"We expected everything to be split between my sister and me. Instead a portion went to you, someone none of us had ever heard of. The magazine was split between my sister and five of my six children. The portion of the magazine that would have gone to my daughter Leslie went to you instead."

"I can well-imagine her disappointment. Does she plan to contest?"

I pulled my head back and crossed my arms over my chest. I imagined a thousand questions marching through her mind, but the emotion on her face offered no insight to what she was thinking. Should I tell her exactly how Leslie felt?

"I'll take that as a yes," she said just as I began to speak.

"No, Ms. Clark." I leaned forward and with my sternest voice added, "My daughter is distinctly unhappy about the will, but this is what my father wanted and we will honor that." The knots in my stomach loosened a bit as I spoke the words, and in my head I heard Pop say, "Let the Golden Rule guide all your actions." The waiter arrived with our food and not a moment too soon. "This is a lot to take in, Ms. Clark. Let's eat while you think."

Only the sound of silverware clinking on our plates or across a knife interrupted the ensuing silence. Sally kept her face down, effectively obscuring my view to her eyes and emotions. She had ordered a barbecue pulled-pork sandwich and fries. The enticing aroma of barbecue almost convinced me I'd ordered the wrong thing. The sandwich was large, and she ate about half before asking for a to-go box and excusing herself to the restroom.

She returned five minutes later. The fastest female bathroom break I had ever experienced. But then it occurred to me she didn't have to fix her makeup or her hair.

"Would you like dessert?" I asked as she sat.

"My belly and brain are full enough, thank you."

The waiter returned with her to-go box, and Karl and I ordered slices of cherry pie ala mode. Meanwhile Ms. Clark moved her leftovers to her to-go box, then turned to Karl.

"Sir, exactly what does ownership entail? Are we talking stock in the company?"

"No, everything is family owned. It means you'll be paid a percentage of the profits. Profits on the magazine are paid out quarterly, on the ranch annually."

"Go on."

"That's all. You spend four weeks at the ranch, fully participating in the daily routine and getting to know the family."

"Four weeks? All at once?"

"Yes," Karl said.

"And if I don't?"

Karl shrugged. "Then no inheritance."

She scoffed. "This is worse than a scam. Do you honestly expect my boss to give me a whole month off?" She shook her head. "This is absolutely bizarre. I don't know what to say, except thanks for dinner." She tossed her napkin on the table and stood. Her belligerent reaction struck me as odd.

I grabbed her wrist. "Hold on a minute! Just sit down and listen."

She stood there glaring down at me.

"Please," I said, doing what I could to soften my tone and releasing my grip on her wrist. Why was this inheritance so difficult for her to accept as real?

She was either as scrappy as a banty hen or stupid as a log. Her plain appearance gave me no clues. She wore sensible black dress pants and a peach cotton shirt that made her clean face glow. Her hair was spiked—maybe she was a bit scrappy. She looked many years younger than the fifty-eight Karl claimed her to be. Finally, she sat back down.

"Pop wanted us to get to know you, and for you to get to know us."

Her brows crinkled, and I could almost see the thoughts banging around in her head like two boxers in the ring.

"Mr. Reynolds felt it essential you understand the hard realities of cattle ranching and a cowboy's life." Karl pushed the conversation forward. "And where your employer is concerned, I can talk with your supervisor. Perhaps you can do your work long distance?"

"Mr. Kandell, the work I do requires fifty to sixty hours per week. I can't do that and participate in the daily routine of the ranch. When do my four weeks begin, and does this full participation include spending time on the back of horse?"

Karl looked to me to answer.

"It can begin anytime you're ready. And yes, you'll spend nearly every day on a horse if you come within the next thirty days. We have cattle to move from one pasture to another before winter sets in. It's best managed on horseback. We'll also spend several nights sleeping under the stars and on the ground. Will that be a problem? Do you have any physical issues that would prohibit that?"

"No. I spent plenty of time sleeping rough when I was in the Corps. However, I haven't been on a horse in over forty years." She gave a nervous chuckle. "Can you give me any figures?"

"Figures?" This from Karl.

"If I'm going to put my butt in a saddle for any length of time, I want to know it's worth it. What are the magazine's current circulation figures, is it solvent? What kind of profits does it generate? What kind of profits does the ranch generate?"

I ruled out stupid as a log. Definitely scrappy and intelligent, but did she have her eye only on the profits? Or did she ask because she wanted to know the loss to our family?

Karl looked over at me. I shrugged. I didn't have all those numbers, but I'd fill in what I could. "Ranching is big business, Ms. Clark. *Cattle and Cowboy* serves that community well. Abby could give you the best answer on the magazine, but I believe they run around a 20 percent profit margin. As far as the ranch is concerned, some years are exceptional, some are horrendous. But Pop didn't become a multi-millionaire because he sold a few head of cattle every year."

"And you're based in Montana, right? The magazine too?"

"Yes, Great Falls, to be exact," I said. She had done some homework, which was more than I could say for myself. I'd only skimmed that two-inch file Karl had accumulated over the years.

"How many people do you employ?" She wiped at the sweat on her still-full glass of water. Nervous or stealthy business acumen?

"About twenty at the magazine. The ranch varies. We take on extra at certain times of the year."

"Do I have to pay my way there?"

"You still think this is a scam." Karl rested his elbows on the table, his fingers steepled against one another. "What will it take to convince you otherwise?"

"Can I fetch you to the airport for a tour of our company jet?" I asked, truly perplexed at her skepticism. "Why are you so skeptical about this?"

"Because only a fool isn't skeptical about something that appears too good to be true."

Ms. Clark looked at me with the same fire in her eyes that Abby had whenever she and I argued. For a moment I felt like a calf facing the branding iron. She dropped her gaze and wiped away the remaining drops of sweat on her glass of water, then pushed the glass aside. Her eyes flitted from one item on the table to another, as if looking for something else to mess with.

"Gentlemen, your news is overwhelming. I'd like to think about this for a day or two and consult my lawyer. What can I do if my boss refuses to give the time off?"

Karl and I looked at each other and then back at her.

"Like I said earlier, I'd be more than willing to talk to him," Karl said.

"I'd love to be a fly on the wall for that conversation," she said.

"As far as I'm concerned, you should be in on that conversation," Karl said.

My hands slammed down on the table, startling Ms. Clark and making the silverware tink on my empty dessert plate. "I'm sorry. This hasn't been easy for me."

She fidgeted in her chair, clearly nervous and upset by my behavior.

"I haven't had time to process Pop's death, let alone think much about this surprise in his will. Don't worry about your boss. We'll make things work. Somehow." I leaned forward across the table toward Sally. "Ms. Clark, Pop sincerely wanted this for you. And so do I. Please don't dismiss it because you think it's a scam or because you're concerned about your boss." Where did that come from? I looked over at Karl, his astonishment at my words clear on his face. But I did truly want this for Ms. Clark, so why should those words have surprised me?

"I know nothing about you. How can I be certain you won't deny the inheritance on some weird loophole and I bust my butt for nothing?"

Her words dripped with cynicism. Undoubtedly, busting her butt for nothing had been a big part of her life. That explained much of her skepticism. Abby had blossomed into a beautiful, loving woman under Pop's love. Though the exact image of Abby, it appeared unforgiveness and bitterness dulled Ms. Clark's beauty. I remembered Karl saying Sally's father was alcoholic. What kind of life had she endured to grow up so plain and bitter?

"We are a family of longstanding Christian heritage. The ranch is managed with integrity and guided by the Golden Rule. We run our business reputably and with integrity," I told her.

"In my experience, the people who tout their Christianity are the worst offenders in actually living it." She rose from the table.

Karl and I followed suit. I pulled a business card from the breast pocket of my shirt. "Here's my card. Call me if you have any questions."

She took the card. "When will you be returning to Montana?"

"First thing in the morning," I said.

"And if your lawyer has any questions, he's welcome to talk with either of us," Karl added. He pulled out a business card from his suit pocket, wrote on it, and handed it to her. "That's my cell number if you need it."

"Thank you very much," she said as she took the card. We watched her walk to the lobby and out of sight. Shoulders back, head high, and confident.

"I think the Marines are about to invade Montana," Karl said.

# Chapter 6

## Sally

I cried out to the LORD, and he answered me
from his holy mountain. Psalms 3:4

As soon as I was out of Mr. Reynold's and Mr. Kandell's line of sight, I pulled my cell phone out of my purse to see if Jen had returned my voice mail. She hadn't. During supper I had excused myself to the restroom simply to call Jen and get a few quick words of advice. I stashed my phone back into my purse and made my way out to the parking lot. The Tasmanian devil whirled and whooshed through my mind. I wanted new direction and purpose in my life, and I got it. Now the question was should I choose door number one or door number two?

I noticed that as Mr. Reynolds had entered the restaurant, he turned white, despite the deep tan of his skin, as if he'd seen a ghost. Why? He seemed to recover after I extended my condolences. As we spoke, his whole demeanor yo-yo'd. Maybe this situation toyed with his emotions the same way it had been with me.

I drove back to my apartment in a daze, nearly running a red light. That would have given me new direction for sure, straight up, but my guardian angels kept me safe. My cell phone rang just as I unlocked my apartment door.

"Great timing, Jen. I'm just walking into my apartment."

"What's this incredible news you have?"

"I've received an inheritance and I need John's advice." I tossed my purse and car keys onto their usual place on the table in the kitchen—the one I used for everything but eating. I fixed a glass of ice water, set it on the end table, then collapsed onto the couch. The warm evening breeze coming through the window only added to my discomfort. Ninety-degree temperatures will do that. I debated whether to turn on the air conditioner but decided against it. I needed the songs of the night to calm my nerves and my racing thoughts.

"John's advice? Why? Your voice mail sounded so frantic. What gives?"

"It's not your typical here's-your-money inheritance. There's a condition I have to meet."

"People can be strange about their estate, can't they? John's expertise is business," Jen said. I could hear her breathing out his name as if calling him to the phone.

"Which is perfect. I've been willed part ownership of a cattle ranch and a magazine." A long silence ensued. "Jen? Jen, you there?"

"Yeah, I dropped the phone."

"Hold on tighter and sit down." I gave her a moment to find a chair. "Multi-millionaire Chase Reynolds, Jr., has willed me 33 percent ownership of his cattle ranch and 10 percent of his magazine *Cattle and Cowboy.*"

"Oh my," was all Jen could say.

"Hello? Sally?" John said. "What's happened? Jen's just sitting there, catatonic like, holding the phone out to me."

"I think the word multi-millionaire has something to do with it. I need you guys's advice."

"There's still time this evening. Why don't you come on over and we'll talk?"

"Wow, Sally. You said you were dissatisfied with your job. God's opened up an amazing door," Jen said as she held their front door open for me.

"I know God always provides, but sometimes in my heart I'm not so sure." I stepped past her and into their house.

"That's your cynicism talking." Jen led the way into the living room and took a seat next to John on the couch. "Have a seat and tell us all about this."

I explained about full participation in the ranch duties, including being on a horse every day and completing four weeks. Then I showed them the info I'd gleaned from the Web about Chase Reynolds, Jr. and *Cattle and Cowboy* magazine.

"I have to get the time off work if this is to move forward. I have to do the four weeks at once or no inheritance." I leaned back in my seat next to the couch and dropped my head back. I felt defeated before I'd begun. "I just don't see Mr. Snyder agreeing to four weeks off."

"I expect you're right about that. He's a real Scrooge when it comes to granting time off," Jen said to John.

"I can't help you there. But didn't you say they would?" John asked.

"Yeah. Mr. Kandell said he'd talk to Snyder. But I've got four manuscripts on my desk that he expects to be done in the next six weeks." I rose from my seat. "Am I crazy to even think about doing this? This just sounds too good to be true."

"Granted, it sounds unusual for sure. But what's there to lose? Four weeks away from those nasty manuscripts and Mr. Snyder?" Jen said. She rose from her seat next to John and approached me. "Go for it, Sally. You've borne so much heartache. The Holy Spirit has prompted me with Isaiah 61:7. Let me go grab my Bible. I don't want to misquote it." She dashed off to her bedroom, returning quickly and already turning to the book of Isaiah. "'Instead of shame and dishonor, you will enjoy a double share of honor. You will possess a double portion of prosperity in your land, and everlasting joy will be yours.' Oh, Sally, what a wonderful word for this very moment in your life. It's God's answer."

"You really think so?"

"Yes!" Jen and John exclaimed in unison.

"Thanks so much for hearing me out on this. My gut still isn't easy about it all, but I'm going to hang on to that verse—and trust God." I drove home, a zillion thoughts crowding my brain.

The next morning I made straight for Mr. Snyder's office.

"Four weeks? Don't be absurd. You've got a pile of manuscripts to wade through and edit," he said without looking away from his computer.

"If you're talking about those four you sent me last week, they're awful." I tried to hide my true disgust. "If I do the editing on those, you might as well put my name on the cover."

"They've been to committee and accepted." Finally he looked up at me. "You will edit them, and you will meet the deadlines."

I balked under his steely blue stare. The man had no heart and no morals. And in that moment I saw my dad. All his vile words and drunken behavior came rushing back to my memory. I never cowered at his words, and I wasn't going to cower now, be it Berkeley Snyder or Chase Reynolds doling out the demands.

I thought about the various manuscripts sitting on my desk. If I had to read one more sordid page…I opened my mouth to protest, but my boss beat me to it.

"No!"

"But I've received an inheritance. I have to go to Montana for all the arrangements."

"Who died?"

"Chase Reynolds, Jr."

"And who is he to you? How come you didn't ask for compassionate time off to go to the funeral?"

"He's a man I've known since 1985." Okay, so I fibbed a little. "I didn't go to the funeral because no one notified me that he died. I can take work with me."

He looked at me, and for one very brief moment I thought he was going to change his mind, but then he shook his head. "No. I want you here. You'll have to arrange to go some other time."

I stood close-mouthed, thinking about the choices facing me: Decline an amazing inheritance and keep working for Mr. Snyder or quit my job and go to Montana. I knew full well that some other time would never come. I didn't think long. "In that case, Mr. Snyder, I quit."

"You can't do that," came his lame response.

"I can. I'm outta here, now." I stood there long enough to see the shock register on his face.

"Today? You have to give notice."

"No, I don't." I strolled out of his office. A wave of fear engulfed me as I strode back to my office.

What did I just do?

But as I gathered my personal items, excitement washed away the fear. No more prima donna authors. No more erotic romance. I was burning bridges, for sure, by so abruptly leaving the authors I was currently working with. I couldn't do that, so I dashed off a brief explanatory email to them all and cc'd Mr. Snyder.

Goodbye job, hello inheritance.

I stopped at Jen's office before leaving.

"Hey, Jen. Just stopped to say goodbye. I just quit."

"You what! You quit?"

I set down my box of personal items and took a seat in the chair in front of her desk. "Snyder gave me no choice. He wouldn't let me take four weeks off. What else could I do? Besides, you know how sick of this job I am."

"Yeah. Can you take me with you?" She chuckled. "Don't forget that plan to start our own publishing business. Maybe this inheritance will open that door wider."

"You might be right." I shrugged. "Can you drive me to airport whenever I leave? I don't particularly want to leave my car sitting in the airport parking lot for four weeks."

"Of course I can."

"I think they're sending their private jet to get me. I'll call you as soon as I know the details." I got up and retrieved my box. "Say my goodbyes to the rest of the office, will you, please?"

"Sure."

When I got home, I called Mr. Kandell. I got voice mail; no doubt they were winging their way back to Montana. I told them I was able to come as soon as they could make flight arrangements, then I spent the rest of the day shopping for boots, some sturdy denims, and a cowboy hat. As I entered my apartment after shopping, my phone was chiming at me. I tossed my packages on the table and pulled my phone from my pants back pocket.

"Hello."

"Miss Clark, this is Karl Kandell. I'm delighted you're able to come so soon. So your boss didn't give you the trouble you expected?"

"He did, but I explained the situation." I wasn't about to tell him or Chase Reynolds that I'd quit my job.

"I've talked with Chase, and he's arranged for his plane to pick you up this Friday around noon. That'll put you here in Great Falls in time for supper. There will be someone at the airport to pick you up and take you out to the ranch."

"How will I find the Reynolds' airplane at Kansas City? I need to know what terminal to go to."

"I'll have to get with you on that information. I'll text you, if that's okay, as soon as I know anything."

"That's fine. Thank you. I guess I'll see you soon," I said, shrugging my shoulders as I spoke and hung up.

I arranged to stop my newspaper and mail delivery and asked Jen to keep an eye on my apartment and water the plants while I was gone. I purchased a couple of timers and set them to automatically turn lights on and off to make it look as if I were home.

At 11:15 Friday morning Jen drove me to Signature Flight Support. Apparently private jets get their own airport space. Here I'd board the Reynolds' jet and fly to Great Falls, Montana. I felt like Genie set free from the lamp.

"Sally, I'm still shaking my head over this. You usually don't take risks," Jen said as she pulled the car up to the curb to let me out.

"I took my share of risks as a kid and while I was in the Corps. I try to keep them to a minimum now." I flashed her a mischievous grin. "The choice was to keep working for Snyder or take this risk."

"I have to admit, I wish I had the guts to just quit."

"If things go south with the inheritance, I have six months of monthly expenses in my savings account. I can always freelance while we work out details and decide if we want to go forward with our own company." I sounded much more confident than I felt. I knew how to act confident, no doubt about that; I learned that game well in the Marines Corps. But deep inside I rarely felt it. Had I made the right decision or stepped into the enemy's line of fire?

"Sally, we can set up that publishing business for sure, no matter how it all ends," Jen said, a big smile on her face. I realized she was as discontent and ready for change as I was. She shut off the engine, and we both emerged and walked to the trunk. I pulled out my two big suitcases and set them on the sidewalk, then turned to hug Jen and say goodbye.

"Thanks so much for dropping me off. And tell John thanks again for his legal advice. Wish me luck." I gave her a long hug.

"No, not luck, but God's favor be with you—His double portion. I'll be praying for you. Give me a call now and then and let me know how it's going."

"I can do that," I said, nodding my head. I grabbed my bags and headed for the gate where the Reynolds' private jet awaited me. As I boarded, a verse from my morning quiet time came to mind. *I cried out to the Lord, and he answered me from his holy mountain.*

Boy, had He answered!

# Chapter 7

## Sally

Lead me in the right path, O LORD, or my enemies will conquer me. Make your way plain for me to follow. Psalms 5:8

I waited at the Great Falls Jet Center for an hour before deciding no one was going to meet me. I prayed for the Lord's guidance.

*Rent a car.*

I went in search of a car rental agency. There were several. "I need to get to Chase Reynolds' ranch, but I don't know the address. Can you look it up for me?" I asked the clerk as he prepared the car rental contract.

"Certainly," he said, and clacked away at his keyboard. "What's your phone number and I'll send the directions to your phone?"

I gave him the number. "Can you print those out as well? I don't know what my reception will be like."

"It can be spotty at times. Smart move," he said. He stepped away from the counter and over to a printer and returned with the directions. I signed the necessary paperwork and he swiped my credit card. "Follow me and I'll take you to your car."

Just after seven p.m. I pulled off a gravel road and onto the blacktop driveway of the Double R Ranch. The gated entry was built of two large sandstone pillars. In wrought iron, the words *Welcome to Double R Ranch* arched across from pillar to pillar. The drive led uphill, and I estimated it to be about half a mile long.

At the top of the hill stood a massive house constructed of logs and what appeared to be granite. The house looked straight out of the 1800s. Even as massive as it was, I found it strangely warm and inviting. Must have been the natural material the house was built with. At that moment it dawned on me. The obituary on Chase Reynolds, Jr. had read multi-millionaire. I was so fixated on cattle ranch I forgot these people were millionaires. What had I gotten myself in for?

I drove slowly toward the house, glancing around at all the other buildings. Was that a tennis court over there? On a cattle ranch? I never realized I had so many preconceived ideas about Montana and cattle ranchers. I parked behind several other cars to the side of the house. Traveling gravel roads for the past ten miles with the car windows down left me dusty (did I mention I don't like air conditioning?). I noticed gray smoke drifting eastward from the back of the house.

"I was getting concerned, Ms. Clark. You were due here over an hour ago." Chase Reynolds' voice startled me, and I jumped slightly at the sudden nearness of this immense man leaning in my car window. "Where's Leslie?"

The musky scent of his cologne chased away my reverie.

"Who's Leslie?"

"My daughter. She was supposed to meet you at the airport."

"Well, she didn't, and I waited for a full hour."

"You should have called. I would have come to get you."

"That hadn't even occurred to me. Besides, I don't think I had your phone number handy." Looking in the rear-view mirror, I hastily rearranged my windblown hair. As I pushed the door open, Chase stepped back a few feet.

"We've killed the fatted calf in your honor. Come and eat. I'll have someone bring in your luggage later."

He offered me his arm, but I stood there glaring at him.

"Just being gentlemanly. The party's in the back," he said. He led the way and I gawked at everything as I followed.

The hickory scent of an open fire, along with the enticing aroma of roasting meat, greeted me as we rounded the side of the house. Twenty-some adults milled around the expansive yard, most sitting at tables covered with the traditional red and white checked picnic tablecloths. Several children frolicked among the group. A side of beef turned on an electric spit, the fire hissing as fat dripped onto the flaming wood.

"I thought you were kidding. You killed that cow just for me?"

"Sure did," he said.

"Don't let him fool you, ma'am. We always start harvest season with a big barbecue," said a young man approaching us. "I'm Chase Reynolds the fourth. It's nice to meet you."

"Hello." I shook his extended hand and flashed a bright smile, hoping it would hide my nervousness. "Chase the fourth? Has the ranch been in existence as long as the family name?"

"Longer. And call me Four like everybody else does." His smile revealed straight white teeth, without a chaw of tobacco bulging from his front lip. Oops, more preconceived ideas? The only horseman I'd ever known was Mr. Campbell, when I was ten. He chewed and it was gross and I nearly gagged every time he spit.

"Gabe, toss me a bottle of water for Ms. Clark. She looks like she needs to wash the dust from her mouth," Four hollered.

I watched as a muscular, blond-headed young man lobbed Four the water. Chase wandered off into the crowd.

"Thank you, and please, call me Sally," I said as I opened the bottle. I liked this young man. Dressed in jeans, a cowboy hat, and a teal John Wayne western shirt, Four was just as handsome as Gabe.

"Everybody!" Four yelled. The crowd grew quiet. Even the children stopped their romping. "This is Ms. Sally Clark."

I gave a confident wave. "Hello, everybody." Some smiled and waved in return, but mostly they sat there, mouths agape. You'd think they'd seen a grizzly bear poised to attack.

"You can go back to eating now," Four said. That seemed to knock the shock out of them, and they turned back to their plates. "Pop mentioned you look just like Aunt Abby. Even forewarned, I find the resemblance astonishing."

"I look like your aunt? Strange, your dad never mentioned it to me."

Chase returned holding out to me a plate brimming with baked beans, potato salad, and beef. I took the plate and thanked him. He led me to a semi-full picnic table and motioned for me to sit.

"This is Linda, Four's wife, and my son Michael and his wife, Hannah," Chase said as he sat. Four joined his wife, and I sat between Hannah and Chase.

"Pop, you weren't kidding when you said Ms. Clark looked like Abby," Linda said. There was a general agreement between those at the table.

"I've heard it said we all have a doppleganger. Over the years, a lot of people have told me I look familiar to them. I seem to have one of those faces," I said, shrugging my shoulders.

"Oh my gosh! You sound just like Aunt Abby, too" said someone at the table behind me.

"No kidding!" said someone else. "You look a lot like, but there are some easy differences, like your hair. But your voice!"

I turned around to see who was talking.

"Those two are my twins, Peter and Gabe," Chase said.

I smiled at each, then turned back to my plate. An uncomfortable silence settled over the table. I was glad for a plate of food to keep me occupied. As I ate, a stream of people introduced themselves. With my mouth full, all I could do was smile and nod my head.

"Ms. Clark, I'm Jake Bonner, ranch foreman."

I looked up to find a man over six feet tall staring down at me. Like most people who spend the majority of their time outside, the sun had tanned his skin to a deep golden brown. A handsome man, with bright blue eyes and brown hair—a deadly combination for me, but I was probably old enough to be his mother. Anyway, a quick glance at his ring finger told me he was taken. "Please call me Sally. All this formality will get old quickly." I wiggled my barbecue sauce-covered fingers, palms up, as an apology for not shaking his hand.

"Out here, Ms. Clark, we call that formality good manners," he said, his voice coldly polite. He looked me over from head to foot. I felt like an old cow about to be slaughtered. If the hired help feels that way about me, I'm doomed. What possessed me to think I could insert myself into the life of this wealthy family? I didn't ask for this inheritance, I only wanted to make a better life for myself. Four weeks, Sally. All you have to do is hang in for four weeks.

"I hope you brought more appropriate clothes." He glared at my sleeveless V-neck shirt and shorts, and then raised an eyebrow at my open-toed slip-on sandals. "Shoes like that belong in the city. Did you bring boots?"

"Mr. Bonner," and I stressed Mister, "I'm not a greenhorn." To a degree, I expected to be received as the wolf among the sheep, but I was determined to remain polite, if not friendly, in the face of any opposition. "I don't understand your contempt. I'm here to simply participate in the daily routine of the ranch, not take it over."

This seemed to bring him to his senses. The corners of his mouth curved upward slightly. Everything about him, from his deep blue eyes to the bulging biceps pressing against the rolled-up sleeves of his plaid shirt, appealed to me. I guessed his age at forty. He could have been much younger, but the sun had done its damage, making his tanned skin leathery.

"Get to know me first, then make your judgment." I wiped the barbecue sauce from my hands, then offered him my right hand. "Truce?"

"Truce." He took my hand and we shook. "I think I'm going to like you, Sally." He released my hand and returned to his table.

"Me, too," Four said. "As my grandfather would say, well done."

At least I had one friend in the family. "Thank you. And my compliments to the cook. Dinner was delicious."

"Now that you're finished, let's go to the barn and find you a horse," Chase said.

"A horse? Now?" My mouth dropped open, and I looked down at my sandals. Chase followed my gaze and smirked.

"Yeah, you know, those four-legged creatures cowboys ride. We keep 'em in the barn." Chase stood from the table, but my derriere seemed rooted to the picnic bench.

"Pop, you can do that tomorrow," one of his sons said.

"No time like the present, son," he said, waving a hand in the air and heading off to the barn.

Reluctantly, I rose from my seat and did my best to run after him. The barn was about fifty yards from the house, an easy distance to jog, but not in slip-ons. I staggered over a few holes in an attempt to catch up and then gave up the effort. I could see him waiting at the barn door, the orange light of the setting sun making him look like a giant crunchy Cheeto (no way could you describe this man as a puffy Cheeto!). He was leaning against the wall, his arms crossed and his Stetson cocked back on his head.

"Is that the only pair of shoes you brought?" he asked as I approached. I couldn't decipher his tone.

"Actually, I brought some bedroom slippers, too. …Of course, I brought others. I expected to step 130 years back in time when the work began, not today."

Chase pulled open the barn door and motioned for me to enter. "First thing tomorrow I'll drive you into town and buy you some boots, work jeans, a flannel shirt or two, and a cowboy hat."

We fell silent as Chase walked through the barn, checking the stalls. Ten stalls on either side of the aisle—impressive—and a horse in nearly every stall. I breathed in the enticing aromas of horse and hay and saddle leather, recalling my days as a ten-year-old in Nebraska. Riding Mr. Campbell's horses had been a godsend for me after my mother died. Being on the back of horse calmed my inner turmoil. Now, as I wandered from stall to stall, perusing all the horses, a smile stole across my lips. I spotted a palomino and headed toward it. The horse whinnied at my approach, then nuzzled me as I stroked its neck and softly spoke to it.

"Be careful," Chase yelled from the other end of the barn. "She bites strangers."

But the horse wasn't the least bit spooked and nudged me as if looking for a carrot or an apple in my pocket. I laughed and rubbed her nose. "Sorry, girl, I haven't got anything for you."

"Looks like the horse has picked you."

I jumped, startled by Chase's silent approach and gentle words in my ear.

"Do you know how to ride?"

"Yes, but like I told you when we met, it's been years since I sat a horse. These are beautiful animals, Mr. Reynolds. Do you breed here or buy?" My childhood riding reminiscences had washed away my frustration at Chase, and I spoke excitedly at the thought of being on a horse again.

"Both. Four manages our horse business, and Michael the cattle. Several of our bulls service ranches nationwide."

"Your bulls service ranches? What does that mean?"

"Service, the term we use for mating. We sell the semen in what's called straws. It's a major part of our ranch income."

"Goodness, seems ranching has as much jargon as the military."

Chase laughed at that. "You're probably right. Getting back to your horse, can you bridle and saddle?"

"I used to know how to bridle; saddle, no. I rode a neighbor's horse when I was ten. Haven't ridden since. He never allowed me to saddle the horses." Then it dawned on me. Chase said the horse had picked me. I looked at the velvety palomino with delight. "I get to ride this horse? What's her name?"

"Sandy. She's one of our best cow horses, though a bit wild. I'm not sure you'll be able to handle her, but she certainly has taken a liking to you."

"Don't be so surprised. Animals sense things people can't." I stroked Sandy's long soft neck. "You know a kind-hearted lady when you see her, don't you, Sandy?"

# Chapter 8

## Sally

You saw me before I was born. Every day of my life was
recorded in your book. Every moment was laid out
before a single day had passed. Psalms 139:16

My phone alarm sounded at five a.m. as usual. I rolled
out of bed, disoriented by the strange surroundings. Oh
yeah, I'm in the middle of Montana about to embark on
an adventure that will determine the course of my future.

I made a quick trip to the bathroom down the hall, then slipped
on my sweats and tennies to go for a run—a habit from my Marine
Corps days I had held onto. Now more than ever I needed the quiet
of my morning run to do some deep thinking and talking with God.
The grandiose surroundings overwhelmed me, and I needed some
hugs from God. I chose Psalm 139 for my morning Scripture reading.
Knowing God was with me wherever I might be brought some
encouragement and confidence to face the day. I laid my Bible on the
nightstand and then made my way downstairs.

As I descended the stairs, I heard muffled female voices coming
from the rear of the house. Probably people having breakfast. I slipped
out the front door and surveyed my running options. The ranch house,
facing west, stood on the crest of a hill. The stunning 360-degree view

captured my attention. To the west, the Rocky Mountains, commanding and formidable, but less attractive than the Bavarian Alps. To the east, a rolling landscape of prairie grass and bluffs. Behind the house, the approaching sun cast the sky a light gray with tinges of pink, tempting me to perch on the corral fence and watch the glorious sunrise yet to come. Down the hill from the house, lamp light shone from the windows of what I presumed to be a bunkhouse. The noise of the horses neighing in the barn confirmed that many others had already risen and started the daily chores.

The blacktop driveway that led to the county gravel road promised the best path for my run. I jogged down off the porch, lost in thought before I reached the last step.

Last night's barbecue had been enlightening to say the least. Four introduced me to his three other brothers but said issues at the magazine had prevented his two sisters from attending. They were to be here today. The Reynolds brothers were handsome, well-mannered young men. The rough life of ranching aged them each differently, and I wasn't sure how old any of them were except for twenty-four-year-old identical twins Gabe and Peter. If any of these young men held animosity toward me, they kept it well hidden. Chase behaved like a cold mackerel most of the night, except for that moment in the barn. Was cold mackerel his usual personality?

All the testosterone around me reminded me of my single status. Single nothing—old maid described me best. Too busy working my way up the publishing ladder. Now even that, too, was gone. Whether Jen and I started a business or not, I now faced starting over.

A semi lumbered by on the gravel road, jerking my thoughts back to the moment. It was a wonder I hadn't run right out onto the road and offered myself as the trucker's first roadkill of the day. That would have made Chase happy. I envisioned him hoisting my mangled body onto that electric spit and eating me for dinner.

I made a U-ie and headed back up the drive. Atop the hill, back lit by the blazing orange rim of sunrise, the Reynolds' estate commanded my view. Solid and impervious, like a guard at Buckingham Palace, daring the world to knock it over. In dying, Chase Reynolds, Jr. had thrust me into this foreign world. I'd seen my share of hostility and foreign cultures during my time in the Corps. Hardship I understood. Time in a saddle I could endure. After the backbiting of office politics in Kansas City, I welcomed the solitude of the prairie with the crickets and cows to lull me to sleep. But nothing in my life had prepared me for this world of wealth and the power it no doubt wielded.

Ten yards from the house, I stopped short. A sea of emotions washed over me. Overwhelm. Doubt. Insignificance. Defeat. I felt like an ant invading a palace banquet. What crazy impulse had overtaken me that day at the office? But I'd been bucking the odds all my life, first through my adoptive-dad's verbal abuse, then as a woman Marine, and then with a new career at the age of thirty-eight. I'd done it before, I could do it now. I took a deep cleansing breath and sprinted the last ten yards to the porch.

I noticed more signs of activity at what I suspected was the bunkhouse and more lights on in windows of the house. I decided against running another mile. Instead, I returned to my room, gathered my toiletries, took a quick shower, and dressed. I descended the stairs and wandered the first floor looking for the kitchen. I finally spotted Chase sitting alone in a dining room at a large table set for four.

"Good morning, Ms. Clark. Glad to see you made it on time for breakfast," he said, a hint of a smile on his lips.

I glanced at my watch, 6:15. "Thank you. I see you are just as rude in the morning as you are in the evening." Something about him pulled the smart remarks from me with the glee a dentist must feel pulling teeth. "Is everyone else late?"

"No, they're out in the barn. One of our mares foaled in the night. But it was rough; we may lose both of them."

That explained the dark circles under his eyes and maybe some of his rudeness. "I'm sorry to hear that." I poured myself a cup of coffee from the carafe on the sideboard that stood behind him. The scents of horse and hay from Chase enticed me more than the smell of the coffee. I'd better take the seat farthest from him or I might find myself leaning toward him to breathe in his earthy scent. In all his aloofness at our first meeting, I had failed to note his rugged handsomeness. Eyes the color of bronze—a first for me to experience. Dark brown wavy hair, graying at the temples. At least six feet tall, fit and trim, no doubt due to the rigors of ranch life. I never found it difficult to admire a handsome man, but that's where it ended. I learned the hard way men wanted only one thing from me.

As I turned from the sideboard, a painting on the opposite wall caught my eye. My mug of coffee dropped from my hand, the mug shattering and coffee splashing across the hardwood floor. Shock riveted my new cowboy boots to the floor. My eyes must have been as big as saucers. There on the wall hung a portrait of…me.

Chase's strong grip on my shoulders brought me to my senses. "Ms. Clark." He shook me gently. "Ms. Clark, are you all right?"

"I…that…why is there a portrait of me on your wall?" I'm on his wall!

Chase turned, following my gaze to the painting on the wall behind him. "Buffalo chips! I forgot that was there."

I pulled my eyes away from the picture and blinked to bring Chase into focus. A servant already busied herself wiping up the mess at our feet.

"Come take a seat," he said and led me to the chair beside his. He grabbed a clean cup, poured some coffee, and handed it to me. "Drink this while I explain."

I took the cup from him and sipped the steaming brew. Is that why he looked so ghostly the day we met? Had my appearance been as much a shock to him as that picture had been to me? People last night had said I looked like Abby, but I shrugged it off. Nothing had prepared me for such an astounding likeness.

Chase sat down in the chair next to me and draped his arm across the back of my chair. My eyes flitted between him and the picture. I had walked into the *Twilight Zone*, but with the proximity of his warm body to mine, it felt more like *Pride and Prejudice*.

"I meant to tell you last night—"

"Really?" Not the smart comeback I was hoping for, but give me a break, I was still in shock.

"Yes, really. The moment just never presented itself. That's Abby, my sister."

I nearly dropped my coffee again. "Four mentioned our likeness last night, and how I sounded like her, but…we could be identical twins! Am I your father's illegitimate child?"

"No!…I…no." He dropped his arm from my chair, leaned back, and shook his head.

"You don't sound very convinced." I took a gulp of coffee, almost oblivious to the burn I felt as I swallowed. I examined his eyes. I could see his doubt. I took a deep breath and plunged forward, glad I could no longer feel the heat emanating from his arm that had been so near my shoulders. "I've heard of doppelgangers, but this is uncanny. I looked just like that at twenty-five."

"If it's any consolation, Abby and I found out by surprise, too. Karl told Abby and me the week after we buried my father that she's adopted." He grabbed the carafe of coffee and refilled his cup, then sat down again. "That's the most any of us knows. But I can't believe Pop would have an affair, much less father a child and then not support it."

"Mr. Reynolds, I…well…that puts a different spin on your rudeness." I determined to keep my smart mouth under control. "I was adopted, but my adoptive mom died when I was ten. Maybe I am your dad's illegitimate child and he was only willing to make it right by one of us. Maybe that's why he willed me what he did, to assuage his guilty conscience." A thousand thoughts raced through my head. Anger churned in my gut. Chase had said they were a family of longstanding Christian heritage. Chase Reynolds, Jr. wasn't anymore Christian than my Christian adoptive father who became a verbally abusive drunk after my mother died. I was convinced Chase Reynolds, Jr. had adulterously sired twins, but embraced only one.

"Why is it people who claim to be Christians are the worst hypocrites I know? You've been like a cold fish since we met in Kansas City. And you and your lawyer have been keeping secrets from me from Day 1."

I bolted from my chair and put as much space between us as I could without leaving the room.

"Secrets? I just forgot to tell you."

"And why didn't you tell me during supper the day we met in Kansas City? Why did your lawyer's letter say I'd received an inheritance but fail to tell me anything about it, let alone the condition tied to it? Am I here long enough for someone to swipe my toothbrush and test my DNA? Will I be refused everything if I'm not related by blood?" I banged my now-empty cup of coffee onto the table and paced the floor, hoping to release my angry energy. Chase sat dumbfounded, glued to his chair. A fleeting look of grief crossed his eyes.

"I apologize, Ms. Clark...Sally. I've handled this whole situation inappropriately. Pop's death was sudden. His will blindsided me...all of us, and then we learned Abby was adopted and might have a twin sister. It's been a lot to take in." He took a long drink of his coffee and seemed to ponder his next words. "Pop was one of the most godly men I know. He told Karl he wasn't Abby's father, and I don't believe for a moment that he adulterously sired you and Abby, and lied about it. I have no secrets and no intention of testing your DNA." He sighed deeply, ran his fingers through his hair, then continued. "I had no idea Karl was anything less than forthcoming about Pop's will. I'll speak to him. I apologize for it all, including my rudeness." He offered a weak smile.

I met his gaze but couldn't read the thoughts behind his eyes. "Apology accepted." I noted a pinkness creeping into his checks, but he held his lock on my eyes.

"What have your kids been told about me? How did you explain the striking resemblance?"

"We told them the truth, that Abby is adopted, and that you could be a twin sister."

The entrance of a maid with a plateful of pancakes diverted our attention.

"Looks marvelous, Rita. Thank you," Chase said, getting up to fix his plate at the sideboard.

"Chase," said Jake Bonner, the ranch foreman, as he entered from the patio door that led to the back yard. "Doc has the mare back on her feet and the foal nursing." He poured himself a cup of coffee and sat down at an empty place at the table. I silently welcomed his entrance. It offered a change in the subject and time for me to think.

"That's great. Has he left already?" Chase asked. Relief washed over his face. Relief about the horse or relief that something offered him a chance to escape me?

"No, he's still out in the barn."

Chase put his still empty plate back on the table. "Excuse me, Sally. I want to grab the vet for a moment before he leaves." And he was out the door.

I turned to Jake. "I heard about the trouble. I'm glad both horses are going to make it."

Jake pulled off his cowboy hat, wiped his brow with his forearm, and hung his hat on the back of his chair. "So are we. That mare's produced a lot of good horse flesh for us. It'd be a shame to lose her."

I heard the front door open and shut, the muffled voices of two women, and the click click of high heels across the hardwood floor. "Daddy?" one of them yelled.

"He's out in the barn, Leslie," Jake hollered to the bodiless voice.

"Is that Clark woman here yet?" A tall slinky young thing entered the room as she spoke. She stopped short when she spotted me. A younger, shorter brunette followed her, their mouths agape. Good thing they weren't holding a cup of coffee.

"Now, Leslie, be nice," Jake said, getting up from the table and giving her a quick kiss on the lips. She returned the peck. Leslie possessed every aspect of beauty I lacked. Her coffee-brown Ralph Lauren jersey dress hugged curvaceous hips. Wavy auburn tresses bounced around her perky, more-than-adequate bosom, and the V-neck of her dress showed her full cleavage to best advantage. She was Aphrodite to Jake's Adonis. She was everything I had once tried to be and failed.

Jake lingered at Leslie's side, his arm curved around her hips. I took a fast look at her left hand. She wore a large diamond ring and corresponding wedding band. Hmmm, must be husband and wife.

"Morning, Emily," he said, releasing his hold on Leslie's hips and giving Emily a friendly peck on the cheek. He turned to me. "Sally, this is Leslie and Emily," pointing to each, "Chase's daughters."

"It's nice to meet you, Ms. Clark," Emily said, smiling sincerely.

"Please, call me Sally. I'm glad you meet you, too."

"Humph," grumbled Leslie. She grabbed a plate from the table and went to the sideboard. Plate filled and at the table, she gave me the once over. What had I done to her to rate this hostility? Then I remembered, I got Leslie's percentage of the magazine.

"I must say, you're older than I expected."

"Leslie!" admonished Emily.

A snide remark wanted to escape, but I bit my tongue. This was the Leslie who had failed to get me from the airport last night. "Will you be spending the day here?" I asked. Dressed as she was, the answer seemed obvious, but I felt driven to converse.

"No, I have a magazine to run—"

"And you intend to keep it that way. I don't blame you, Ms. Reynolds. I would probably feel the same way if a total stranger got what I believed was mine."

The men of the Reynolds clan began filtering into the room and the ordeal of the night commanded the conversation. I finished my coffee and managed some scrambled eggs and hash browns, then snuck out to the barn to see the new foal and to regroup.

As I entered the barn, the earthy scents of the leather, hay, and horse again tickled my childhood riding memories. Mr. Campbell's barn, my sanctuary when Dad was drunk. Dad? My adoptive father, and he never let me forget that it was only to placate my mother that he ever agreed to my adoption. I shook my head to cast his memory aside and sought out Sandy's stall. When I approached, she whinnied and nodded her head as if to say good morning. I began to think Chase lied about her disliking strangers.

What a morning, and it was only 7:30. "Hey, Sandy. At least you're happy I'm here." She nickered and nodded her head again. Like always, I had jumped into the deep end. I'd quit my job in a fit of frustration, thinking I'd just inherited a fortune. Remember, Sally, I scolded myself, if it looks too good to be true, it probably is. The Reynolds' ranch and mansion proved a fortune existed, but I had to spend four weeks in this semi-hostile environment to gain the inheritance. But then why should this be any different than the rest of my life? I did all I could to prove I was worth Dad's love. I worked my buns off in the Corps to prove my worth. Now here I was again, having to prove myself.

Mr. Pendrake came to mind. I smiled at his memory. He was the only man I'd ever met who loved me for who I was. Not a man-woman kind of love, but a godly, fatherly love, the *agape* love the Bible talks about. I'd never known a better man—the father I wished I'd had. He looked beyond my age and saw past the hard edges and cynicism fifteen years in the Marine Corps had carved into my personality. He and his wife had become my mentors.

*I saw you before you were born. Every day of your life was recorded in my book. Every moment was laid out before a single day had passed,* the Holy Spirit whispered to my spirit.

"Father, Your love for me touches every page of the Bible. In my head, I know You love me. Why can't I ever feel the depth of that love in my spirit?" I glanced around, hoping no one had heard my brief words of prayer.

Sandy nudged my shoulder; she seemed to sense my dejection. I stroked her neck as best I could over the stall gate. "You're right, girl. I'm thinking negatively. I'll be right back. I'm gonna go greet the new little one."

# Chapter 9

## Chase

*People with integrity walk safely, but those who follow*
*crooked paths will slip and fall. Proverbs 10:9*

"I don't know about the rest of you, but I'm not allowing this Clark woman to steal my inheritance," my daughter Leslie said as I entered the dining room for the second time that morning.

"*Your* inheritance? It was never that, so exactly what do you mean?" I asked. Leslie jumped, startled at my appearance. Her face looked guilty, as though she hadn't intended for me to hear what she'd just said.

"Daddy, that 10 percent of the magazine should be mine, not that woman's."

Only Leslie called me Daddy. To the rest of the kids, I was Pop, just like my father had been to me. They called their grandfather Poppie to avoid any confusion between the two of us. "Leslie, did Poppie ever tell you the magazine would be yours?" I asked her.

"No." She pursed her lips into a pout. Her spoiled-brat behavior struck me again as it had at the reading of Pop's will.

"But he always told me how proud and glad he was when I took over as managing editor. Poppie started the magazine; Emily and I have worked there before, during, and after college. We deserve it."

"But, Leslie—" Emily tried to protest.

"But nothing!" Leslie yelled, rising from her place at the table so abruptly she knocked her chair over doing it. Her face reddened with anger as she picked up the chair and shoved it under the table. I had never seen her that upset except as a two- and three-year-old.

"Calm down," I said. "An inheritance isn't about who deserves what. And you will treat Ms. Clark with the same respect we treat everyone."

"Respect? She's a thief and the daughter of a killer."

"What?" resounded from several in the room, including me.

"Her father's a con artist and serving a life sentence for murder."

"That doesn't make her a thief," Peter said.

"She's been arrested three times for theft." Leslie walked over to Abby's picture and stood staring up at it.

"How do you know all this?" Michael asked before I could.

She turned to face the group seated at the dining table. The redness drained from her cheeks. "I did my own investigating. What was Poppie thinking? Did her resemblance to Aunt Abby cloud his judgment?"

Things just kept getting worse and worse. "You let me take care of any investigating that needs done." I scanned the room. Emotions ranged from calm to grief to rage. "I'm saying this to all of you. You will treat Ms. Clark politely. And nothing said here this morning is to leave this room. Now, everybody, as soon as you're finished with breakfast, go about your business for the day."

The boys rose from the table and shuffled out the patio door toward the barn. Jake pulled Leslie to a corner of the room. They stood talking in whispers. Leslie, my first born, commanding and confident in everything she took on, but headstrong. A lot like me in too many ways.

"Pop, it'll be okay," Emily said. She gave me a teddy-bear squeeze and reassuring smile and then began to clear the table. Most of the plates were still topped with food. Apparently everyone had lost their appetite.

Four approached me and pulled me toward the other side of the room, away from Jake and Leslie.

"Pop, remember, what you just said applies to you, too."

"What do you mean? Of course, I'm going to go about my business for the day."

"I was referring to treating Ms. Clark with respect." Four paused, his eyebrows raised as he looked at me. "I've never seen you be rude to anyone. But last night you were terribly rude to her. All night. What gives?"

"I don't know," I said, shaking my head. "I'll be seeking God for an answer to that, but the situation has been remedied. Ms. Clark called me on the carpet already this morning while you were all out in the barn."

"This has been hard on us all, but I can't imagine what it's been like for you. First Poppie's death. Then Poppie willing a portion of the estate to a total stranger. Then learning Aunt Abby is adopted and that the total stranger is identical to Aunt Abby." Four searched my eyes for understanding. "We all do weird things when we're grieving."

"How'd you get to be so wise? If you see me misbehaving again, bring it to my attention." I patted Four's shoulder, then gave it a reassuring squeeze. "I love you, son. I'll be in my office if anyone wants me."

Four smiled, nodded his head, and left for the barn. I walked over to Emily and gave her a kiss on the forehead.

"Thanks, hon, for helping clean up in here." I glanced over at Leslie and Jake still conversing. I hoped Jake could talk some sense into her, but neither looked very happy.

Questions bombarded me as I walked to my office at the far south end of the house. I had missed my quiet time with God because of attending the foal's difficult birth.

For a long quiet moment I stood looking out over the prairie of the family ranch. Golden rolling hills stretched for miles, dotted by our black Angus as they grazed. Great-great-granddad had started the ranch with longhorn cattle. The family made the switch to Angus when Pop took over. I drew in a deep breath, thankful the ranch was still in family hands, then turned and sat down at my desk. My wife's picture stared up at me. Her hazel eyes sparkled, and the cool morning breeze from the window behind me seemed to tousle her flowing auburn hair across her face.

"Karen, I miss you. You'd know how to handle Leslie. Put in a good word for her up there, will you?" Five excruciating years had passed since Karen's death. Would the ache ever go away?

An image of Sally came unbidden to my mind. What a stark difference between Karen and Sally. Physically as opposite as Yin and Yang. But, as I was learning, they both possessed the same fiery spirit, facing life's challenges with grit and determination. Guilt gnawed at my gut. Where was that coming from?

*You've treated Sally with contempt.*

"Contempt, Lord? I've been rude, yes, and I apologized. I repent and apologize to You now. But I haven't despised her." I waited to hear Holy Spirit's response, but only silence met me.

I shook Sally's visage from my mind and turned to the task at hand. I pulled some paper and a pencil from the desk drawer and jotted down Leslie's tidbits of info. Should I talk to Karl or simply confront Sally about it? I grabbed the phone and dialed Karl's number.

"Hello," Karl answered.

"Karl, Leslie confronted us with some unnerving facts about Sally this morning. I need you to find out what's true, if you can."

"Okay. Shoot."

"Her arrest record and whether or not her father is in prison."

"If you'd read my file, you'd know she has no record."

"I know, I know, I should have read the file. But Leslie apparently did some investigating on her own. She says Ms. Clark has been arrested three times for theft. Can you look into that? And what about her father? Was there anything in the file on him?"

"What does her father have to do with anything?" Karl asked.

"Yeah, that's pretty much what Pete said too. I just want to know, okay?"

"I'll look into it, but it wouldn't hurt to get Sally's side of the story, if you haven't already."

"No, I haven't. Sally did mention something this morning that concerned me. Said your letter had been…less than forthcoming. Was there a particular reason you didn't say what the inheritance was and list the conditions in the letter you sent her?"

"I felt it would come across like a scam." Karl paused and I could see him in my mind's eye pinching the bridge of his nose like he often did. "Given her initial words at our meeting in Kansas City, seems no matter what I said, she would have viewed it as a scam."

"You're probably right about that. She strikes me as very bitter. If the moment presents itself, I might ask her why that is. The next four week's present a wild ride. I might have to brush up on my bronco skills."

Karl laughed. "Give her time."

"I will. For now, let me know what you find out about her dad and Leslie's claims, okay?"

"All right."

I hung up the phone and went in search of Sally. Her bedroom door was wide open and the room empty. The dining room was also empty. I headed for the barn.

I found her leaning against the rails of Midnight's stall, observing the new foal. "Sally, I'd like to talk to you for a minute," I said as I approached her from behind.

"The foal is beautiful, and so lively. Hard to believe he nearly died," she said as she watched the foal frolic in the stall with his mother. I smiled down at her. The royal blue of her long-sleeve western shirt made her eyes sparkle. Or maybe the smile emanating from them accomplished that.

"Let's go somewhere a bit more private," I said, even though the barn appeared empty. I didn't want to risk someone overhearing the conversation.

"Sounds serious. Am I late again?" she asked.

"Late again?" I thought briefly about what she could mean, then it dawned on me and I snickered. "I was only joking this morning, and last night, I was concerned about your safety."

"You're a hard man to read. The way you sound, I just figured I did something else wrong," she explained.

"No, nothing's wrong. It's just a conversation no one else needs to hear." I led the way out of the barn and over to an empty corral. I pushed my Stetson up off my brow and looked down at her, observing her fresh-off-the-rack clothing. "I see you do have appropriate clothes and boots."

"Yeah, like I told Jake last night, I'm not a greenhorn."

"How many pairs of jeans and shirts did you bring? I can drive you into town to purchase more if need be."

"I've got four pair of jeans and about ten shirts. I assumed I'd be able to do laundry a few times during the next four weeks."

"Of course. That should do you. Let me know what you spent. I'll reimburse you. In the meantime, some unpleasant news about your background has come to light. I'd like to hear it from you."

"Could you be anymore vague?"

"Your father?"

"He's in prison for murder if that's what you mean. What bearing does that have on me?"

"None. All the same, I'm sorry to hear that's true. It must be hard on you."

"No. He's only my adoptive father, and he spent my childhood making that point abundantly clear. He never wanted me. Said he gave in to my mom's desire for a child. He went to prison after I joined the Marine Corps. I don't know the details of the crime, just that he was convicted of murdering his business partner." She sighed and took a seat on the corral fence. Maybe she felt the added height gave her an edge over me now that I had to look up to meet her eyes.

"I'm sorry. I can't imagine growing up unloved and unwanted."

"My mom loved me very much. After she was gone, I held on to my memories of her. It helped."

"All the same, it explains some of your cynicism."

"Don't try to psychoanalyze me. Anything else you need to know?" she said, looking down.

"Is it true you were arrested three times for theft?"

"What?" she exclaimed, dropping from the fence, hands on her hips, and her face red with outrage. "Did you bribe the police chief in Scottsbluff to release my sealed juvenile record?"

"No!" I hollered back at her. "What's with you? First you accuse us of scamming you, now I'm bribing the police. Why do you jump to the worst conclusions?"

She dropped her arms to her side, took a few halting steps toward the barn and then turned back to me. A quizzical expression creased her brow. "Because that's what life doles out. I sensed resistance from you the moment I met you at the restaurant in Kansas City. I got more last night during supper, and not just from you."

Her resemblance to Abby struck me and for a brief moment I leaned toward her, my arms willing me to hug and comfort Sally as I did Abby whenever she hurt. Sally's words revealed she'd experienced more than her fair share of heartache. As much as I wanted to comfort her, instead I turned away and leaned over on the fence railing. This woman is not your little sister. Hugging her just now would not be a smart move.

Abby brought sunshine wherever she went. Her goodness drew out the best people had to give. But Sally? She seemed to expect the worst, and…that's what I had been giving her. I turned back to face her. She stood tall and proud, as if she was back in the Marine Corps being reprimanded by her commanding officer. With her scrappy attitude I wondered how often that might have happened.

"Sally, I apologize, again. I've been putting my foot in my mouth since this situation began."

Her postured relaxed a bit. My apology must have surprised her.

"Yes, I got into my share of trouble as a teen," she said. "It was my way of dealing with my father's alcoholism and verbal abuse. My senior year, I got caught shoplifting for a third time. The judge sentenced me to jail. As I sat in court waiting for my case, I listened to the sentences he handed out to the others in front of me. He offered one guy a choice, jail or the military. I asked him why I couldn't have that same choice. That's how I ended up in the Marine Corps."

If a gene for pluckiness existed, she had it.

"You questioned the judge about his ruling? That took courage…or stupidity. It obviously impressed him." I chuckled and shook my head. The frustration I felt drained away and pity took it's place.

71

"I don't want your pity. I don't need your pity."

Were my feelings that obvious?

"I just want fair and decent treatment for the next four weeks. What happens after that is anybody's guess."

"Hey, Sal," someone hollered. We turned our attention toward the voice. Gabe stood waiting in the barn. "I've been lookin' all over for you. It's time for horse lessons."

"Any more questions?" Sally asked.

"No." I nodded toward Gabe. "Better get at it. We hit the trail on Monday."

"Hit the trail?"

"We'll be rounding up several herds to move them to different pastures before winter sets in."

"What does that entail?"

"About ten days out on the prairie, in the saddle, sleeping on the ground. It'll be a lot like it was in my granddad's day."

"Okay, thanks," she said. She jogged the ten yards to the barn, and she and Gabe disappeared inside.

I headed back toward the house in search of Leslie. I hoped she hadn't gone back into town. She certainly hadn't dressed for working at the ranch for the day. I found her at the tennis court, practicing her backhand volley against the machine. How had she learned about Sally's juvenile record? I bristled at the thought that she had bribed someone. I thought I raised my children to know better. Still her pouty behavior at the breakfast table this morning shocked me. With me at the ranch year-round and her in town running the magazine, our lives had grown apart.

I remembered Karl saying Pop had made the change in his will just six months ago. Had he witnessed something in Leslie's behavior or attitude that prompted him to not give her a portion of the magazine? Had he witnessed the kind of behavior I was just now noticing?

"Leslie!" I headed to the machine and shut it off.

"Hi, Daddy."

"I want to talk to you." We walked over the bench at the side of the court and sat down. "Your behavior this morning disturbed me very much."

"Daddy, I'm only trying to protect what rightfully belongs to the family."

"How did you find out about Sa—Ms. Clark's arrests?"

"On the Internet. All for the low price of $12.95."

"Don't be smart." I stood and looked down at her. Her Gucci sunglasses hindered my view of her eyes. "Sealed records are sealed for a reason. They're not available for $12.95 or any other price. This is a person's life you're playing with, not your doll's."

"I'm not playing, Daddy. This Aunt-Abby-look-alike duped Poppie somehow, and I intend to make it right." She stood and took a few steps away from me.

"Retract those claws, young lady, and change your attitude. She did not dupe Poppie. This inheritance came as much of a surprise to her as it did to us." Leslie's catty behavior left a bitter taste in my mouth. "It's business as usual while she's here. No more investigating and no more disrespect."

"About business as usual. I've decided to join the roundup."

"Leslie, how—I've never seen you so upset about anything." I sighed. "Remember, Ms. Clark will be here four weeks. If she doesn't complete those four weeks, her share of the magazine goes to you. Remember as well, that when Miss Clark dies, her share reverts to the family. We're not losing anything permanently." I was immediately sorry I spoke those words, but I hoped they would calm Leslie's fears. It did. I saw the tension in her body release. I felt distinctly uncomfortable talking about Sally dying.

"When she dies it all comes back to us. I forgot about that. It does make me feel better, but I still want to observe her."

I removed her visor and kissed her forehead. "As long as you're nice."

"Yes, Daddy." She smiled at me and jogged back onto the court.

Leslie had a short fuse. She held the county record for temper tantrums as a three-year-old. She'd learned to control them as she grew, but stress sometimes got the better of her. Was this childish, selfish behavior what brought about Pop's decision?

I made my way back to the house. Now I would have two pigheaded women to watch out for during the roundup. What a miserable ten days this could turn out to be.

# Chapter 10

## Sally

Keep me safe, O God, for I have come to you for refuge.
Psalms 16:1

How had Chase Reynolds found out about my juvenile record? How much or how little did he really know about me? I would have to think about that later. Right now, Gabe, or was he Peter, commanded my attention. I jogged toward the barn where he stood waiting.

"Everything okay?" he asked. "Things looked a little intense out there."

"Just discussing a bit of family history. Are you Peter or Gabe?"

"Gabe. I wear a brown hat; Pete's is cream." Twins Gabe and Peter, two blonds in a family of brunettes, sported stunning glacier blue eyes. They were numbers four and five in the sibling chain, with the easy-going personality to match their birth order. Like Four, they treated me as a welcome guest.

"Pop's asked me to show you how to groom, saddle, and bridle Sandy. After that, it's a lesson in roping."

He led the way to the tack room where he handed me some brushes and a bridle and then lifted a saddle from a sawhorse.

"First thing you want to do before you saddle any horse is to make sure she's clean. Any dirt in her coat will be like gravel on her skin when you saddle her," he said as we walked to Sandy's stall. "Hang her bridle on that nail," he said, tilting his chin up toward a nail in the post. He placed her saddle on the stall gate, then opened the gate and led the way in.

He handed me one brush after another as he showed me how to first curry and brush her before saddling her. "I've never seen Sandy so receptive. She won't let Leslie close enough to even offer an apple." He reached out a hand and stroked Sandy's forehead with the back of his fingers.

I reached for her saddle but failed in my attempt to pick it up. I hadn't expected it to be so heavy. "Wow, how heavy is this thing?"

"Around thirty or forty pounds. Never weighed it. Will that be a problem?"

"I'm not used to picking up that kind of weight. If I was lifting it to carry, I'd be fine. But I'm not so sure about lifting it up to Sandy's back."

"I'll show you a trick that should help." He showed me how to use my knee to boost the saddle up and then lay it down on the saddle blanket rather than allowing it to drop roughly onto her back. Not an easy task for short people like me. As I stood next to Sandy my eyes were level with her back. I stood 5'5" tall. How tall did that make Sandy?

Sandy skittered a bit as I made my first attempt and failed. She showed amazing patience with me as I made a second attempt.

"Third time's a charm," Gabe encouraged me. I smiled at him, positioned the saddle against my knee and hoisted the saddle up and onto Sandy's back. Gabe was an apt teacher and didn't make me feel like some idiot city slicker at a dude ranch, even though that's exactly how I did feel. He explained the importance of making the girth tight, but not too tight, and then showed me how to tighten it and test it.

"Once you've saddled her enough times, you'll get the feel of it."

As the morning wore on, we laughed and talked as if we'd known each other all our lives. Maybe he was interacting with his aunt Abby instead of me. It didn't matter. I concentrated on his instructions and relished being on a horse again.

As we finished the morning, he explained the roundup.

"We'll spend several days rounding up our herds. We pasture several herds in different places during the summer, but for winter we move them all to one pasture that makes winter tending easier. You'll probably be very sore for the next several days. Remind me and I'll give you a bottle of pain killer to help get you through."

"Thanks. I appreciate that."

When it was time for lunch, Gabe showed me how to first look after Sandy before we walked up to the house to eat.

The servants had set out food on the sideboard again, and everyone wandered in and ate as they had a chance. Leslie attempted a stare down, but I refused to play. She had shed her Ralph Lauren attire and donned a tennis outfit. She spoke only to her siblings. Fine by me.

When Chase entered the dining room, Gabe bragged to him about how quickly I learned. I felt my cheeks grow hot as Chase stared at me. I couldn't read the look in his eyes and that frustrated me. As an MP I learned to read body language and a person's eyes. I utilized those skills daily and they had served me well. Why couldn't I read him?

I looked over at Gabe, hoping to force Chase to look at someone besides me. "That's only because you're a good teacher, Gabe." I glanced back at Chase still staring at me. Is that how he looks at cows he's about to slaughter? I squirmed a bit in my chair. Would I always feel like the cow to be culled from the herd?

"I seem to have met all the family except Abby. Where is she?"

"She's in Michigan, checking out a new printer for the magazine. She'll be back in a few days," Chase explained.

"I'm excited to meet her, though a bit nervous, too. I imagine she feels the same. It isn't every day you discover you have an identical twin, by birth or not." I looked up at her picture on the wall. Our resemblance was uncanny. I couldn't imagine we were anything but true twins. Would it be wrong for me to request a DNA test? A gnawing desire to know for sure had sprouted.

Everyone remained silent, focused on eating. I decided to be done with lunch. "I'll meet you back at the barn, Gabe. I'm going to tell the cook thank you for my lunch." I rose from my chair and left the room.

"I thought she'd never finish," I heard Leslie hiss as I rounded the corner to the kitchen. The temptation to eavesdrop on their conversation entered my mind. In that moment of hesitation I heard Chase's response, "I warned you this morning about your rudeness."

I licked my finger and made an imaginary score mark in the air. Sally 1, Leslie 0.

Sunday morning the family went to church. I stayed behind to soak my already sore muscles in a hot bath. Thankfully, my daily three-mile run kept me fit, but my arms and shoulders burned like fire. I'd spent a good deal of Saturday learning riding and handling techniques, then how to rope a cow. My arms were doing most of the work.

Gabe also instructed me on how to handle the cattle during the roundup. Oddly enough, I looked forward to this activity. I hoped the tense atmosphere so apparent in the house would dissipate out on the range. Wishful thinking?

After my soak, I meandered to the barn, the one place I felt truly welcome. Several horses I'd never seen now occupied the corral. Sandy was in her stall.

"Hi, Sandy. The action starts tomorrow. Are you ready?"

She whinnied. I brushed her down, then visited the new mother and her foal. I could get used to this. What was life on the ranch like during a normal day? The place was a beehive of activity. Was this the norm or were they doing extra in preparation for the roundup? How much of the life of a cowboy had really changed in the last 150 years?

I decided to call Jen. With the one-hour time difference, I knew they'd be out of church by now.

"Sally, hello!"

"Hi, Jen. Thought I'd give you a call while the family isn't around to eavesdrop."

I heard her scoff. "Are things that bad?"

"No, mostly it's the oldest daughter. I got her percentage of the magazine. I think she feels robbed."

"Ouch! I can imagine. So tell me all about the place."

"The magnificent Rockies to the west, green rolling hills to the east. The silence! The ranch is about fifteen, twenty miles outside of Great Falls. I am definitely a country person, Jen. No traffic noise, no sirens, no screaming neighbors. And no Mr. Snyder."

"Best benefit of all." She laughed. "What's the family like?"

I told her about the six children and Chase. "Chase the fourth is the first son, but second born. They call him Four. He's been really nice. In fact, all the kids have been nice except for Leslie. She is so different from the others. Hard to believe she's from the same gene pool."

"So what have things been like so far?"

"They kick off harvest season with a big barbecue. Friday when I arrived, they had roasted a side of beef over an open fire. Delicious. I spent yesterday on a horse, learning stuff. I'm already sore. I should have brought a bottle of ibuprofen. I expect I'll be plenty sore for several days."

"John's had time to look through the details in the will. He found the stipulations a bit odd, but nothing that warrants concern."

"Odd isn't the word for it. Chase's sister is a dead ringer for me. I think we might be twins. During the barbecue Friday night, several mentioned how similar we looked. But when I spotted her portrait on the wall…Jen, I'm not kidding. We could pass for identical twins."

"Oh my goodness. I bet that was a shock."

"I dropped my cup of coffee when I saw her portrait. I still haven't met her; she's out of town."

"Do you think they have hidden stipulations to all this? Are they asking for a DNA test?"

"No, I did ask about that. Chase said he has no intention of doing a DNA test. Turns out Chase's sister, Abby, the lady I look like, was adopted. But he's also convinced that his dad didn't father either of us through an affair. Strange though. If we are twins, why did the man adopt only one of us? Mom told me I was adopted, but never mentioned a twin. I've told you Dad always made it clear he didn't want kids. I wonder if he said no to twins and forced Mom to adopt only one of us? That would explain why Mr. Reynolds adopted only Abby."

"That's all water under the bridge, as they say. You're God's child, and He's been looking out for you, even if it doesn't seem that way to you. Trust in Him." Jen always had an encouraging word for me.

"I do trust God. Lately it's been tough."

"No matter how all this turns out, God will lead the way as long as you seek His guidance. You know that. Pray in the Spirit and listen for His voice," Jen advised me.

"You're right. Deep down I know all that, but the devil is working hard to convince me otherwise. Pray for me, every day. The next several days I'll spend ten or so hours a day in the saddle. And I'll be sleeping under the stars."

"Hey, you're a Marine, you can handle it. And if that Marine Corps discipline fails, remember you can do all things through Christ who strengthens you."

I took a deep breath and let it out slowly as Jen prayed for me and we hung up.

I had my head in places it didn't belong. God had opened an amazing door, but I had allowed Leslie's barbs to penetrate my spirit. Keep your eyes on Jesus, Sally. If all this goes south, you still have your friends and apartment in Kansas City and the potential to start your own company with Jen. I pocketed my cell and walked back to the house. The sun warmed my face and a cool breeze caressed my arms. I reached the house in time to greet Chase and the twins as they returned from church.

"Feeling better after your soak in the tub?" Chase asked as I approached him in the driveway.

"Yes, thank you. I'm going to be sore in places I haven't noticed since I was in boot camp. Is there anything I need to prepare today? Am I going to have to wear the same pants and shirt for the next ten days?"

"Of course not. You'll have only saddlebags, though, so pack as light as possible. Roll your clothes, instead of folding them. And there are some things you need to be aware of," Chase said as we all walked to the front door.

"And those are?"

"Safety."

I gave him a questioning look.

"Much of Montana is habitat to the prairie rattlesnake, and they'll be looking for a warm place at night. So, keep your blanket rolled until you're ready to climb in. Once we've camped for the night, don't go off hiking on your own. Stick to camp. When you need a privy—day or night—avoid rocky outcroppings. At night, don't wander far outside camp. You won't need to; it's pitch dark and campfire light doesn't reach far. We haven't had much issue with wild animals for several years, but you never know. Montana is home to plenty of bears, mountain lions, and coyotes."

"Wouldn't they be more likely to go for the cattle than a person?"

"Yes. We carry rifles, and we set a guard at night."

"Is it worth it?" I asked.

"Of course it's worth setting a guard. We don't want to lose any cattle."

"No, I meant considering the dangers, is doing the roundup by horse really worth it? Or has it become a tradition that outweighs common sense?"

He shrugged. "This isn't a tradition; it's a necessity. Been doing it since I was a kid. Never gave the dangers any thought. For the terrain, doing it on horseback is the easiest. It's all part of living in Montana, and it keeps us grateful for what we have today."

"Besides snakes, are there any other venomous things I should know about?"

"The black widow and hobo spiders, and the typical bees, wasps, and hornets. You seem nervous. Are you allergic?"

"I dealt with venomous creatures in the Middle East. I like to know my enemy."

"Coyotes give us the most problem. Rest easy. God watches over us. Let's have lunch and afterward I'll show you the state website so you can read up on snake and bear safety."

Lunch was a loud event with everybody ensuring this and that had been done in preparation.

"Sally, as soon as you're done eating, saddle Sandy and we'll get in a few more lessons," Gabe told me as I finished off the last few bites on my plate.

"Sure thing." I finished, went to the barn, and saddled Sandy. After waiting another twenty minutes for Gabe, I went searching for him. He was still eating.

"Gabe, you going to be done with that meal today or tomorrow?" I asked, a big smile on my face.

"Sorry, Sally." He smiled sheepishly, wiped his mouth, and rose from the table.

"Did you have any trouble saddling Sandy?" he asked as we walked to the barn.

"Not at all."

Not ten minutes later, I found myself eating dust. Sandy's saddle had slid loose, dumping me straight to the ground.

"Sally!" Gabe yelled as he jumped off his horse and rushed toward me. "You okay?"

I stood, brushing the dirt from my face. "Yeah, I'm fine. What happened?"

Gabe grabbed Sandy's reins and pulled her over. He reached for the saddle now hanging precariously down her side and lifted it back into place. "You didn't get the girth tight enough," he said and began adjusting it.

"I was pretty sure I had, but lesson learned." I mounted Sandy after Gabe finished with the saddle and our afternoon progressed smoothly.

When I crawled into bed that night, I ached all over, but I had one more thing to do. I pulled out my laptop and did research on the wildlife of Montana on the site Chase told me about. Encountering a bear didn't appear too likely, but I read about how to behave should I face one. I also read about the prairie rattler Chase mentioned, which was more likely. I should have brought my own pistol from home, but even if I'd thought to bring it, the airport security would have confiscated it.

As I laid my head on the pillow, I prayed I didn't meet any critters, wild or otherwise.

# Chapter 11

## Sally

In You, O Lᴏʀᴅ, I put my trust; Let me never be ashamed;
Deliver me in Your righteousness. Psalms 31:1 NKJV

After two full days in the saddle, every muscle from my neck down burned with pain. When we made camp Tuesday night, I was afraid I wouldn't be able to walk once I dismounted. Is this how cowboys get bow-legged? I dismounted in slow motion, then stood to steady my land legs. I leaned my head against Sandy's side and took several deep breaths, hoping fresh oxygen would carry away even a little of the pain throbbing in my body. This might have been a breeze when I was twenty, but at fifty-eight it was no picnic.

I untied my sleeping roll and saddlebags and dropped them to the ground, then released the saddle cinch and buckles. I must have been moving imperceptibly because Michael appeared at my side, taking pity on me. He handed me the reins to his horse and pulled Sandy's saddle off before I could object.

"Thanks, Michael. I'm beat," I admitted and gave him a smile.

"Go straight to bed after dinner. Sleep will help." He smiled back and left to tend to his own horse. Among the boys, Michael was the quiet one of the family. Four carried the family name, but Michael bore the Chase resemblance. Knowing I was old enough to be his mother,

I admonished myself for finding Michael so attractive. I had long ago resigned myself to the fact that men weren't attracted to a woman with hair shorter than theirs. Who was I kidding? My short hair didn't deter them. My lack of beauty did. All men wanted from me was a romp in bed. They married the beautiful and busty women. I missed on both counts.

Most of the time I was content to be single. At the Reynolds' ranch, handsome men aplenty surrounded me, and my single status yowled in my head like a cat in heat. I had silenced the alarm on the biological clock several years back. I sighed and shook the thoughts from my head. Stay focused on your goal, Sally. The inheritance is what matters.

Before supper, I sought a privy behind a tall scrub oak some five yards from camp, grateful the descending darkness offered some aid to privacy. I hadn't taken five steps back toward camp when Leslie appeared in front of me.

"You witch!" she shrieked through gritted teeth. Her right hand slapped me full force across my face before I ever saw it coming. Never mind that nearly every muscle in my tired body barked at me. Why not add this cheek, too?

"I have no say about the inheritance, but I'm not going to stand by and watch you steal my husband out from under me," she spat.

Dumbfounded, I stood there for a moment gathering my thoughts. "What are you talking about?" I felt a warm trickle at the left corner of my mouth. I gave it a quick lick and tasted blood.

"Stay away from Jake."

A coyote howled in the distance as the night began to settle. I remembered the diamond—now absent from her left hand—and the kissed greeting the morning Leslie arrived at the ranch house. "I have absolutely no interest in Jake."

"I see the way he looks at you. And you flirt back."

"I'm fifty-eight. Probably old enough to be his mother. And I do not flirt." Me, flirt? What a laugh. How Leslie had managed to observe Jake eying me was a mystery. She had skipped breakfast this morning and ridden with one of the other ranch hands all day yesterday and today.

But I noticed how Jake looked at me, and I didn't like it either. I'd ridden with him today. Dealing all day with his nauseating chewing-tobacco spit stripped me of my appetite, and his wanton stare left me feeling violated.

I brushed past Leslie on her right and headed back to camp. She grabbed my upper arm and pulled me around to face her, but I was ready for her this time. My right arm went up instinctively, prying loose her grip without effort. I maneuvered her thumb and wrist into a jujitsu lock—nothing too painful, mind you, just enough to let her know who was boss. Sally 2, Leslie 0.

"If you don't like the way Jake looks at me, talk to him, not me." I scowled at her and maintained my hold on her wrist as I watched the defiance ebb from her face. I released my hold and stepped back. She jerked her hand to her chest, rubbing her wrist in an effort to smooth away the pain.

"Just you wait. We all wanted to contest Poppie's will, only Daddy said no," she huffed and threw me a wounded grizzly bear look. "My brothers might act nice toward you, but no one really wants you here."

I did my best to hide the emotions washing over me at her words. I didn't want her to think she had succeeded in a verbal slap.

"You run to Daddy-dearest with your complaints, but I'm going to pretend this never happened," I told her, then dragged my sore butt back to camp. I listened for her footsteps behind me, crunching in the dry brush, but heard nothing.

Leslie's words taunted me as I made my way back to camp. I had to give her credit; she had scored one with her words.

Contest the will? No one wanted me here? Her brothers were merely acting nice? My interactions with the boys had seemed sincere. Could sincerity be faked? Is this what I could expect for the next four weeks?

Were any of her words true? And what did she mean with "only Daddy said no"? That he was the only one of the clan who didn't want to contest the will or that they weren't contesting simply because Chase had said no?

My cynicism roared like a lion. One life lesson I had learned well over the years: Most people treat you nice because they want something from you. How far into enemy territory had I stepped? This amazing opportunity began to look more and more like a huge mistake.

My life had become the *Twilight Zone* meets *Gunfight at the O.K. Corral.* What had Chase said? "The roundup is the closest we get to the hard realities of Great-great-Grandpa's days of ranching, and it keeps us grateful for what we have today." Lucky Great-great-Grandpa. He only had mountain lions, bears, and blizzards to face, not Leslie Reynolds.

When I stepped from the brush into camp, Cook's beef stew bubbling in a large black kettle over an open fire smelled inviting enough to quell my chaw-induced nausea. Had we gone back in time? Not that I'm complaining; food cooked over an open fire tastes amazing.

I withdrew to my little western-style bivouac, sat down on my blanket, and leaned back into the soft lambskin of my upturned saddle to rest until supper was ready.

Last night Michael had shown me how to prop up my saddle and use it like the back of a chaise lounge to sleep in. We all slept by the cook fire next to Cook's Jeep Wrangler; Leslie and I on one side of vehicle, and Chase, Michael, Jake, and three other cowhands on the other. Two men, among the six of them, rotated guard duty through the night, armed with a rifle, watchful of coyotes and mountain lions. Leslie better be careful; she might get shot by mistake.

I licked the bloody corner of my mouth, then wiped it clean. I hoped no other signs of redness or bruising would force me to lie about what had happened.

How could Leslie even imagine I was flirting with Jake? I had at least fifteen years on the man. Yes, he was handsome with his dark brown hair, blue eyes, and strong square jaw. I'd found him attractive when I first met him that night at the barbecue, but that attraction died a quick death when a chaw of tobacco took residence in his left cheek the moment the roundup began. How did Leslie reconcile her perfumed, sophisticated, corporate lifestyle with his nasty tobacco habit and wet-dog scent?

The sun had dipped below the horizon and now cast a violet hue across the camp. The dipping temperature nipped at my shoulders. I pulled my fleece jacket from my saddlebag and draped it over me. I was not a stranger to sleeping outdoors, but admittedly, that had been in the early days of my time in the Corps. Decades of living with the luxury of a bed every night had softened me a bit. My derriere growled at me. I closed my eyes and rolled onto my side. Then my stomach growled. Which would win out, my hunger or my tired, aching body?

"Sore, are we?" Chase said, looking down at me. I opened one eye and looked up at him. He had changed his clothes and looked refreshed, as if he had just showered.

"If by *we* you mean my left and right buttock cheeks, then yes, *we* are sore." I cautiously sat up. "Where ya hidin' the portable shower?"

He laughed for several seconds, then drew in a deep breath and recovered himself. "Glad to see you have a sense of humor left at the end of a long day. I think you must have missed the call to supper. You going to eat?"

"As long as I can do it standing up."

"I won't stop you."

"Would you help me up, please?" I reached out a hand. His warm hand in mine sent tingles up my arm. As I stood, we came face to face for a brief moment. Reflections of the campfire danced in his bronze eyes. When his right index finger softly wiped at my lip, my stomach did a flip flop. His brows furrowed as he tried to focus on the dark liquid in the fading light.

"Have you been nibbling at Cook's stew or is this blood?"

"I tripped over a branch when I was looking for a privy."

"Branches scratch, not split your lip."

I held up my hand to stop any further protest he may have. "I'm fine." I headed toward supper and away from Chase. He fell in behind me. I looked for Leslie as I approached the chow line, but didn't see her.

"Has anyone seen Leslie?" Chase asked. When the only answer he got was no, he left, ostensibly to search for her.

Uh-oh, Daddy's angry. I wondered what had transpired between them for him to conclude Leslie had been the one to cause my split lip. What a spoiled little brat she was. Had I been her mother I might have returned her slap for acting like such a child. What would Chase say to her? It didn't matter. She had suffered my warning.

I pushed her out of my mind and turned to supper, wolfing down two bowls of Cook's delicious stew with some bread. Before I finished, Chase returned, but without Leslie. Wrinkles of anger creased his forehead. I finished eating and handed my dishes to Cook. I was eager to get back to my sleeping roll and get eight hours of exhausted sleep, oblivious of my pain. The singing of a cowhand lulled me and the cattle to sleep. When Leslie crawled into bed, I didn't know, and I didn't care.

# Chapter 12

## Chase

Some people make cutting remarks, but the words
of the wise bring healing. Proverbs 12:18

Michael, I'm getting too old for this," I told my son as I poured some coffee from the tin pot that hung over the campfire. Dark still reigned the morning, but the sun would rise before 6:30. "I'm stiff as a board this morning."

"Come on, Pop. We only spend this kind of time on horseback twice a year. We're all bound to be sore."

"It's nice to know I'm not the only one who hurts," Sally said, as she wobbled to the cook fire to get coffee.

"Massaging your muscles helps. Remind me before we break camp and I'll show you some stretches that will help, too," Michael offered.

"No saddle sores, I hope," I said. Sally looked bright-eyed, if not bushy-tailed.

"No, just sore muscles." She stretched from side to side. "What's on today's agenda? I'm rather enjoying this."

"Really? You enjoy sore muscles?" I asked.

She laughed. "That I'll pass on. No, I love being on the back of a horse. It makes me feel...I don't know, independent."

"Makes me feel one with nature," Michael said.

"You'll ride with Jake again today," I told her. "But today won't be as long as yesterday. We'll be up near Hunting Bear Cliff. There's water there for the cattle and us, if you want to take a bath in the river."

"What river?"

"The Teton. We'd prefer the Missouri, but it's on the wrong side of the highway," Michael said with a smile.

"Sounds enticing. I can just imagine a bath in the Big Muddy, with cows." Sally looked down at her dust-covered jeans.

"The Big Muddy?" Michael asked.

"Missourians nickname for the Missouri River, because it's so muddy. Rather wide, deep, and fast moving, too. Sure wouldn't want to attempt a bath in it," Sally explained.

"In Montana the Missouri isn't muddy, just cold. So is the Teton." I poured myself a second cup of coffee. "Eat up, everyone," I hollered. "We break camp in an hour."

I put Jake with Sally, and Michael with Leslie. The rest of the hands partnered up on their own. Once we rounded up the cattle, we'd drive them to our wintering pastures. Four, Pete, and Gabe remained at the ranch to keep things running there, accessible by a two-way radio I kept in my saddlebags. On the range, the radio was a much more reliable tool than cell phones. I spent the day ensuring everyone was doing okay. Poor Michael, his ears looked red from dealing with Leslie's complaints. I could hear her from thirty yards off.

"Leslie, quit your griping," I told her as I rode up next to her at about ten that morning. "That's all you've done since we started two days ago. You're the one who insisted on coming. If you can't hack it, you have no right to judge Sally's performance."

"I'm not judging her performance."

"You said you wanted to watch her. Why else but to make a judgment of her?"

"Judge not, lest ye be judged," Michael said.

"Very funny," Leslie said, smirking at Michael as she spoke.

"I wasn't trying to be funny. Poppie had his reasons for doing what he did, and I'm beginning to understand them."

"What do you mean by that?" she asked.

"Since the day the will was read, you've been behaving like a spoiled two-year-old," Michael answered. "Maybe Poppie noticed that bratty behavior long before I did."

I was glad Michael said it. From him it would carry greater weight. A sibling's reprimand comes through in a way a parent's doesn't. How would Karen have approached this?

"I have not been acting bratty," she said. If she hadn't been on a horse, I was certain she would have stomped her foot.

Michael laughed. "I can see your foot stomping in that stirrup. By the way, what was in that letter from Poppie that Mr. Kandell gave you?"

"I haven't read it yet. And even—"

"Haven't read it?" I interjected.

"What's in that letter is no one's business but mine," she sniped.

"That's true, but don't be disrespectful. Read it, and soon," I reprimanded her. "Hopefully it will give you an attitude adjustment."

"Nothing in that letter is going to change my opinion of Sally Clark. She doesn't belong here." Leslie sat tall in the saddle, her posture defying my words.

"Poppie determined otherwise. Now, stop acting like a two-year-old or you'll find yourself over my knee."

She stared at me and I could tell she was assessing just how serious I was about spanking her. "I'm grouchy because I'm so sore. Can't I at least ride with Jake?"

"We're all sore. I don't hear anyone else but you complaining. Seems to me you said Sally would never last ten days in the saddle. You haven't lasted two! She's fifty-eight and you're thirty-five." I took a deep breath and plunged on. "I've seen nothing Christ-like in your behavior for quite some time. Maybe it is that bratty behavior that changed your grandfather's mind about you."

A hurt look crossed her face, yet I could see her fighting not to pout.

"I'm sorry to be so abrupt. I'm just very disappointed in you right now, Leslie. And no, you can't ride with Jake." I glanced over at Michael. His imploring look said it all.

"Ride with the remuda. Just don't chew their ears off like you have Michael's. I don't want to hear another complaint out of you. You could always go back to town and give up this ridiculousness."

"I'll stay. I'll do better. I promise. Thank you, Daddy." She blew me a kiss and galloped off.

"So, Michael, what's she been like this morning?"

"Pop, I might as well have been out here alone rounding up these cattle. She just plodded along, not doing anything but complaining."

"What's your impression of Sally so far?"

"I haven't been around her much since we started. It's obvious she's sore, like the rest of us. I helped her get Sandy's saddle off last night, but she didn't ask for my help, and I haven't heard her complain."

Jake had given me the opposite impression about Sally's behavior during their day together. "I'd like input from all you kids as time goes by. So keep your ears and eyes open, will you?"

"Sure, Pop." Michael gave me a quizzical look.

"Question?"

"Just wondering why you want our input. It's not like anyone pronounces their approval over her. Isn't it just a matter of Sally completing the four weeks?"

"Sort of. She has to actively participate in the daily activities. So, I'd just like to hear everyone's opinion. I can't observe her 24/7. She'll be doing all the things you kids have done growing up. Each of you will spend time with her. I'd like a complete picture. I can't get that without input from each of you."

"OK, you got it."

"Should I replace Leslie for today or can you handle things?"

"I'm fine. Send someone to check up now and then."

"I can do that. I'll see you later." I reined my horse to the right and rode to check on the other men. After that I spelled Jake for an hour and sent him forward to meet George at the anticipated camping ground for the night.

Sally looked tired, but she performed well and worked with the cattle like she'd been doing it for months, not two days. Leslie looked as out of place here on the range as a robin in winter, but not Sally. She seemed as much a part of the prairie as the sagebrush. She sat tall in the saddle and handled Sandy like she'd been riding all her life. Her cheeks glowed. Her eyes shone bright. Her lips were red.

Plain Jane had disappeared.

"I like to watch the sunset when I can. Care to join me?" I asked Sally as we finished eating supper that evening. She looked a bit surprised at my request.

"Sure. Just let me get my jacket. The temperature dips rather suddenly once the sun goes down."

"I'll go with you. I have to get my rifle."

We strolled through the camp, retrieved what we each needed, and then I led the way to Hunting Bear Cliff. "You look fresh and clean. Did you bathe with the cows after all?"

She chuckled. "No, but I managed a sponge bath."

I offered her a seat on one boulder and I took a seat on another. "These stones mark where my great-grandfather met with Chief Hunting Bear 150 years ago. He named the place Hunting Bear Cliff to memorialize the meeting. Not the official state name, but that's what we've always called it." I gazed east out across the prairie to the Bear Paw Mountains.

"Is there Native American in your heritage?" Sally asked.

"My grandmother," I replied. After that, we fell into an uncomfortable silence as we watched the sun dip below the mountains. Truthfully, Sally watched the sunset. I watched Sally. She didn't at all resemble the woman I had met barely a week ago in Kansas City. Her cowboy hat sat cocked back on her head and a scruff of her short hair poked out in all directions. The fading sun cast a golden glow on her face. A gentle smile swept her lips. How like Abby she was, yet so different, too. Their voices were identical, and more than once I caught myself with Abby's name on my lips. It struck me like a frog's tongue to a fly that I often expected Sally to act like Abby, but she rarely did.

"What is she like?" Sally asked.

I blinked. "You mean Abby?"

"Who else? You've been staring at me for the last five minutes like you were peering into another face."

"I'm sorry; I was." I hopped down off the boulder and took a deep breath. I had missed most of the sunset. "I see Abby when I look at you. I hear her when you speak. I expect you to act like her, and when you don't…well, I get frustrated."

Sally turned her attention away from me and back to the last rays of gold shooting upward through the mountain valleys. "Not the spectacular color we have in Missouri, but nice all the same." She pulled her knees up to her chest and wrapped her arms around them.

"Are you cold?" I asked, but wondered if I made her feel vulnerable.

"No, I'm fine. Just resting."

What was I thinking, asking her out here?

"Chase, why did you really ask me out here?"

"How do you do it?" I scoffed. "That's twice in the last five minutes you've read my mind." My face grew warm with embarrassment. That nagging heaviness I'd felt the day she arrived at the ranch chewed at my stomach.

"Something I learned as an MP. Usually helped to relieve a tense situation." Sally's eyebrows gave a Groucho Marx wiggle and a mischievous smile pulled at her chapped lips. Her flippant manner calmed the turmoil raging inside my head. I stepped over to her.

"We'll be camping here all day tomorrow, a hub as we gather the last of the cattle. I imagine you could use a rest."

"If a rest means gaining the feeling back in my butt, that might not be a good thing. Better to be numb all the time. Would you help me down, please? I don't trust my legs to hold me." She released her knees and held her hands out to me.

I grabbed her hands and she slid off the boulder. I felt the warmth of her body against me as we momentarily stood next to each other. "Your hands are cold." I kept my hold on her hands to warm her.

"That's why coats have pockets," she said, looking up at me. She pulled her hands away and shoved them into her pockets. Darkness had descended. I could barely see the outline of her face, let alone the emotion that might be playing in her mesmerizing eyes. How long did we stand there looking at one another before she spoke?

"Chase, you still haven't told me why you brought me out here."

"Because I don't know the answer." I shrugged. "To get know you better. I think that's what Pop intended in bringing you here. We'd better get back to camp." I pulled my flashlight from my pocket and turned it on.

"You're a strange man, Chase Reynolds the third," she said to me as we headed to camp.

I turned to face her, training the light on her face. She stood with her arms crossed, that same mischievous smile on her lips. "I could say the same about you, Sally Clark."

"At least I'm not rude one day and seductive the next."

"Seductive?" That was a slap in the face. "I'll grant you rude—and I apologized for that—but I haven't been seductive. I told you, one minute I see Abby, the sister I love and hug every day I can. The next I see you."

"Yes, Sally Clark, thief, interloper, the burr under your saddle. I expect hugging me is similar to embracing a cactus."

"Don't be ridiculous," I said. "You're no cactus. You're a beautiful woman with clean natural skin that glows and eyes that flash with determination. A woman who meets life with grit and a sense of humor."

"I learned determination and grit at an early age. The Marine Corps developed them further."

"You might think the world is out to get you, but it isn't, and neither am I."

"I have yet to see any evidence of that."

"I'm sorry you see it that way. Probably any explanation I offered, you'd call an excuse. What has made you so cynical?"

She picked her way through the brush. "This total darkness takes some getting used to. It's freaky not being able to see my feet."

Ignoring my question. Should I let her? No, I couldn't let this pass.

"Stop," I said, grabbing her shoulder and turning her around to face me. "I want to understand you. Help me."

We stood staring at each other. Darkness shrouded Sally's face.

"Are we going to stand here staring at each other all night or are you going to answer me?" I said.

"I'm tired; I hurt; I want to go to bed, not discuss my life."

"Look, part of Pop's purpose in all this was for us to get to know you. How can we do that if you act like a clam?"

She took in and released a quick exasperated breath. "Okay, then. When I was a very little girl, my father said he loved me. But the truth came out when my mom died. I bore his verbal abuse nearly every night. Too many people in my life who said they cared, betrayed me. That's why I'm cynical."

"I'm sorry."

"Don't be. Just know it takes a lot for me to trust people. Now can we get back to camp while I can still see my hands?"

"Of course. I've grown up with this kind of darkness. The lights of Kansas City kept me awake nearly all night. Remember, you can sleep in tomorrow. We'll be camped here all day," I reminded her.

"I'm a morning person. Normally wake up between five and six o'clock. When's breakfast?"

"Not till seven, but there'll be coffee by 5:30."

When we arrived back at camp, a general chatter moved throughout the group. Seemed most intended to stay awake longer than usual. I spotted Jake and Leslie off by themselves, looking very upset with each other.

"Thanks for sharing the sunset with me. Good night," Sally said and wandered off to her side of camp.

"Good night," I called after her. I realized it probably took a lot for her to tell me about her father's betrayal. But she said too many people had betrayed her. Who else in her life had wounded her? Did Pop know about any of it? To know Sally better I'd need to read Karl's file on her.

# Chapter 13

## Sally

He led me to a place of safety; he rescued me
because he delights in me. Psalms 18:19

Day five of the roundup dawned crisp and clear. As I lay in my bed roll, I looked over at Leslie. Still sound asleep. Undoubtedly, she wasn't any more used to this rugged activity than I was. My body most distinctly appreciated yesterday's day of rest.

I cast aside my thoughts and braced myself for the chilly air that would assault me the moment I crawled out from under my blanket. Having acclimated to the 90- and 100-degree temperatures of Missouri summers with morning temps in the 80s, I found Montana mornings downright chilly. Seemed the Missouri lows equaled the Montana highs. I had no idea what the temps were; I only knew it felt chilly to me.

Each day the camp sprang to life at 5:00, more than an hour before sunrise. Chase, Michael, Jake, and the other cowhands completed morning tasks while Cook fixed breakfast. This allowed us to start the day's work with the cattle as soon as the sun rose. We made camp at night prior to sunset, using the last rays of light to set up camp and settle the cattle. Cook drove back to the ranch each day and prepped what was needed for the night's meal and the following day's breakfast.

Cook also provided pre-packaged granola bars and such that we ate for lunch.

The aches that screamed at me each morning as I climbed from bed had finally disappeared with last night's sleep. I scrambled over to the cook's Wrangler for my cup of java and breakfast and to warm by the fire. Only the campfire offered light.

"Ah, Spam, the caviar of potted meat," I heard Peter say as I approached. Yesterday while we were camped all day at Hunting Bear Cliff, Gabe had driven Pete up to join us. He stood watching Cook open another can of Spam. Six other cans lay empty in the trash barrel, their contents now sizzling in a cast iron skillet crusted by years of cooking over an open fire.

"Pete, you have such refined taste." I laughed. "I'm grateful to these little piggies for my breakfast, but it gives me heartburn." Cook had served Spam twice already.

"Taint my cookin'. 'Tis all the mustard ye bury it in givin' ye heartburn," Cook groused at me. In five days, I still hadn't figured out the ethnicity of Cook's accent.

"With all the fancy camping equipment that exists these days, Cook, why do you cook over an open fire?"

"Always cooked that way when we went campin' as kids. Fancy stuff is nice, but nothin' tastes as good as bein' cooked over a campfire."

"Morning, Sally," Michael said as he approached the cook fire. "You're on drag with me today."

"Drag?"

"Rear of the herd. Roundup is done; now we move the cattle to our wintering pasture."

"Okay, I'll be sure to wear my bandanna."

"Bring a spare," he warned me with a smile.

Cook beeped the Jeep's horn to signal breakfast was ready. Everyone gathered and wolfed down their meal. I gobbled down a slice of Spam, some scrambled eggs, and a biscuit. I grabbed three biscuits and several slices of Spam for my lunch on the trail and wrapped them in a napkin. I hoped my hard work herding cattle would counteract the calories I munched down every day. Once back at my bivouac, I shoved my lunch into my saddlebags, then rolled up my blanket and headed to the remuda to retrieve Sandy.

I'd ridden with Chase the first day, and then with Jake the following two days. All I really did was shadow them as they rode the range, plucking cattle out of the nooks and crannies of the hills. I considered my performance satisfactory thus far. I asked questions when I could, eager to learn about cattle and ranching. Oddly, I felt at home. Several times the thought that I had been born in the wrong century ran through my mind. Of course, if I'd been born in the nineteenth century, I'd be herding a wood-burning stove and a passel of children instead of cattle.

Each day as I tended to the cattle, I began to realize how wound-up the daily stress of my editing job made me. Out here on the open range with the rugged beauty of the Bear Paw Mountains to the east of me, rolling prairie on the another, and the overpowering Rockies on the west side, peace reigned. No boss clamored at me to meet deadlines. No phone demanded my attention twenty times a day. I had no access to the outside world at all—I'd been advised to leave my cell phone at the ranch. Probably wouldn't have been able to get a signal and even if I stashed it in my saddlebags, I'd be concerned it would fall out as I retrieved other items.

Today the Montana sun caressed my face with its gentle warmth, and the prairie breeze offered me its sweet scents. One hundred mooing cows, snorting horses, hyah-ing cowboys, and untold other baying and chirping critters suspended me in time, carried me into a world I thought only existed in western movies. I found myself yearning for this simplicity of life, a simplicity I had never experienced until now.

The darkness of night could be a bit disconcerting. If I walked ten yards from camp, I couldn't see my feet. But the stars! Never had I noticed so many. They glittered down at me each night as if they were trying to tell me campfire stories of cowboys long ago.

As I reached the remuda, Sandy met me. "Good morning, girl. I sure am going to miss you when this is all over." I grabbed her halter and led her back to camp, though I think she would have followed me without it. She looked as grungy as I felt. The cleanliness I achieved after my sponge bath in the Teton River two days ago had deserted me the next day. Lucky Sandy. She only had to work four hours before getting turned loose to the remuda, while I saddled another horse and continued to work. Her backside got relief, mine didn't.

"Guess, I'm official, Sandy," I said as I curried her down. "My backside isn't sore anymore." She whinnied a congratulations. "Did you spend the night rolling in the dirt? You're filthy." Dust covered every golden inch of her satiny coat. I checked and cleaned her hooves, then saddled and bridled her. She stood calmly while I strapped on the saddlebags Chase had given me to use and then tied on my blanket.

"Hey, Sal, you ready?" Michael asked as he rode up.

All the men had taken to calling me Sal. I guess Sal fit a ranch hand, and Sally a saloon girl. I mounted Sandy, and Michael led the way to the rear of the herd. I hoped my time with him would afford me a chance to ask him all the questions I had. He spent our first hour together instructing me how to handle the rear of the herd and what to watch for. Finally we settled into an easy walk behind the cattle.

"How did you manage to be so different from your father?" With my bandanna over my face and the moos of the cattle, I had to yell the words to be understood.

"I don't follow you."

"You reflect Christ, like the Bible teaches us. Your dad? …I guess most of the time he's been nice to me, but there are times when he does the opposite of what I expect." I kept my eyes roving over the cattle and the countryside as we talked. Never had I seen so many miles and miles and miles of rolling prairie—not even in that stretch along I-70 in western Kansas that so many of my friends complained about. Above me, the deep blue sky seemed just as endless. Now I understood how Montana earned the nickname Big Sky Country.

"You mean he's a hypocrite."

"No, though he did seem a bit rude during our first meeting and the night of the barbecue. He's been better the last few days, but—"

"Hyah," Michael hollered and slapped his coiled lasso against his leg. A wayward cow bellowed its disapproval but moved a bit faster all the same. "Sal, I've noticed Pop's not quite been himself. Poppie's death was so sudden, and I think his death has shaken Pop nearly as hard as Mom's death did."

"So he's not on top of his game?"

"Exactly."

I noticed a cow lagging and wandering off so I prodded Sandy and rode over to the left of the herd to guide the cow back. He was an obstinate black beast, but each time he attempted to turn away from the herd, Sandy stepped forward to block him. Stubborn as the cow was, he was a welcome diversion to the mulish Leslie. She hadn't spoken one word to me since the night she slapped me. That was probably a good thing.

After a few minutes of playing tag with me, the cow rejoined the herd. Sandy did all the work. All I did was holler and wave my rope. When I took my place at the rear of the herd again, Michael was off in the other direction doing the same thing. At this rate, it would take us all day to have a five-minute conversation. After several minutes he rode up beside me again.

"When did your mother die?" I asked.

"Actually, I hadn't thought about it, but it's been five years ago this month."

"So another death on top of scarred grief. That gives me a better perspective. Except for some friends in Kansas City, you and your brothers are among the few Christians I've ever met whose actions match their words."

"I learned it all from Pop. He's passionate about living his life for Christ, and he encourages that passion in us every day. You know you might also consider that except for your hairstyle, you look just like Aunt Abby. Sometimes I have to catch myself to not call you Aunt Abby. Maybe Pop's struggling in the same way."

"You're probably right. That would explain the abruptness of his behavior at times. He did tell me he expects me to act like Abby."

I could see only the smile in Michael's eyes as he looked over at me. Dust of the trail grayed his blue bandanna. His sweat mixed with dirt created streaks of mud down his neck. Even with my bandanna over my mouth, I could taste dirt and feel its grit between my teeth. I ran my tongue over my teeth, gathered some spit in my mouth, then leaned to the side, lifted my bandanna, and tried to spit out the dirt. I heard Michael laughing.

"Breathe through your nose and you won't get so much dirt in your mouth."

"Then it all gets stuck in my nose and I can't breathe. Do you think your grandfather had an affair that resulted in me and your aunt Abby?"

He jerked back on his reins, his horse's head rearing up in objection.

"Sorry, I didn't mean that to be a slap in your face."

He relaxed and prodded his horse back into action. "I don't believe that for a moment!"

"Neither does your dad."

The sun, now directly overhead, beat down on us, though it was nothing compared to the typical August ferocity of Missouri. All the same, sweat trickled down my neck and the middle of my back. Michael lifted his hat and with a bandanna he pulled from his jeans pocket wiped the sweat off his brow, then wiped his neck. I did the same. First thing I was going to do when this ended—take a long soothing bath. It might take an hour of soaking just to loosen the caked-on dirt and dust.

I smiled my thanks, but my bandanna got in the way. "Thank you."

"You're welcome. Anytime you wanna talk, I'll listen."

We were just about to ride out to gather wanderers when a shot rang out.

"Is that a signal of some sort?" I asked him.

"No," he said as he scanned the area. Another shot rang out and a cow about five feet ahead and to the left of me fell to the ground. The herd bellowed and began to run.

"What's happening?" I yelled, trying to rein in Sandy, but she refused to stop and pranced in a circle.

"Stampede!"

# Chapter 14

## Sally

God is our refuge and strength, always ready to
help in times of trouble. Psalms 46:1

S tay to my left and follow my lead," Michael hollered at me,
then urged his horse into a gallop. He veered off to the left of
the stampeding herd. Sandy took off on her own accord but
responded to the leading of my knees. I pressed first my right knee and
then my left into her sides to fall in behind Michael.

My left hand clutched the reins, and both hands gripped the saddle
horn in my effort to stay on the horse. My knuckles turned white. I'd
never ridden so fast. The cattle bawled. Their hooves pounded, creating
a thunderous roar and a cloud of dust that obstructed my view. I feared
my horse or Michael's would hit a hole and both horse and rider would
crash to the ground. The fear nearly rivaled facing a terrorist's rifle.
At least in that case, I had a weapon to defend myself. Right now all I
could do was call out to Jesus for help. And I did just that.

I searched the cloud of dust for Michael. I could hear his voice
but failed to see him. A froth of sweat appeared on Sandy's neck. The
canteen that hung from my saddle horn bounced and thumped against
Sandy with the rhythm of her gallop, banging into my left knee every
now and then. I hoped my saddlebags were tied securely. The rapid

pace of Sandy's breathing pushed against my legs. My legs tightened around her heaving rib cage in an effort to stay securely seated in the saddle. The pace of my breathing matched Sandy's.

How long would the animals run? How did you stop a stampede?

Then almost as suddenly as it had begun, the stampede ended. I have no idea how long it lasted, but it felt like an hour. The herd continued to bawl but paced in place. We reined up our horses and looked for other ranch hands. Sandy's sides heaved in and out as she worked to catch her wind. I did too. Michael jerked off his hat and wiped the sweat from his face with his forearm.

"Stay here. I'm gonna look for Pop," he yelled. He pulled his rifle from its leather scabbard. "Here." He held it out to me. "Keep this handy and yours eyes peeled for coyotes."

I took the rifle from him, and he cantered southeast toward the head of the herd. Sandy still seemed skittish, jerking her head up and down. I leaned over and patted her neck wet with sweat.

"Easy, girl. It's over." I scanned the range for cows that may have run off, but also for whoever had fired those shots. Nothing. Ten minutes passed and Michael still hadn't returned, then from the south I spotted a rider approaching.

"Sal, are you all right?" Pete asked once he rode close enough.

"I'm a little shaky. One of the cows got shot. That's what started them running."

"I heard the shots. Wasn't Michael with you?"

"He rode ahead to find Chase. Said I should wait here." I looked back to where I knew the cow lay and wondered if it was dead. "That cow might not be dead. Does it just get left like so much roadkill?"

"No, of course not. Ride with me and show me where it is."

I prodded Sandy and we headed northwest at a canter. We had covered about a mile or two when we heard a faint groaning of the animal drifting across the prairie. Pete urged his horse into a gallop and we covered another three quarters of a mile in short order. We dismounted and he handed me his reins. He approached the injured animal with caution, stopping five feet from it. The cow's tongue hung from its froth-covered mouth and a pool of blood had formed from under its belly.

"I expect he'll die soon," Pete said, returning and taking the reins to his horse. "Keep your distance. I'll see who I can find to help." He mounted and galloped off, leaving a cloud of dust in his wake.

I loosened the girth on Sandy's saddle to give her some relief and sat down to rest. Who had fired those shots and why? Surely cattle rustlers had died out with the Wild West. Michael had seemed as surprised as I when the rifle shots pierced the peacefulness of our day. Countless hours on the firing range taught me to distinguish the difference in sound between a pistol and a rifle. And a rifle afforded a discreet distance. As I mulled it over, I realized how close Michael and I had come to being on the receiving end of that second shot.

An hour later I still waited. I rose from my seat in the dirt to get a drink from my canteen. The strap had become twisted with all the gyrating the canteen had done during the stampede. The sun now dipped halfway toward the horizon. I hoped I didn't find myself out here alone come sunset. Soon after, Michael rode up.

"Hey, Sal. You doin' okay?"

"Thought maybe I'd been forgotten."

"Sorry about that. One of the ranch hands got thrown from his horse during the stampede." He dismounted.

"Is he okay?"

"Broken arm. Coulda been a lot worse though." He handed me his reins and turned to inspect the animal.

"It's dead," I told him. The beast had ceased its agonized breathing ten minutes after Pete had ridden off to find help.

"It's a he, a steer. Females are called cows," Michael explained with a smile. He went over to it all the same. He gently placed his hand on the animal's ribs and felt for its breathing. Once convinced it was really dead he began rubbing his hands over it as if feeling for something.

"What are you doing?" I pushed my Stetson onto the crown of my head and wiped the perspiration from my forehead.

"Looking for the entry wound." Not having found it, he rose and walked over to his horse. He pulled a walkie talkie from his saddlebag. "Michael to Pop, come in."

"Go ahead, Michael," came Chase's voice.

"We lost the steer. Send the truck."

"Got it. I'll radio the ranch. How's Sally?"

"She's good. Over and out." Michael shoved the walkie talkie into his back pocket. "This certainly is a first for me," he said, shaking his head.

"The stampede or the steer getting shot?"

"Both."

# Chapter 15

## Sally

Protect me from wicked people who attack me, from murderous enemies who surround me. Psalms 17:9

We camped there that night. The cattle had run about five miles during their stampede. But in that stampede they had also burned a lot of energy. Michael decided it was best to let them rest and calm down.

The cattle weren't the only critters upset. Agitated, questioning whispers carried through the camp. Chase had driven back to Great Falls to the hospital with Peter and the wounded man, leaving Michael in charge. A deputy from the county sheriff's office arrived in camp just as supper was ready.

"Sam, good to see you," Michael greeted the man as he arrived. "You're just in time for dinner. Or did you plan it that way?" He chuckled, patted the deputy's shoulder, and then they headed toward me. "Sal, this is Deputy Sam Lone Wolf. He's here to ask some questions about today."

"Nice to meet you, deputy." I shook his hand.

"Let's take this conversation somewhere private," Deputy Lone Wolf said and led us to a spot away from the group waiting for their meal. He dug a pen and small notepad out of his shirt pocket. "Michael, why don't you start."

"Can't tell you much, Sam. There were two shots. The second downed the steer."

"What direction did the shots come from? Could you tell?"

"From behind us I think. Sal, what do you think?"

I closed my eyes and tried to recreate the moment in my mind. "I'm not familiar with how the open prairie affects sound, but I'd say from behind and to my right."

"That would make it from the northwest of us. We were heading southeast," Michael said.

The deputy scribbled down the info.

"How far apart were the shots?" the deputy asked.

Michael and I looked at each other and shrugged. "At least fifteen or twenty seconds. We had time to react to the first shot, and I asked Michael if it was a signal of some sort."

"Did either of you see anything or anyone?"

"I didn't have time to look. I was too busy reacting to the stampede," Michael said, shaking his head.

"I didn't see anything either, before or after the stampede, and I had plenty of time to look around after it was all over."

"What time did all this happen?"

"Sometime between one and two o'clock," Michael said.

"Ms. Clark, would you mind getting me some coffee?" the deputy asked.

"Of course not." I hoped they wouldn't say anything important while I was gone and kept looking back over my shoulder as I headed over to the cook fire. They were deep in conversation, and I knew the deputy had sent me on an I-need-to-get-rid-of-you errand. It took some discipline, but I sat and waited a few minutes before walking back with his coffee.

"Thank you," he said, taking a sip of the cook's strong brew.

"Are you done asking Michael the questions you didn't want me to hear?"

The deputy sputtered, spitting out some coffee. I laughed. "Sorry, Deputy, I didn't mean to make you choke."

"She was an MP with the Marines," Michael said by way of explanation. "Is that all you need from us?"

"For now anyway."

"Be sure and grab yourself some dinner before you leave."

"Thanks, Michael." He turned to me. "Nice to meet you, Ms. Clark. If you remember anything, let Michael know, and he can reach me." He shook my hand and headed off to question the others. Michael and I headed for the chow line.

Most of the hands had finished supper and scattered for the night. After filling our plates and taking a seat near the campfire, I broached what I knew would be a sensitive subject. "Michael, who from the group carries a rifle during the day?"

"All of us. Wild animals don't restrict their movements to nighttime."

"Those shots weren't meant for a wild animal. They were too long. Well, I suppose a hunter would shoot at a distance, but gut level, I think the shots were intentionally for us. Are most of the hands decent with their aim?"

"Hmm, I think so, but I'm not sure. Are you saying someone was trying to shoot our cattle? And what do you mean the shots were long?"

"After fifteen years of handling weapons, you learn things. The sound of the shot seemed much too far for a hunter or someone protecting themselves from a wild animal attack. Does the Reynolds' family have any enemies who would do something like this? Are there any disgruntled former employees?"

Michael's startled reaction told me Deputy Lone Wolf had probably asked the same things. "You believe someone killed that steer on purpose? That's ridiculous. Maybe the shooter thought he was aiming at a coyote."

I figured the chances of that were about a billion to one, but I'd already been accused of thinking the worst of the Reynolds clan. I didn't want to give him that impression. I'd had a lot of time to think while I was out there. Alone. In the middle of nowhere. Babysitting a dead cow—oops, a dead steer. This shooting was intentional, not accidental. But maybe the sun had fried my brain.

"Sal," Michael mumbled through a mouthful of food. "More than likely, it was a tourist hunting elk."

"A tourist? Pretty stupid tourist not to know the difference between a cow and an elk. My first thought was rustlers, actually. Does rustling still happen? In my world, people shoot people." I shook my head and pushed the food around my plate. "Sitting out there alone today, I had a lot of time to think. I just don't think this was some random hunting accident."

"I expect your experiences in the military and life in a big city tend to push your thoughts that way. I'm certain it was nothing more than an accident." Michael had first shift guard duty that night and shuffled off to watch the herd as soon as we finished eating. I borrowed a rifle from one of the ranch hands and a flashlight from Cook and wandered off to watch the sunset. Maybe that would calm my nerves.

As I walked from camp, I considered the possibility of someone wanting revenge against the Reynolds and Chase's words about a longstanding Christian heritage. Certainly, those two things didn't jive. I understood Michael's insistence at it being an accident. Admittedly, when Chase interacted with his children and employees, he was respectful, commanding, and confident. But with me, he seemed nonplussed. Chase speechless? Only with me, like a giant oak morphing into a sapling.

Leslie had kept her distance since our encounter that second night out. I could understand someone wanting revenge against her. So why shoot at the cattle or at Michael and me? I attempted to extend understanding to Leslie; she was grieving. She was shocked by her grandfather's will and the revelation of my existence. That shock applied to the whole family, but the boys readily accepted me, almost with open arms. I grew more confident Leslie had lied about them only acting nice.

I'd walked only a few yards from camp when I heard hushed voices. I stopped and listened with the intent of moving in the opposite direction.

"I told you, she can't inherit anything if she's dead."

"But—"

"No buts. You'll be richly rewarded."

I stood frozen to the spot. I tried to identify the voices but the best I could do was to determine they were male.

"Now get back to work."

I heard the rustle of the prairie grass. I hunkered down, hoping not to be seen as they parted ways. When all was silent again, I stood.

*She can't inherit anything if she's dead?* They're talking about me! And someone would be richly rewarded for ensuring I turned up dead. I remembered Leslie's words, *just you wait.* Was she behind this? Was everyone treating me nicely because they knew I wasn't going to be around much longer? Was the whole family in on a plot to kill me?

Get a grip, Sally. If they felt that strongly about the will, they'd just contest it, not kill you.

All the same, I now believed today's bullets had been meant for me, not the steer. Someone had tried to kill me but failed. Then I remembered the incident on Sunday with Sandy's saddle coming loose. Maybe someone had messed with the saddle when I had gone to find Gabe.

This revelation wreaked havoc on my mind.

Who could I trust? Would the deputy believe me if I told him? Probably not. The banter between him and Michael made his friendship with the Reynolds family obvious. Nope, he wouldn't believe me.

"Heavenly Father, that bullet was meant for me. What do I do now?"

*You are my beautiful warrior daughter. I brought you through Desert Storm. I rescued you from every trap and protected you from deadly disease. I'll bring you through this. Instead of shame and dishonor, you will enjoy a double share of honor. You will possess a double portion of prosperity in your land, and everlasting joy will be yours.*

I took a deep breath, breathing God's words deep into my spirit.

"Thank You, Father, for Your words of encouragement." By now, darkness encroached. I pulled the flashlight from my pocket, switched it on, and made my way back to camp.

To avoid snakes climbing into bed with me, I kept my blanket rolled up, as Chase had advised, until I was ready to lie down for the night.

While I probably didn't need to sleep with my boots on, I did anyway. Previous experience in the Middle East had taught me caution in all things. Every possible danger out here in the wild now became a potential threat to my life, and I determined to be more cautious.

Whatever came my way, God would bring me through to the other side, to where His grandest blessings awaited.

# Chapter 16

## Chase

Truthful words stand the test of time, but lies
are soon exposed. Proverbs 12:19

Peter, do you have any idea where those shots came from?" I asked as the two of us waited in the Great Falls hospital ER waiting room.

"No, sir. I barely heard them. I just know that suddenly the cattle were stampeding."

"Have there been any reports of the coyote population getting out of control?"

"No. I talked with the game warden early Monday morning before we started out. He said things had been pretty calm all summer."

"Chase Reynolds?" a man in a white coat called out. I stood and approached him.

"I'm Chase Reynolds," I said, extending my hand in introduction.

"Dr. Jordan." He shook my hand. "Your man is going to be fine. Fortunately the break in his arm is a minor one. We've set it and given him some pain killer, but he'll be on light duty for the next several weeks."

"Okay, thanks. Are you keeping him here for the night?"

"No, he's free to go home. He'll be out soon." The doctor shook my hand again and returned to the ER.

"Well, that's good to hear," I told Peter. "I saw him go down. It could have been a lot worse." I grabbed my Stetson from the chair. "Listen, I want you to wait here. I'm going to head over to the sheriff's office. I'll see you back at the ranch later. Check in with Michael as soon as you get there. Find out what they've been able to figure out about all this. Probably was just hunters."

"I doubt it. Elk season doesn't start till tomorrow and you know private land is off-limits to hunters."

"Excellent points. Maybe we have an out-of-state hunter who ignores the law."

"How you gonna get to the sheriff's?"

"I'll call a taxi. See you later." I pulled my cell phone from my shirt pocket as I walked toward the front of the hospital.

As I waited for the taxi, I thought through the afternoon's sequence of events. I'd heard the shots, though barely. I heard the thunder of hooves before I saw the wave of black rushing forward. Then I saw Randy's horse go down, Randy with him. Thank God the animals had begun to slow by then or Randy might have been trampled. As I assured that Randy and the horse were okay, Michael rode up.

"Pop! Everyone all right here?"

"Thankfully, yes. I think Randy broke his arm, but nothing more serious. Do you have any idea what started this?"

"A shot that downed a steer. He was still breathing when I rode off, but I don't expect he'll live."

"Wasn't Sally riding with you? Where is she? Is she okay?"

"Calm down; she's fine. I left her on drag. That steer, it was five feet from her when it went down. She's got my rifle if she needs it."

"Like that'll do her any good. She probably couldn't shoot the broadside of a barn. You shouldn't have left her alone."

"Pop, she was an MP. A Marine. She could probably outshoot us all."

"Oh, yeah. I tend to forget that. I've radioed Gabe to drive out so we can get Randy to the hospital. Go check and see if anyone else is hurt."

And off Michael rode to get it done.

Five feet from Sally. That disconcerted me. I hadn't seen a single coyote or bear all summer. If there'd been one, Michael and Sally would have spotted it long before anyone else. Michael would have handled that kind of situation. And like Peter said, hunting season hadn't started and the shooting occurred on private land.

Had the shooter been aiming for Sally? I didn't want to go there. I couldn't.

My visit with the sheriff was short. I reported what had happened but held back my suspicions about it not being an accident. Maybe that was wrong of me. Only the family knew the stipulation in the will about Sally's share in the profits reverting back to the family when she died. I refused to believe any of my children would want to kill her.

I grabbed a taxi home. By then it was dinner time. I'd missed lunch, probably everyone on the trail had, too, since the stampede occurred just prior. I made my way to the kitchen.

"Rita, make a plate for me and keep it warm, will you, please. I've got more pressing matters."

"Chase! What are you doing here? I mean, there's plenty of food, but what…?"

"Had to bring Randy into the hospital. He's fine, minor break to his arm. He'll be on light duty for a while, so if there are some things he can help with around the house, let me know."

"Will do," she said and turned back to her work. I made my way to the barn office. Pete was at the desk.

"Pete, you're back. Didn't expect to see you this soon. Did you get Randy settled?"

"Yeah, his wife was pretty upset when she first saw him, but once we assured her it was a minor break and he was fine otherwise, she calmed down. I told him to take the weekend and relax and call Monday before driving out. No sense him being here if there's nothing for him to do."

"Check with Rita. I told her to put him to work."

Pete nodded. "You want me to replace him on the roundup?"

"Yeah. Figure it out yet tonight and let whoever know. Gabe can drive us back to the group first thing in the morning. Have you heard from anybody at camp?"

"No. Just got back myself. Haven't had a chance to radio Michael."

I grabbed the radio. "Chase to base camp. Come in." I waited for a response.

"This is George; go ahead, Chase."

"George, is Michael or Jake around? I need an update."

"Michael's talkin' to Deputy Lone Wolf at the moment. Not sure where Jake is."

"Let Deputy Lone Wolf and Michael know I want to talk with them." I waited while George passed on the message.

"Hey, Pop. How's Randy?" Michael said as he came on the radio.

"Minor break. He's home resting. Give me an update."

"Things are pretty tense. I've doubled the night guard, in case there's a bear in the area. I think Jake's talked to everyone, and they all say they didn't shoot at anything. Probably a hunter or a nearby rancher."

"A nearby rancher wouldn't hide what happened. He'd apologize, then pay salvage for that steer and take him home. How's Sally? Pete told me she was only five feet away when it went down."

"She's a little shaken, but overall I think she's fine."

"Good. I'm staying home for the night. Gabe will drive us up tomorrow morning. Don't start out until we get there."

"OK, Pop. Here's Sam."

I waited while Michael handed the radio to Sam.

"Sam here, Chase. How can I help you?"

"What have you found out so far?"

"Not much. Michael and Ms. Clark both agree the shot came from behind them. I'll have our people scour the area, see what we can find."

"Michael mentioned local ranchers and while I don't think it was one of them, it could have been one of their kids or grandkids. Can you check?"

"Sure, Chase, but I get the feeling you think this wasn't an accident."

"No, not at all. But Pete said hunting season doesn't open until tomorrow. I'm just concerned about some crazy hunters. I've reported the incident to the Cascade County sheriff as well. You might connect with them."

"Jurisdiction falls to us here in Chouteau County, but I'll give them a call in the morning. Michael's still standing here. Do you need to talk to him again?" Sam said.

"No, we're good. Thanks, Sam. Over and out."

I set the radio down and turned to leave the office.

"Pop, what else could this be other than an accident?" Pete asked before I could leave. "Why would someone intentionally kill one of our steers? We're good people."

I smiled at his comment. We are good people. People clamber to work for us because we pay well and value our workers. We have a good reputation across the state. "You're right. An accident of some kind. In all the years we've been doing this, we've never had an incident like this. It's unnerving."

The next morning, Gabe, Pete, Al, and I set out at five o'clock sharp. I wanted a report on the status of things before we started the herd once more toward winter pasturing. We arrived in time for breakfast.

"Michael, how'd it go for the night?"

"Fine, Pop. Do you want to make up the few miles we lost yesterday?"

"I hadn't thought about that. Too many other thoughts crowding my mind. You're our cattle manager. It's your call. I've got a brief announcement and then I'd like you to let the group know your plans. I'd like you with Sally again today, but riding right point."

"Do you think she can handle that?"

"She'll do fine. She doesn't need to do anything but watch and follow you." I poured a cup of coffee, then had George beep the horn. I waited while everyone gathered.

"Yesterday's incident is behind us. We don't know where those shots came from, but you know how ignorant tourists can be when

they're hunting. So, I want everyone to keep your eyes open. Michael."
I stepped back and allowed Michael to move forward.

"We lost a few miles yesterday, but there's no need to hurry. Another day won't impact us either way. Better to not fret the cattle," he said. "If it takes an extra day, then so be it. We'll take our usual pace."

As Michael spoke, I searched the group for Leslie. She stood at the very fringe, looking rumpled and disgruntled. I pointed my finger at her and then at myself. I saw her shoulders drop in frustration, but she started toward me.

"We break camp in thirty minutes. That's all. Thank you," Michael said. I watched the group disperse and Leslie's slow approach toward me.

"Good morning, Daddy," she said as she reached me.

I pulled her over behind the Wrangler where we had a bit of privacy. "Hear me and hear me good. You'll pull your weight today. You're wrangling, and no more repeats like the other day, whining to ride with Jake. If I see otherwise, you're out of here."

She looked at me for several moments, her face displaying hurt. But in her eyes I could see her calculating my mood.

"Yes, Daddy."

# Chapter 17

## Sally

Keep me safe, O God, for I have come to you for refuge.
Psalms 16:1

I munched down my breakfast as I surreptitiously watched Chase and Leslie talking behind Cook's Jeep. Chase's posture reminded me of my dad when he was bawling me out. Chase jabbed his finger in the air toward Leslie several times. When he was done talking, Leslie stomped off. Not a happy camper.

When I spotted Chase walking toward me, I trained my eyes on my breakfast.

"Sally?"

I looked up. "Yeah?"

He crouched down next to me. "How you doin'?"

"Fine." I shrugged. I sensed tension in him, but he didn't strike me as someone who could be easily unsettled. I couldn't imagine him being troubled by stampeding cattle. "By the looks of you, you're not so good."

"That's what four hours of sleep will do to you. Michael tells me you handled that stampede pretty well yesterday."

"I don't know about that. Never ridden that fast on a horse before. I'll be honest; I was scared."

"Listen, I've put you on point, riding with Michael again. All you have to do is follow him."

"Whatever you say."

"I'll see you later." He stood, smiled down at me, and then made his way around to each ranch hand.

I finished my breakfast, retrieved Sandy, and prepared for the day.

Riding point thrilled me. Certainly no dust to eat. Granted all I did was keep up with Michael, but I realized the skill this position required. The cattle seemed to bellow more, maybe they wanted a day of rest after stampeding.

I reveled in this lifestyle, and my "hyahs" at the cattle that day contained a joy that bubbled up from within me. So what if someone was trying to kill me. If I was going to die, I'd die with my boots on, like any good Marine. And it didn't matter that they were cowboy boots instead of combat. Besides, God had my six. He had promised me a double share of honor and a double portion of prosperity. That was a promise for here and now, not just when I entered heaven.

"You certainly seem to be enjoying yourself," Michael said.

"I am. I feel so alive. I think God should have made me a cowboy in the 1800s."

He laughed at that. "God knows what He's doing. He made you for today. And His purpose for you is for today, not for the 1800s."

"My purpose? I've asked God to show me that, a lot. But I've never been 100 percent confident I heard Him correctly."

"I've never met anyone with such a determined spirit as you have. You're a warrior, Sal. Part of God's army. You're meant to be leading the charge."

"I know I'm a warrior, and I understood who the enemy was during Desert Storm. But now?" I said.

"The war I'm talking about is in the spiritual realm. The enemy is out there, like a roaring lion, seeking whom he may devour. God loves you and He's proud of you. You're his beautiful warrior daughter, and you're right in the middle of His will for your life."

"Wow, where did that come from?" I asked. His words permeated my spirit like a flaming sword. How could Michael know God had called me His beautiful warrior daughter just last night? And did that mean someone attempting to kill me was part of God's plan? No doubt the enemy wanted me dead.

"A word of knowledge the Holy Spirit gave me just now."

"I don't know quite what to say or how to respond."

"It's your choice to accept those words or not."

"I know about the devil and him wanting to devour us. But God saying I'm His beautiful warrior daughter? Daughter, yes; warrior, yes; beautiful, no."

"Do you think of Aunt Abby as beautiful?" Michael asked.

"Yes, she's very beautiful. What's that got to with anything?"

"Are you not identical to her?"

"Yes, I am, but—"

"No buts, you are just as beautiful as she is," he insisted.

"My life experiences have taught me otherwise."

"It's time to overcome that false belief. Beauty is more than what's on the outside. It's what's inside radiating outward that brings beauty. Like I said, you have a determined spirit. From what I've seen so far, you have a heart that seeks after God. As you identify false beliefs and replace them with God's truth, that beauty will shine forth."

"I…thanks. I'll give all that some long thought." What false beliefs did I hold and how were they impacting my life?

Michael flashed an encouraging smile, then galloped after a cow (or was it a steer?) headed in the wrong direction.

A warmth permeated me as I pondered his words. Did God really feel that way about me? He said so last night. I knew in my head He loved me, but I had never experienced being loved, except by my mother. That was so long ago, I had nearly forgotten how being truly loved felt. God, help me experience Your love within my spirit, not just know it in my head.

# Chapter 18

## Chase

Fools think their own way is right, but the
wise listen to others. Proverbs 12:15

Clear skies and decent temperatures blessed the day. I had skipped breakfast and now my belly was yelling at me. I rode to the remuda to see if Leslie had something I could snack on. It would be a good way to check in on her as well.

I scanned the horses but didn't see her anywhere. I spotted Joe and rode over to ask him.

"Where's Leslie?"

"Don't know. She rode off to find a privy about thirty minutes ago."

"And you didn't notice she hadn't returned? Something could have happened to her."

"Sorry, boss. She's a big girl. She knows how to take care of herself. She had a rifle and bear spray."

"Which way did she go?"

"Behind us," he said, jerking his head in that direction.

I headed northwest, shaking my head as I rode. This roundup was quickly earning "the worst ever" title. "Leslie!" I yelled into the expanse of prairie.

No reply. I rode a ways on. "Leslie!" Still no answer. I scanned for a dust trail. Nothing. I checked the sky for buzzards. Nothing, and for that I thanked God. "Holy Spirit, show me where she is." I reined up my horse and sat quietly, listening for Holy Spirit's answer.

*Jake.*

I had Jake on left point, opposite of Michael and Sally. I spurred my horse into a gallop. The moment I spotted Leslie next to Jake, I reined in. How should I handle this? Surprise her now or follow her and see how long she rides with Jake? I growled at myself for allowing her to come. I urged my horse into a lope and caught up with them.

"Leslie!"

"Daddy! What are you doing here?" she said innocently.

"I run this outfit, remember? You're supposed to be with the remuda. Now get your butt back there, and tonight, you're going home."

"But, Daddy, I had to—"

"But nothing. Now go."

She stared at me momentarily, defiance in her eyes, then rode off.

"Jake, what's going on? What was she doing here?"

"Said she missed me."

Uncomfortable with Jake's tone of voice, I scrutinized his face. "She may be your wife, but while she's out here she works for me and is under my authority. You know that full well."

"Yes, sir. I—"

"Get back to work," I commanded and rode off to check on the drag riders.

The rest of the day passed uneventfully. As evening arrived, most ate supper and retired to bed. Leslie and Jake were both conspicuously absent. I wolfed down my meal and left to find them.

"I don't know why you came, Leslie. All you've done is complain and connive," I heard Jake say as I approached them. Connive? I stopped short. It was wrong to eavesdrop, but these circumstances demanded it.

"I came to keep my eye on you. I've seen you flirting with Sally. And it's not the first time I've seen you flirting with another woman," Leslie snapped.

"Don't be ridiculous. I don't flirt with other women, and I didn't flirt with Sally," Jake insisted.

"I mean it, Jake. I believe the evidence of my own eyes. If I catch you again, I'll file for divorce, and I'll see to it that Daddy fires you."

Jake grabbed her upper arms and jerked her toward him. "Don't you threaten me. I'll do as I please."

Time to intervene. I stepped forward into their line of sight, watching Jake as I did. Jake dropped his hold on Leslie as if a snake had bitten him.

"Hey, you two. Missed you at supper." I pretended not to have noticed the tension between them. "Did you get anything to eat?"

"I wasn't hungry, Daddy, besides, I'll get some decent food when I get back into town."

"Excuse me, I've got first shift guard duty tonight," Jake said and tromped off. I watched him leave, then turned to Leslie.

"Is everything all right? You two seem upset."

"It's fine. Nothing I can't handle. ...Daddy, would you please reconsider sending me home?"

"No. I think that's best. You go have a long hot soak in that jacuzzi of yours and then get a good night's sleep in a soft bed. Tomorrow go back to the magazine and ride herd over that big desk of yours. It'll be more comfortable and a lot less dirty. With you out of the office, who's been minding your duties?"

"Matt."

"The one who's sweet on Emily?"

"Yes, that's him. How am I getting home?"

"Gabe should be here soon. I radioed him early today."

Leslie drew in a short breath and exhaled just as quickly. I struggled to read her mood, her normal confidence absent.

"Earlier today? You decided to send me home whether I complained or not?"

"You made your choice when you left your position this morning and rode with Jake."

"I tried to tell you. Joe gave me a message to deliver to Jake."

"Joe gave you a message to deliver?" An outright lie, I knew. Joe said Leslie had ridden off to find a privy. Should I ask her what the message was? How deep a hole would she dig? "And did you deliver it?"

"Of course."

"Gabe will be here soon. Gather your stuff."

"Okay. I guess I'll see you sometime after you get back." She leaned up and gave me a peck on the cheek.

"Wait for Gabe at the Jeep." I kissed her cheek and gave her a hug. "I've got other things to check on. Bye, hon." I left to find Michael.

Tomorrow I'd make a point of watching how Jake acted toward Sally. Clearly, Leslie was upset. She'd witnessed inappropriate behavior from Jake before and not just with Sally. I didn't like it. Jake's threatening, abusive behavior toward Leslie just now disgusted me. I'd never seen him behave that way toward anyone, let alone Leslie.

# Chapter 19

## Sally

You will trample upon lions and cobras; you will crush
fierce lions and serpents under your feet! Psalms 91:13

As the roundup drew to a close, I dreaded its end. Eleven days
and around one, maybe two, hundred head of cattle. I couldn't
tell. I saw a waving sea of black. Every moment thrilling in
its own way. Except for the stampede and the dead steer—that I could
have done without. Chase had paired me with Pete, Michael, and Jake,
with a wide variety of duties. I kept a vigilant watch over my shoulder
for potential trouble. But despite the hazards, I'd learned a lot and had
grown not only a deep respect for what the family had accomplished,
but also for the work of the cowboy and rancher.

After Leslie left the roundup, Jake's behavior toward me turned rude
and aggressive. At times, his chaw spit came close to landing on me.
My comments about it only served to make him madder. I'd decided
to keep a close eye on him. He might feel as cheated as Leslie about
missing out on the profits from the ranch and magazine. After all, they
were husband and wife.

Tonight was our last night out. Tomorrow, I'd sleep in a soft bed
again. My body rejoiced in that idea, but my head refused it. Warmer
temperatures blessed the day. I draped my jacket over my saddle,

grabbed my blanket instead, and retreated from camp to watch the sunset, the same as I had each night since Chase had taken me to Hunting Bear Cliff. I'd brought a flashlight, intending to stay and watch the stars paint their velvet black canvas. I spread my blanket and stretched out.

A peace I'd never experienced settled over me. I felt at one with this land, this simple lifestyle free of today's modern conveniences.

"Father, lead me. What is it You have for me? Why have You brought me here of all places?" I sat listening for His still small voice in my spirit. Nothing. Maybe I was asking the wrong questions. Michael said I was a warrior. God said I was His warrior daughter. But I'd had my fill of fighting battles while in the Corps.

"The thought of returning to the noise and violence of KC makes me cringe. I've inherited profits in the ranch and the magazine. But nothing has been said about staying here to actually be a part of this family. I think I could get to like that. You've brought me to a crossroads, heavenly Father, and I don't know what road to take from here. If I'm Your warrior, what war is it You want me to fight? Please show me the way."

I knew for certain I would return to Kansas City only long enough to find somewhere new to live. But where? And what of Jen? What about our plans to start our own publishing company? Would they be willing to leave Kansas City? I couldn't ask that of them. "You're not at that bridge yet, Sally," I said to myself. "Focus on today. You've got at least two more weeks to put into this effort."

At least I didn't have to return to erotica fiction and Berkley Snyder.

A rustling in the brush startled me and I turned to find Chase standing there.

"May I join you?"

"I guess so. I'll even share my blanket if you want." I took a deep breath and willed myself to relax. I'd let my guard down for a moment, but it could have been a very costly moment. That rustle in the grass could just as easily have been a bear or a human killer. I scooted over and Chase took a seat, cross-legged, on a corner of the blanket.

"You looked a million miles away. Something troubling you?" Chase asked.

"I was just thinking about the fact that I don't want this to end."

"The sunset?"

"The roundup. I can't explain it, but I feel like I belong here. The peace, the beauty this place offers. It makes my life in Kansas City look feeble in comparison. I grew up in a small rural community. I never realized how much I missed it until now."

"So why are you living Kansas City?"

"I moved there for the job." I pulled my knees to my chest and rested my chin on my knees. The sunset cast its final rays. "Now that this is done, what do the next two weeks entail?"

"Good question. What do you want them to entail?" He stretched out his legs, leaned back on one arm, and looked at me. His face held sincerity, as did his voice.

"I was just asking God that question. Mr. Kandell stated I share in the profits, but the will never said anything about becoming an actual part of the ranch. I'd like to learn more about running the ranch, but if everybody expects me to leave after my four weeks is done, learning about ranching seems a moot point."

"You mean you want to stay?" Chase said, his voiced laced with incredulity.

"Yes. I know that must seem silly. I'm still trying to figure out why your father wanted me here for four weeks if it wasn't to stay eventually, to be a part of the family." I rushed on before Chase could interrupt me. "I haven't met Abby yet, but it appears she and I might really be twin sisters. I don't want to go back to Kansas City and leave behind a sister I always wished I had. I grew up an only child, and now, I'm suddenly a part of a very large family."

Chase sat silent, his face blank of emotion. What thoughts raced through his mind at my words? I could hardly believe I'd spoken them, let alone even thought them.

"I'm sorry. I have no right to insert myself into your family. Forget I said anything."

"No, no. It's not that. I'm just surprised. I've struggled with that aspect of Pop's will as well. That he wanted you to stay and become a part of the family, part of the ranch, never crossed my mind."

"I can imagine Leslie's response." I rolled my eyes. "She'll love that."

Chase laughed. "No doubt. But don't let her intimidate you."

"She doesn't." I shrugged. "I came out here tonight seeking some answers from God, but I haven't heard any."

"They'll come when He's ready for you to take the next step. I wanted a chance to let you know before we headed home tomorrow that you've been amazing. You do seem to belong here."

"Belonging here. That only complicates things. A friend in Kansas City and I talked about starting our own publishing business. But I dread going back to KC. Traffic and sirens and cement." I shook my head and sighed.

"With God, you'll figure it out. ...Listen, tomorrow's tasks will get a little hectic. The boys will load the horses onto trailers, and we all head back home."

"How do all of us get back?"

"Most of the hands will ride back in the pickups towing the horse trailers. But Gabe is driving up in the ranch van for everyone else."

"Did all the cattle make it, except for the one that got shot?"

"As far as I know. We'd better head back to camp and let the night critters have our space."

We stood and I gathered up my blanket. We walked back to camp in a comfortable silence. It seemed we had finally made peace with one another.

I didn't feel sleepy, but maybe once I lay down, I'd feel different. I grabbed my jacket from off my saddle, heard a rattle and a hiss, and felt a sting on my right arm. I didn't have to look at my arm to know what had happened. The angry snake rattled more, poised to attack again. I stepped back out of its reach.

"Chase!" I yelled but kept my attention on the snake. Certainly didn't need him slithering off into someone else's bed or advancing toward me for another tasty chew on my arm.

"What's happened?" Chase said as he jogged up next to me. He grabbed my arm.

"That's what happened." I nodded toward the rattler. "Sure wish you had your rifle with you."

About that time Michael showed up. He did have a rifle and promptly shot the critter. "I'll radio the police to send an ambulance," Michael said.

"Sit down." Chase pulled a handkerchief from his back pocket and wiped away the blood oozing from the bite. "How are you feeling?"

"Startled. And it hurts, a lot, for such a tiny wound. How poisonous is that snake?"

"Enough to kill, but you'll be fine. We're only fifteen or so miles from town. The ambulance won't take long." He used my bandanna to wipe away the blood oozing from my forearm. "How'd this happen?"

"It was under my jacket. I didn't notice anything when I picked it up. That was enough to make the snake mad though. Bit me before I even knew it was there. Seems odd, it being there after all this time on the prairie and no other wild animals causing any problems."

"Yeah, we've been fortunate." But the look on his face said more.

"I can tell by your look you're not telling me something."

He shook his head. "Just concerned for you and watching for signs of a reaction to the venom. Try and relax. The faster your heart pumps, the more that venom makes its way through your system."

It wasn't long and I heard the faint sound of the ambulance siren.

Chase whisked me into his arms as we watched the ambulance pull up. The EMTs jumped out and pulled a stretcher from the back of the ambulance. Chase softly laid me on the stretcher. In short order, the ambulance rushed me to the hospital in Great Falls, Chase and Michael watching as we drove off.

During the drive more symptoms settled over me. "Hey guys, I'm beginning to feel nauseous and lightheaded."

One of the attendants patted my shoulder. "That's expected. Here's a vomit bag. We'll be at the hospital in no time."

But I was vomiting and covered in sweat before we ever arrived.

As I lay in a hospital bed...in the dark...in the wee hours of the morning, my mind whirled with questions. I had just begun to believe no one was really out to kill me, but now, my suspicions came raging back. Someone put that snake under my jacket. I was certain of it.

Once the ER doctor had administered an antivenin, I recovered quickly. The doctor all but guaranteed I could leave in the morning, and I didn't want to do anything to put that in jeopardy. As I lay in the hospital bed, I began to meditate on Psalm 23 to calm my mind.

"The Lord is my shepherd." He takes care of me, watches over me.

"He makes me to lie down in green pastures." Yup, I'd been doing that for the last ten days. But Satan had snuck in. He'd snuck into the Garden, too. Why should here be any different?

"Yea, though I walk through the valley of the shadow of death, I will fear no evil." Shadows can't hurt me. Jesus is my refuge and strong tower and...

"Good morning, young lady," a nurse quipped as she entered my room. Her cart of medical equipment clanked as she approached my bed. "I've come to check your vitals. If all's well, you can have breakfast and go home."

I pushed myself to a sitting position and held out my left arm. She placed the blood pressure cuff and pushed the button on the machine. As it pumped the cuff, she swiped a thermometer across my forehead. "How are you feeling?"

"Ask me that after I've had my coffee." I chuckled. "Just kidding. I feel okay. My arm hurts a bit, but overall, my body is saying a big thank you for having a bed to sleep in."

"A bed to sleep in? You aren't homeless, are you, dear?"

Dear? Was I back in Missouri? Why did people use terms of affection on perfect strangers?

134

"No. I've been on an old-fashioned cattle roundup. Sleeping on the ground. That's how that nasty rattler bit me."

She patted my shoulder and wrote some things on my chart. "Your vital signs are good. Let me take a look at your bite."

I held out my right arm and she gently removed the bandage. I looked down at the bite and shrugged. "Looks fine to me," I said.

"Yes, it looks excellent. You're a fast healer, Miss Clark."

"The Lord is my healer."

"Amen to that, honey."

I watched her as she dressed my wound with a clean bandage. "I don't have any way of getting back to Reynolds' ranch, and I don't know how to contact them. Can someone look up the phone number for me so I can call them?"

"Let me check at the nurse's station to see if there are any special instructions. Your breakfast should be here soon." She left the room.

I climbed out of bed and traipsed to the cabinet, hoping to find my clothes. Good, they were there. I grabbed them and went to the bathroom. When I came back out a tray of food was sitting on the tray table. I sat down on the edge of the bed and pulled the table close. I lifted the cover to find a fried egg, hash browns, and two slices bacon. Yummy. I'd had enough of Cook's Spam to last me till next year.

Just as I finished, there was knock on the door.

"Come in." I watched as the door opened and a man entered.

"Good morning. I'm Dr. Jordan. Your numbers look great," he said as he perused the chart in his hands. "The nurse is writing up your discharge papers as we speak. Four will be here to get you in about an hour."

"Four? You say that like you know him."

"Oh yeah. The Reynolds family is well-known. Good people." He smiled and peeled back a portion of my bandage. "This looks excellent. No redness at all. The nurse wasn't kidding when she said you heal fast."

"Considering all the dust and dirt you scrubbed off my arm last night, I'm glad, too. Any special instructions before I leave here?"

"Keep it clean. Take it easy for a few days. Here's a scrip for pain medication. Get it filled and don't wait until you're in pain to take it. If you start feeling bad, come back." He replaced the bandage and placed some fresh tape over it. "It was nice to meet you, Miss Clark. You take care."

"Thank you, doctor."

He smiled and left the room. I leaned back on the bed.

In truth, I welcomed establishing a daily routine again. I liked being on a horse each day and being on the range, but I hadn't been able to get in my daily three-mile run or have my daily Bible reading and quiet time with God. I desperately needed both. I glanced at the clock: 7:39. I had an hour to kill before Four arrived.

*Kill.*

Not my best word choice given the circumstances.

# Chapter 20

## Sally

*He will cover you with his feathers. He will shelter you with his wings. His faithful promises are your armor and protection. Psalms 91:4*

The drive back to the ranch was a short one. Four and Emily plied me with questions about how I felt and my night in the hospital. "I'm fine, really. I'm sure there's something much more interesting we could talk about, like when am I going to meet Abby?"

"Our pilot, Steve, is bringing her in from Minnesota at noon today," Four said. "She'll be at breakfast in the morning."

"Good. I'm so excited about meeting her. Speaking of the magazine, how come you're not at the office, Emily?" I asked.

"I thought you might like a bit of female companionship this morning, that's all."

"That was very thoughtful of you. Thank you." I squeezed her hand to acknowledge her kindness.

"So, Emily, is the rumor I hear correct? Are congratulations in order?" Four asked.

"If you're referring to my engagement, then yes, the rumor is true," she said with a big smile.

"Who's the lucky guy?" Four said. "You're the most eligible bachelorette in Great Falls. Every guy in town has been after you."

"Don't be ridiculous. You know perfectly well that Matt and I have been dating for over a year."

"Congratulations," I offered. "Is he one of the ranch hands? I don't recall meeting anyone named Matt."

"He's one of our journalists at the magazine. He asked me out on a date the first week he worked there. I don't know why he took so long to ask me to marry him. Do you have a boyfriend waiting for you to come home, Sally?"

"No. Men aren't interested in a woman unless she's under thirty-five. I passed that mark ages ago."

"Hey now, don't forget there's a man present," Four said. "And if you want to talk in cynical generalizations, I'd say it's mostly men over forty-five who only look at women under thirty-five."

"Yeah, you might be right about that, mid-life crisis and all that," I said. "Guess I'd better start looking for someone under thirty-five, equality of the sexes and all." We all burst out laughing. When our laughter subsided so did the conversation. We rode the rest of the way in silence.

I retreated to my room as soon as we arrived.

My saddlebags lay on the bed. I headed immediately to unpack them, but then pulled up short as I reached out. Who had brought them here and was there a "surprise" inside? I felt a bit guilty for suspecting that one of the Reynolds children might have planted a rattler in one of the pouches.

I stood staring at it.

Nope. I'm not opening either pouch.

The feeling someone was out to kill me clutched at my throat. I left the room to find Chase or a ranch hand. Except for servants in the kitchen, the house was empty. I made my way out to the barn and nabbed the first guy I could find.

"I've got a favor to ask. Have you got a few minutes," I asked.

He shrugged. "I guess so. What do you need?"

"I need someone to check my saddlebags for rattlesnakes."

He laughed, but swallowed it down quickly when he saw my raised eyebrows and the anger in my eyes. "You're serious."

"Darn tootin'. What's the saying, 'Once bitten, twice shy'?"

"Oh, yeah, I heard somebody got bit. That was you, huh?"

I nodded and turned back to the house. He followed.

"Joe, where you goin'?" someone hollered. I turned and spotted Jake standing at the barn door.

"Miss Clark wants me to check her saddlebags for rattlers," Joe hollered back.

"Don't be ridiculous," Jake yelled and jogged toward us. "Get back to work," he told Joe and jerked his hand over his shoulder, his thumb pointing toward the barn.

"Sorry, Miss Clark," Joe said and made his way back to the barn, head hanging.

"You need something, you ask Chase," Jake grouched. "I don't want you interrupting work with silly errands."

I took a deep breath in an effort to remain calm. "I have no idea how my saddlebags got to my room. They were sitting next to my jacket. What's to say a different rattler didn't crawl in for a cozy sleep?"

"Snakes don't travel together. They're lone creatures. Who knows how many hands have picked up those bags. If there was a snake in them, it would have protested long before now. I've got work to do. Go find Chase to open your bags," he said, scoffing. "Never met a scaredy-cat Marine before!" He started laughing at that thought and stomped off, laughing all the way back to the barn.

"And a good day to you, too," I said under my breath. Since the night Leslie left the group, Jake's attitude toward me had grown mean. Better that than constant advances.

Where my saddlebags were concerned, maybe I was being silly. Scaredy-cat Marine, indeed. I had stared down situations Jake probably couldn't even imagine. I headed back toward the house and my room.

I stood there. By the bed. Just staring at the bags.

"Something wrong?"

The voice startled me and I jerked around toward it.

"Sorry, didn't mean to startle you," Chase said from my doorway.

"I know it's silly, but I'm concerned there might be a snake hiding in one of those pouches." I explained to him what I had told Jake.

"Guess if I was you, I'd be a bit skittish, too. I'll check." He walked over to the bed and smacked each pouch, then stopped and listened. He did this several more times. "I think we're good." He unbuckled each pouch then proceeded to dump the contents on the bed.

Out plopped a snake among my other things. Chase and I both jumped back from the bed. The snake just lay there, as though dead. We stood staring at it for several moments.

"Why isn't it moving? Is it dead?" I asked.

Chase stepped closer and examined it from a safe distance. Then he grabbed a book from the bookshelf in the room and threw it at the snake. Nothing happened.

"Hmm, it must be dead," Chase said. He approached the bed and cautiously reached out to grab the snake. "Wait a minute…" He jerked the thing from the bed and whipped around to face me. "This is fake!"

I stood frozen to the spot.

"Sally! Are you okay?" He threw the fake snake to the floor.

"What a dumb question to ask! I'm livid."

"I asked because you're face is ashen and dripping with sweat." He reached his hands out toward me and cradled my shoulders.

"I had a run-in or two with venomous creatures when I was in the Middle East. Was real sick. Guess it bothered me more than I realized." I collapsed into the chair behind me. "I'll be fine."

"Can I get you anything?" He knelt beside me, concern etching his face.

I leaned forward, resting my elbows on my legs and burying my face in my hands. "Wow." My pulse pounded in my ears. I sat breathing deeply for several seconds, then leaned back in the chair as I calmed. "Guess I'd better report this to my VA doctor. I was totally panicked."

"Do you suffer from PTSD?"

"Never been diagnosed as such. But like I said, I'll let my VA doc know about this."

"Malmstrom Air Force Base sits on the east side of Great Falls.

Maybe you can see a doctor there."

"Thanks for the suggestion, but it isn't necessary, really. A fake snake. Who would do something like that and why? Is this your idea of a practical joke?" I leaned forward, almost nose to nose with him.

Chase stood, putting his fists on his hips. "There you go again, assuming the worst of me. How can I get it through that thick head of yours I want you to have that inheritance as much as Pop did?"

I looked up at him and wondered if I should tell him about the whispered conversation I'd heard the night of the stampede. I stood from the chair and glared up at him. "My thick head knows otherwise. Let me tell you." I moved to the door, then turned to face him. "First, Sandy's saddle comes loose while I'm in it and dumps me to the ground. Second, a steer gets shot not five feet away from me. Next, a rattlesnake finds its way under my jacket and a fake snake into my saddlebags. Those things alone should be enough, but let me add one more." I paused for effect, but it was lost on Chase.

"Go on. I'm waiting."

"The night of the stampede, I went to watch the sunset. On the way out of camp I overheard part of a conversation between two men. 'She can't inherit anything if she's dead,' one guy said. The other tried to protest. 'No buts. You'll be richly rewarded.' Now tell me someone in this family isn't out to get me."

I stomped over to the bed while Chase stood dumbfounded beside the chair, staring at the fake snake on the floor. As I began gathering my dirty clothes from the bed, Chase grabbed my arm and pulled me around to face him.

"Why haven't you said something about all this before now?" he grouched.

I pulled my arm free from his hold. "Because I didn't know who I could trust. ...I still don't."

Chase's angry expression softened and his shoulders slumped. He sighed and ran his fingers through his hair. "You can trust me. Let's keep this information between the two of us here at home. As soon as you're up to it we—you and I—will report it to the sheriff. For now, I think a day of rest for you is in order."

"O…kay," I said. Where was the snappy comeback when I needed it?

"I'll ask Rita to draw you a hot bath. You can soak and relax as long as you like."

"That sounds great." I stood staring at him. Maybe he wasn't so bad after all. "Thank you."

He grinned, nodded his head, retrieved the fake snake from the floor, and strolled out the room. The rock in my stomach disappeared and peace settled over me. My level of trust in Chase eked up a bit. The final test would be when we sat before the sheriff to report my claims.

# Chapter 21
## Sally

I will say of the LORD, "He is my refuge and my fortress;
My God, in Him I will trust." Psalms 91:2 NKJV

As Chase scooped up the fake snake and left my bedroom, the peace that passes understanding washed over me. The kind I'd read about so often in the Bible. Chase's concern cemented the fact that someone intended to kill me. I plopped down on the bed as that thought sunk in. As I sat there, the Soldier's Psalm flashed into my mind. My commanding officer in the Middle East had all Marines under his command memorize and quote Psalm 91 on a daily basis. Not one Marine had been killed or injured during his tenure. I quoted it out loud now to counter the enemy's attack on my peace.

"I will say of the LORD, '*He is* my refuge and my fortress; My God, in Him I will trust.' ...Surely He shall deliver you from the snare of the fowler." God had not brought me here to let me be killed. He promised me a double share of honor and a double portion of prosperity. I took a deep breath and pushed aside the enemy's fear tactics.

Right now, I had eleven days of grime clinging to my body. A long hot soak sounded wonderful. Rita informed me when the bath was ready, and I lounged in the tub for a long time, careful to keep my right arm out of the water. I tried not to think about anything. Every time the thought of someone trying to kill me entered my mind, I resisted it and meditated on Psalm 91 and Isaiah 54:17, "No weapon formed against you shall prosper, And every tongue which rises against you in judgment You shall condemn."

After my bath, I made my way to the kitchen and asked for a sandwich, then retreated back to my room. I ate the sandwich and then lay down to catch up on the sleep I'd missed last night.

"No weapon formed against me shall prosper. Not stampedes, not bullets…not snakes…not panic…attacks, and not…Leslie Reynolds."

When I awoke, darkness had descended. I grabbed my cell phone to check the time: 4:30 a.m.! Guess I was more tired than I realized.

The doctor had ordered rest, so I skipped my morning run. Tomorrow, for sure. I dressed, took a long deep breath as I left my bedroom, and made my way to the dining room. Empty. "Duh, Sally, what did you expect at this time of the morning?" I told myself. Even the servants were probably still sleeping.

Today I'd meet Abby! An excited nervousness coursed through my veins. It isn't every day you meet the twin sister you never knew you had. I went back to my room and grabbed my Bible from my suitcase. Yesterday's panic attack concerned me. I needed the peace and calmness of spirit I so often found during my quiet times with God. I also wanted to maintain that peace that passes understanding that had washed over me yesterday afternoon.

I read from Joshua. As I read verse six, it leapt off the page at me. "Be strong and of good courage, for to this people you shall divide as an inheritance the land which I swore to their fathers to give them." Divide as an inheritance. Was this an answer from God? Was He assuring me the inheritance was mine?

I had a goal to achieve. I'd survived Dad's verbal abuse and fifteen years in the Marine Corps. I wasn't going to let a snake bite get the best of me—or someone trying to kill me. I determined once again I would conquer this challenge Chase Reynolds, Jr. had deposited in my lap. At six o'clock, I laid my Bible on the bedside table and walked back down to the dining room. As I reached the entryway, I paused. Why couldn't this first meeting with Abby happen between just the two of us rather than with the whole family gawking at us? Hoping to identify who was already in the room, I listened for any conversation. All I could hear was the chink of silverware on the china.

"Good morning. We missed you at supper last night."

I spun around, startled, yet again, by Chase's voice. "Chase. Good morning. I wish you'd stop sneaking up on me." I gave him a weak smile. "Sorry about supper. I took a nap and slept clear through to 4:30 this morning."

"Are you feeling okay? You seem a bit jumpy."

"I'm nervous about meeting Abby. But I'm excited too. Is she in there? It's the crowd of family looking on that bothers me most."

"I hadn't even given that a thought. I'm sorry. Abby might feel the same way. I haven't spoken to her since we left on the roundup." He stuck his head around the entryway and perused the room. "She's not in there. How about I show you to my office, and I'll find Abby and bring her there? Then you two can officially meet and get past some of the awkwardness before facing the rest of the family."

"That would be very nice. Thank you."

He took me by the elbow and led the way to his office. "I'll be back in two shakes of a calf's tail," he said, clicking on the light to the room and then quickly leaving.

I took the opportunity to examine the room. Built-in bookcases lined one wall—be still my heart! I love books. Most of the shelves were full of ancient-looking tomes. No doubt a collection of the generations of Chases. A large desk made of a dark red wood I didn't recognize commanded the room. Behind the desk on one side were french doors, on the other a large picture window. Along the wall across from the desk stood two leather chairs with a small rectangular table between them. The room oozed masculinity. Why shouldn't it; it was Chase's office.

I walked to the picture window, though what I expected to see, I don't know. At 6:00 a.m. the sun still hadn't risen, but a pre-dawn gray tinged the horizon.

I heard a noise at the door and turned from the window to see who was there. Chase stood in the doorway. "Sally, this is Abby." He reached out his arm and Abby stepped into view. Seeing her there was like looking into the mirror, but not quite. She wore her hair long and pulled back. A small amount of makeup adorned her face, and she appeared a bit heavier than I was. I don't know how long we stood there silently making our own observations of each other.

"I'll leave you two alone. If you need me, I'll be in the dining room," Chase said, and left.

Abby and I stood glued to our places for a moment longer. Then a big smile broke out on Abby's face and a tear dripped down one cheek. She rushed toward me and caught me up in a hug.

"Sally, I'm so thrilled to meet you. Welcome to the family." She released her hug and stepped back to observe me. "How could anyone doubt we're twins. No one wonder Pop was so taken with you. I can't imagine why he and Mom said nothing about meeting you."

"I understand from Chase that until now you didn't know you were adopted. I expect that had something to do with it."

"Yes, you might be right. Would you like to sit or take a walk as we talk?"

"I'd prefer a walk. We could watch the sun rise." I stepped to the french doors, and we walked out into the coolness of the morning, Abby leading the way.

"I'm excited you're here. Tell me all about yourself," Abby said.

I shrugged. "Not much to tell. My mom died when I was ten. Dad took her death pretty hard. Turned to alcohol. I joined the Marine Corps when I graduated high school."

"What was that like? Did you see a lot of the world? I've never been abroad."

We reached the corral next to the barn. I climbed the fence and took a seat. The horizon now shone scarlet with the advancing sun. Horses in the corral whinnied and approached me. I reached out and rubbed their foreheads. Abby took a seat next to me.

"I served in the Middle East and a couple places in Europe. Paris! It's an amazing city with such history. You've got to visit it sometime. When

I heard about the fire at Notre-Dame Cathedral, it really upset me. All that history and architecture. I'm glad they're restoring what they can."

"Let's visit it together. You could be my guide. Maybe Chase would join us and we can experience Paris like Mom and Pop did."

"I've let my passport expire, but yeah, I think I'd like that. You know, as foreign as my time overseas was, being here among your family is more foreign to me than that ever was."

"Why? We're ordinary people," Abby said.

"Ordinary! Far from that. The life of a rancher isn't ordinary. And you live in the lap of luxury. This beautiful home. Servants that manage the daily household tasks. Miles and miles of land. Hundreds of cattle. I've been alone most of my life. I can't imagine growing up with a brother. And there are all Chase's kids. Such a big family."

"Yes. I've had a wonderful life. ...I'm sorry yours seems to have been...otherwise."

"It's been okay. Saw lots of places while in the Corps, learned a lot. It's served me well throughout my adult life." I needed to change the subject. "Tell me about you. Married? Kids?"

"Never married. Couldn't find a man like Pop." She laughed, and shoulder bumped me. "I've been quite content to be single. I'm very active in my church—I sing in the choir—and I love running the magazine. I understand you're an editor at a publishing house. Do you like it?"

"Yes, I do. A friend and I are thinking about starting our own publishing company. I'd like to see how things run at the magazine. Could I get a tour?"

"Of course! I think we're going to get along famously."

Our conversation fell silent as we watched the sun rise and the horses playing in the corral. I felt...I couldn't identify the emotion in my gut. Good, bad? No. Empty. Why had I felt so alone all my life? That it was me against the world.

All these attractive men around me accentuated my singleness. Like excising a boil, they had lanced the loneliness I'd been suppressing for decades. Now it gushed to the surface like a drill striking oil. A boil would heal, but how could I heal my loneliness?

"Has this all been a bit overwhelming for you?" Abby broke the silence.

"A bit? No, a lot." I scoffed. "For the most part, everybody has been very kind."

"That's good. But your face says there's more. I want our relationship to start on a positive footing. I know we've only just met, but I sincerely want to know if there's something wrong."

"My emotions are acting chaotic today. I think I'm just worn out. Between the roundup, the stampede, and getting bit by a rattler, I need some recovery time."

"No doubt. Leslie is still grumbling about sore muscles and she only lasted, what, five days?"

I sighed and looked over at her. It had been me against the world for much too long. I was alone because I never opened up to let anyone in. Now, suddenly, I had twin sister. I didn't want to shut her out. Maybe it was time to take an emotional risk and stop being the stolid Marine. "I've been an emotional basket case since yesterday. I've felt all alone since my mother died. Like it was me against the world. My time in the Corps only accentuated that. Right now, inside, I feel like my life is being rototilled."

"Rototilled?"

"Everything is all mixed up, like a farmer tilling the ground before he plants. I always wanted a sister. And looking at you, it's like looking in the mirror almost. I'd love having a sister." I knew I was afraid to get hurt if I reached out for this relationship, but I couldn't tell that to Abby. "If we're twins, why didn't your dad adopt us both?"

"I've been wondering the same thing. I wish I had an answer."

I sighed again and hopped off the fence. "My emotions are raging. I'll blame the rattler. I apologize."

Abby hopped down. "Don't be silly. There's nothing to apologize for." She stood staring into my eyes as though searching for something. "You believe you're unlovable and unworthy, don't you?"

I stood dumbfounded. I'd never thought of that, but the moment she said it I knew she was right. Somehow this family had a direct pipeline to God! First Michael gives me a word from God, and now Abby seemed to have inside knowledge about my life.

"Sally, God loves you! You are worthy simply because you are God's child." She pulled me into a tight hug. "You're not alone anymore. You've never really been alone; God is always with you."

A few tears trickled down my cheeks. After a gentle cry, I pulled back from her hug and took a deep breath. Get a grip, Marine. "Thanks. I'm okay now. I'm still going to blame these chaotic emotions on that rattler." I wiped my tears with my shirttail and smiled. I had to get my emotions in check. I could see the train wreck coming if I got too attached to this family despite my desire to embrace them.

"You can blame it on the rattler, but in doing so, you're denying the fact that the Holy Spirit is revealing and healing a deep wound in your life. You do have a born-again relationship with God, right?"

"Yes, I do."

"Then acknowledge His working in your life." She took my face in her hands and looked me straight in the eye. "God wants me to tell you 'Be strong and of good courage, for to this people you shall divide as an inheritance the land which I swore to their fathers to give them.'" She dropped her hands from my face.

"Wow! That's the exact verse God showed me this morning during my quiet time."

"Then no doubt it's confirmation of a message God needs you to hear. Everything's going to be fine. God has things in control. He loves you, and so do I. As far as I'm concerned, you're a part of this family." She gave me another hug and a smile.

I felt a warmth within my spirit and wondered if, for the first time ever, God's love had permeated to my spirit.

# Chapter 22

## Sally

*Why are you cast down, O my soul? And why are you disquieted within me? Hope in God; For I shall yet praise Him, The help of my countenance and my God. Psalms 42:11 NKJV*

Chase stood from his chair as Abby and I entered the dining room. He might be rude at times, but he was always the gentleman. A rude gentleman. Is that an oxymoron?

"Good morning, ladies." He acted as though he hadn't already seen us this morning. "Abby, was your trip successful?"

Abby gave him a quick kiss on the cheek.

"Yes, it was. Thank you. Did you boys leave anything for me and Sally?" she said, looking at the heaping plates of food that sat in front of both Gabe and Peter.

"Ah, come on, Aunt Abby. We're not that cruel," Gabe said. Abby chuckled.

"Come on, Sally. Let's see what Rita cooked for today." She grabbed a plate from the table and made her way to the sideboard. I did the same.

"What's on the agenda for today now that you've put the cattle to bed?" I asked as I finished putting some hash browns on my plate.

Chase began to laugh. "Put the cattle to bed." And he began to belly laugh.

"What's so funny?" I asked. I looked at Abby. She shrugged. Pete and Gabe seemed just as clueless. Finally, Chase brought his laughter under control.

"I just had this wild image of the cows and their calves climbing into bed, and Sally pulling a blanket up over them and kissing them goodnight." And he began to laugh again. Now that everyone else had the picture, laughter burst out around the table. While everyone had a good laugh, I set my plate down next to Abby's, then filled a cup with coffee, and took a seat.

"Okay, so we didn't really tuck those black beasties into bed, but we did finish the roundup. Do we get to rest a day or two?" I asked. "Where are all your other children?"

"As bachelors, Gabe and Peter still live here. Everyone else has their own homes. Four and Michael are already out in the barn," Chase said.

"I guess I assumed everyone lived near enough to join here for breakfast every day." I felt the tension exit my body at the news that Leslie lived in town. A respite from her constant "looks could kill" glares that she had dispensed during every meal on the roundup.

"On a working ranch, there is no rest," Chase explained, wiping tears of laughter from his eyes. "I needed that laugh. 'A merry heart doeth good like a medicine.' Do you need a day to recoup? Didn't the doctor say you were to take it easy for a few days?"

"Yes, he did, but I think a day will suffice. Is there some kind of plan for me for the next couple weeks? I mean, I'm sure your dad had a purpose for me to be here for so long."

"Since Pop didn't tell us anything about this, we really have no idea," Abby said, between mouthfuls. "Maybe the three of us can discuss it after breakfast." She pointed her fork toward Chase.

"Sounds good," I said. "I know I don't want to sit around doing nothing. Assign me some chores or something."

"Maybe she can help us with the foals, Pop. They seem drawn to her the minute she shows up at the barn," Peter said.

"Really? I hadn't noticed that," Chase said.

"That's because you weren't there. Surely you noticed how Sandy treats her," Peter said.

"Yeah. Sandy isn't even that nice to Aunt Abby," Gabe said.

"Sandy isn't mean to me," Abby protested.

"I didn't say she was. I just meant she treats Sal in a way she doesn't you," Gabe explained.

What did that mean that this horse treated me better than anyone else in the family? What did that say about me? That I was more attractive to horses than to people? I didn't know whether to laugh or cry at that thought.

"Let's finish breakfast, then we'll discuss things in my office like you suggested, Abby."

I finished my meal amidst routine family conversation. With a full stomach and a cup of coffee, my emotions steadied out. Whatever had gotten into me? I'd have to talk with God about that tonight at bedtime.

Trepidation filled my stomach as we entered Chase's office. That feeling of a calf to slaughter washed over me again. How many times would my stomach flip with that thought? Only Chase prompted it. Should I tell him how he made me feel? At least I had two blessed weeks without Leslie's constant presence. Then I remembered there was Jake to deal with. As rude as he was yesterday, would he ignore me or get even meaner? Or would he resume his advances toward me now that Leslie wouldn't be around to observe him?

Sally, you made it through the Middle East mess; you can make it through this. But in wartime I understood the rules of engagement and who the enemy was; here, it was anybody's guess about both. My enemy? In my opinion, Leslie headed that category, with Jake running a close second. But would they commit murder? Clearly, someone had attempted to kill me. I needed to remind Chase about visiting the sheriff. I'd have to get him alone, or could I create a plausible excuse?

*Remember the message I just gave you through Abby and keep your eyes on Me just like Peter did when he walked on the water toward Jesus.*

Yes, Father. Thank you for the reminder. I'm never alone; You're always with me. Abby has accepted me as her sister, blood or not.

"Abby, have you had an opportunity to give this any thought?" Chase's words drew me back to the here and now. He took a seat at his desk.

"Not much. That press trip occupied my mind." She pulled one of the leather chairs against the wall closer to Chase's desk and sat down. "Pop wanted us to get to know her."

I pulled a chair next to Abby and sat down, looking questioningly at Chase for his response to Abby.

"I seem to remember someone saying something about her learning about ranching and the cowboy life," Chase said.

Abby shook her head. "I wish Pop had talked to us about this. Maybe he intended to."

"How would that change things?" Chase asked, leaning back into his black leather chair.

"Not change, just give us an idea of his intentions. Then we'd have a better feel for what she can do during her stay."

"You know," I stood quickly from my chair, "I think I'd be a lot more comfortable if I just left the two of you to discuss this on your own." I turned to leave the room.

"Nonsense. Sit back down. This is about you," Abby said to me, then turned to Chase. "We need to pray about this, and we need to ask Sally her thoughts."

Chase bolted forward in his chair, leaning his forearms against the edge of his desk. "You're right. I haven't been thinking clearly since the day Pop died. Maybe Pop did mean to tell us. I'm sure he didn't expect that heart attack. But now Holy Spirit can tell us." He looked at me. "Would you be too uncomfortable praying with us?"

"I'd be fine with that." I made eye contact with him as I spoke. His eyes held such pain.

"Abby, why don't you lead us?" Chase shifted his elbows to the desk, clasp his hands, and leaned his head down on his hands.

Abby and I bowed our heads and she began.

"Father, thank you for this amazing gift You've given me, to meet a sister I never knew I had, and a twin sister at that. I'm in awe of how You work in our lives. All the same, this has been rather overwhelming to us. First Pop's death and then learning about Sally and that I'm adopted. We don't know what Pop intended, but You do. You're the One who told him to do it. Reveal Your intentions to us."

I drew in a deep breath and released it. This had to be worse for them. Grieving their loss and then finding out about me. That put things in a different perspective for me. In all this wild ride, I continually failed to remember they were deeply grieving. Maybe in that, I also misread their intentions toward me.

Abby sat quietly, listening for an answer, I expect; so did Chase. I had rehearsed a myriad of scenarios all throughout the roundup. A bolt of realization flashed through my mind. In the past ten days, I had discovered how at home I felt in a saddle and out on the plains. Life in the big city meant crowded sidewalks and crowded streets, the stench of vehicle exhaust, heat radiating off the cement in summer, and my car sliding around on icy streets in winter. No, I needed and wanted more simplicity to my life and to make a home in the country or at least in a much smaller town than KC. And God had opened the door to heal my wounded heart.

"Father, give us Your wisdom. Guide us. Help us to rest in You and to simply get to know Sally," Chase said. "Thank You, Lord. In Jesus' name, amen."

I looked up at Chase who was looking at me with those penetrating bronze eyes. He sighed and leaned back in his chair again. "Abby, did you get any particular direction?"

"All I sensed was normal routine."

"Me, too," Chase said, nodding his head as he spoke. "Sally, what about you? Did the Holy Spirit speak anything to you?"

"I…" I looked from Chase to Abby, then back at Chase. "No words specifically, but a realization. I want to simplify my life. It's time to leave Kansas City."

"The country life does seem to agree with you." Chase smiled. "And that helps. For this first week, let's try to get back to normal, at least, start to find a normal without Pop. Sally, would you be comfortable helping Gabe and Peter with the foals?"

"I'd like that very much."

"Okay then. In a week, we'll reevaluate. How's that sound to you, Abby?"

"Like a good idea. But I'm going to work here at the ranch with Sally. I can't get acquainted with her if I'm living in town and working at the office every day. I know that's not the normal routine for me, but like you said, Chase, we're finding a brand new normal."

And so, my four-week trial continued.

# Chapter 23

## Chase

The wicked are trapped by their own words, but the
godly escape such trouble. Proverbs 12:13

As Abby and Sally left my office, I sought the Holy Spirit again. "God, why did Pop die? My spirit is heavy with grief. It's as though you've ripped off the scar forming on my heart from Karen. Do you want me in a perpetual state of grief? Is that how you keep me humble and dependent on You? I'm not sure I like it. In fact, I know I hate it.

"God, help me understand. Forgive my anger. It's not for me to question Your will or Your actions. But I need Your grace to endure. Show me the way. I want to be obedient to Your Word and Your will. I need to be strong for Abby and all the kids. I can't do that without You."

*Remember, my son, My grace is sufficient. Lean on Me, not on your own understanding. I am doing a work in Sally's heart and yours. Open your heart to her.*

"Open my heart to her! What does that mean?"

*In your presence she feels like a cow to be culled. Allow yourself to see her for the woman she is and not an interloper. You have allowed Leslie's complaining to taint your view.*

"Oh, God." I dropped to my knees, God's words resonating within my spirit. "I'm so sorry. I hadn't realized. Thank You. You are such a wondrous God and worthy to be praised. I worship You, O Lord. Guide me each day as You have today and all the days before and all those yet to come."

*Show her you're trustworthy. Take Sally to the sheriff as you said you would.*

"Yes, Lord." I rose and made my way to the barn, first to find Four and Jake, then Sally.

I found Jake in the barn office along with Four.

"Good, you're both here." I pulled a chair next to the desk and sat. "Abby, Sally, and I just met to discuss Sally's duties for this week. Pete and Gabe suggested at breakfast that she work with them and the foals. I agreed. Do you have any objections to that, Four?"

"Not at all. She does seem to have an affinity with the horses."

"Jake? What about you? Any objections?"

"Yeah. She did nothing but complain those days she rode with me during the roundup. I don't want to listen to more. She'll only get in the way."

"But she'll be working with Pete and Gabe, not you. And they suggested it, so they must not have any complaints about working with her," Four said. He appeared as upset by Jake's opinion as I was.

"Abby will be here, too, working alongside Sally, so they can get better acquainted. Business as usual, Jake. With your duties, they won't get in your way. All the same, let me know if there's any problems." I scrutinized Jake as I rose from the chair and put it back. Jake's brow was crinkled in anger and his jaw was clenched. Was Leslie's complaining affecting him the same way it had been me? No doubt Jake had to put up with Leslie's complaining more than I did. But Jake's terse words to Leslie and grabbing her arm that night during the roundup? No, that spoke more to his own desires. A deep foreboding settled in my spirit as I left the barn to find Sally.

I walked to the foal training area to find Sally. She was perched beside Abby on the corral fence, watching and listening to something Gabe was explaining.

"Hate to interrupt, gang, but the sheriff needs to talk with Sally," I said as I approached them. "Abby, if you want, you can ride into town with us and I'll drop you off at the office until we're done."

"I'm not dressed for the office. Why don't I go with you to the sheriff's?" Abby asked.

I wasn't prepared for that question. How could I discourage her without creating suspicion? "Have you had a chance to talk to Leslie about your being here at the ranch for the next couple weeks?"

She and Sally climbed off the fence and brushed the dust from their pants.

"No, I haven't. I guess this would be an ideal time. Let me grab my purse and my phone. I'll meet you at the truck." Abby jogged to the house while Sally and I walked to where the truck was parked.

"Why does the sheriff want to talk to me?" Sally asked.

"He doesn't. We need to talk to him, remember? You're feeling up to it, aren't you?"

"Yeah, I'm fine."

"Good. Just remember, I'd like to keep this between us two. I especially don't want Abby to know. It'll be too upsetting for her. She'll hover over you like a mother hen. From what I've seen of you so far, I don't think you'd be very comfortable with that."

"You're right about that." She grinned, but then it quickly disappeared. "I don't feel comfortable keeping secrets from her. She welcomed me into the family so readily this morning. Said she wanted our relationship to start on 'a positive footing.' I do too, and keeping secrets is hardly that."

"No, it isn't. I'm sorry to put you in that position, but right now all we have are suspicions. Let's talk to the sheriff and see what he advises."

Sally appeared dissatisfied with that answer, but she held her tongue as we climbed into the pickup and waited for Abby.

"Let me get this straight, Chase. You're saying that shooting wasn't just an accident?" said Sheriff Terry Daniels.

"That's right."

"And you're basing that on what?" Sheriff Daniels asked.

"Sheriff, I heard—"

I held my arm out in front of Sally to stop her. She had nearly bolted from her chair as she began to speak.

"I had my suspicions the day of the stampede. I should have told you then, but I didn't want to entertain the thought that someone I knew could be trying to kill Sally."

"That's understandable," Sheriff Daniels said. "Obviously things have changed, because you're here. Give it to me again, but this time give me all the details."

"Pop willed a third of the ranch and 10 percent of the magazine to Sally. Five of my children got 10 percent of the magazine as well. But Leslie got $200,000 instead of 10 percent like the others. She threw a hissy fit over that. We were all perplexed at Pop's will; none of us knew Sally Clark. But Pop's will also stipulated Sally had to spend four weeks at the ranch." I turned to Sally and nodded for her to tell her observations.

"Since arriving at the ranch," Sally began, "I've tumbled to the ground because of a loose saddle, a steer was shot, I got bit by a rattler, and we found a rubber snake in my saddlebags the day I got back from the hospital. All those things might seem like accidents—or a practical joke—except for two things. One, it's too many accidents all at once, and two, I overheard part of conversation stating 'she can't inherit anything if she's dead.' When the second party in that conversation tried to protest, he got encouraged with 'you'll be richly rewarded.' If that doesn't sound like a plan to kill me, I don't know what you'd call it."

"Yes, I agree." The sheriff rocked in his chair for a bit.

"Face it, Chase, there are only two logical suspects. Only Leslie and Jake have any real motive to get rid of me," Sally said.

"Yes, the same thought has occurred to me."

"The voices I heard sounded like men, but I was hearing the conversation at a distance. The 'you'll be richly rewarded' does sound like someone outside the family is taking those pot shots at me."

"Should I put an officer in there to keep an eye on you, Miss Clark?" the sheriff asked.

"I know how to take care of myself. I don't need police protection," Sally protested.

"With respect, ma'am, you're not twenty anymore and could easily be overpowered by a man."

I watched Sally, expecting her to jump out of her chair. Her body tensed, but it seemed she was working to control her temper.

"Sheriff, I run three miles a day, every day. I'm a Marine. I expect I could hold my own even against you."

I watched a smile slowly come and go on the sheriff's lips. Somehow, the thought of Sally and Sheriff Daniels battling it out forced a smile to my lips. Given what I had seen of her performance during the roundup, I expect she could hold her own. "Besides, Terry, a deputy at the ranch would disrupt things too much," I said.

"Oh, I see," Sally turned on me. "What does it matter if I get hurt, but let's not interrupt the smooth flow of your day!"

I huffed but tried to remain calm. "That's not what I meant. How do we catch a killer if he knows we're onto him? A deputy at the ranch would tell everybody something fishy is going on."

"It's not up to you to catch the would-be killer, Chase. That's my job," Sheriff Daniels said. "Keeping Miss Clark safe is my primary concern."

"I'll keep an eye on her. If she's never alone, I think she'll be okay," I said.

"I wasn't alone when that steer got shot," Sally said.

"No, but you were out in the wide open. Those conditions don't exist at the ranch. But no morning run."

"No way! That run serves my peace of mind as much as it does my body," Sally argued.

"I'll let you two settle that later. For now, I'll connect with Chouteau

County Sheriff's Department about the shooting. Who took the report that day?"

"Deputy Lone Wolf," I said.

"Okay. I'll apprise him of the developments and we'll revisit his investigation. We'll get to the bottom of this, rest assured," Sheriff Daniels said.

# Chapter 24

## Sally

For the mouth of the wicked and the mouth of the deceitful
Have opened against me. Psalms 109:2a NKJV

*L*ongstanding Christian heritage indeed," I mumbled as I climbed into Chase's pickup as we prepared to leave the sheriff's department.

"What did you say?" Chase said as he slid into the driver's seat.

"I said, longstanding Christian heritage indeed."

"Being Christian doesn't mean we're perfect."

"I know that. I'm just tired of Christians who tout their Christianity but fail miserably at living it." I looked over at Chase staring at me. He said nothing, then turned his attention to starting the pickup and driving back to the ranch. I turned toward the window.

*Sally, you're letting your father's behavior taint every relationship you have. King David sinned time and again. That didn't make him any less a man after My own heart. You are not without sin. Judge not.*

I sighed and willed my body to relax, then silently answered God. Heavenly Father, You're right, of course. I'm so sorry. I struggle to understand Your love for me, and I'm sorry to say I expect You to turn on me, too, just like Dad did. Please heal that wound.

I wiped away a stray tear and watched the scenery go by. Chase drove without attempting conversation. I suppose he was deep in thought like I was. When we stopped to get Abby, she immediately discerned the tension between me and Chase and kept silent for the drive to the ranch.

When we arrived, I headed straight to the barn.

"Sally, tell Gabe I'll be out in a few minutes," Abby yelled after me. She probably planned to grill Chase about what was going on. What would he tell her?

The next day Chase refused to allow my morning run. Instead, he offered an evening ride to watch the sunset. I agreed on one condition, that there be no conversation between us unless I initiated it. My morning run was my solace. I communed with God and listened for His guidance for the day. My time with God fed my spirit. I didn't want Chase's presence to steal that from me. His agreement surprised me.

Abby had not approached me about the tension between me and Chase. Maybe she was waiting for me to initiate that conversation. Her behavior toward me remained on an even keel. I did my best to act as though nothing was wrong. Not easy when you know someone is trying to kill you.

As Tuesday arrived, my spirit had regained some peace. I lost myself in working with Gabe in training the foals. Okay, mucking out stalls I could do without, but it was part and parcel of ranch life.

"Sal! Come here. I need to talk with you a minute," Jake hollered from the door of the tack room.

I looked at Abby, then at Gabe.

"What could he want?" Abby asked.

I shrugged my shoulders, then walked the length of the barn to where he stood.

"Five of the men have just reported the cinch on their saddles was cut. That'll easily cost a couple hundred to repair. What do you know about it?"

"Why should I know anything about it?"

"Toby said he saw you coming out the tack room and a few minutes later when he went in to get his saddle, he discovered the damage."

"I went in to get curry combs. Are you accusing me of doing the damage?"

"Yes. I was in there earlier this morning and all was fine."

"Why would I do such a thing?"

Gabe and Abby approached us.

"What's the problem?" Gabe asked.

"Five saddles have been damaged. And I think she did it. Look at this mess." Jake stepped aside and we all peered into the room.

"Don't be ridiculous," Abby said. "She's been with me all morning."

"Were you with her when she went into the tack room?" Jake demanded.

"No."

"Well then," Jake said.

"Well then, nothing," Gabe said. "Report this to the police and let them investigate."

"I will as soon as this conversation is over. And I'm keeping my eye on you," Jake said, pointing his finger at me. He turned, walked back into the barn office, and slammed the door behind him. Abby, Gabe, and I returned to where we were exercising the foals.

"Why did he accuse you?" Abby asked.

"Because apparently I was spotted coming out of the tack room just before the damage was found."

We returned to our work.

Later, at lunch, we got a full accounting from Jake.

"It's five saddles, Chase. All damaged in the same way, the cinch cut clear through," Jake explained as he filled his plate.

"Well, get them to Buckholz to repair," Chase said.

"Already have. Sent Joe into town with them this morning." Jake scowled at me as he sat at the table, directly across from me.

I briefly grinned at him then turned my attention to the food on my plate.

"Any idea on who did it?" Chase asked.

"Sally. She was the last person seen coming out of the room. If it wasn't her, she'd have seen the mess," Jake said.

Chase looked over at me.

"The tack room looked fine when I was in there," I said, my hands raised in surrender. "It wasn't me."

"I didn't say it was," he said.

"The straps were strewn all over the floor! How could you not see that?" Jake said.

I dropped my silverware on my plate. "Like I told you this morning, because when I was in there, everything was fine. Which means the damage was done after I left."

"Or that you did it!" Jake said.

"Now hold on, Jake," Abby said. "Why would she do something like that? Why would anyone?"

"For the same reason someone hid a rattlesnake under my jacket," I blurted out. I slapped my hand over my mouth the moment I said it. "I'm sorry, I shouldn't have said that." I looked around at everyone sitting at the table. Everyone but Jake sat there shocked. Jake just scowled.

"Sal, Deputy Lone Wolf assured us that was an accident of nature," Gabe stated.

Palpable tension filled the room.

"I said I was sorry." But no one returned to their food. They sat there staring at me, and I was left to wonder what they each might be thinking. No one spoke another word. We finished eating and returned to our respective duties, but the afternoon conversation was subdued. Only Abby spoke to me as though nothing had happened.

For the following two days, nothing but tension filled the air. I plodded about my work all the same but prayed in the Spirit every moment that didn't demand my focused attention. When Thursday dawned, I wanted and needed my morning run. I'd missed all my runs since the roundup had begun. The sun blazoned the eastern sky with hues of magenta then fiery orange. Magnificent. A run would energize me and improve my mood. Not only did my run keep me physically fit, it kept my emotions positive. But I had promised Chase I wouldn't run, and if I was going to complain about unChristian behavior, I certainly couldn't renege on my promise.

I spent most of the day mucking out stalls. Abby had been called into the office. Everyone stayed busy. The ranch functioned like a well-trained squad of Marines out on maneuvers. Still, the tension in my shoulders increased. My teeth ached at day's end from clenching them all day. I watched the machinations of the ranch and wondered what was normal. What had Mr. Reynolds' duties been before his untimely death? Everyone seemed tense, but maybe I was projecting my own tension onto them.

Friday dawned with the realization that today marked three weeks since coming to the Double R Ranch. I pulled on my sweats, slipped quietly out of the house, and jogged to the far corral. I climbed the fence to watch the sunrise. As I sat there, I meditated on the verse God had given me from Joshua, divide as an inheritance the land. I believed more than ever God intended me to have this inheritance.

As sunrise ended, I prepared to return to the house. Sitting there on that fence even the most inept sniper could have snuffed me. I hopped down and scoped the area. Nothing out of the ordinary. The smell of bacon and sausage enticed me the moment I stepped into the house. I took a quick shower, dressed, and skipped down the stairs, ready to greet the day with my usual bright-eyed and bushy-tailed manner. One more week, Sally. One more week and it's home free.

The first evidence of a tainted day announced itself as Chase, Abby, and I returned from picking up the repaired saddles in town.

"What is that horse doing there?" Chase exclaimed as we all observed a horse prancing along the driveway. He slowed the SUV to a stop. "Abby, take the wheel. I'll hop out and get her." He shifted into park and slipped out of the seat. Abby left her seat next to me in the back and went around and climbed in behind the steering wheel. She pulled out slowly, and I watched as Chase approached the horse, grabbed its halter, and led it back to the barn.

As we arrived at the house, more horses and several foals greeted us in the driveway.

"Whatever happened? These horses should all be in the corral next to the barn," Abby said. She quickly parked the SUV and got out to round up the animals. I slipped out of my seat to help, glad they each wore a halter.

"What's going on!" Chase hollered as he approached the house with the other horse. He jogged to the corral, the horse complying with the quickened pace. Chase came to an abrupt stop about five yards from the corral. He looked around at Abby and me. "The gate is open. Who was out here last?"

"I have no idea," Abby said.

"I came out at sunrise. All was fine then, and I didn't see anybody else around," I said, as I helped herd the animals back into the corral. Chase shut the gate after the last animal entered.

"Let's get lunch. And first thing after breakfast tomorrow morning, Abby, I want to meet with you, Jake, and Four. Too many *accidents* have occurred for my comfort level. It's time to get to the bottom of all this."

# Chapter 25

## Chase

Truthful words stand the test of time, but lies
are soon exposed. Proverbs 12:19

As Saturday dawned, my gut churned. Troubled thoughts filled my night. First the stampede and dead steer. Then Sally getting bit by a rattler. Then damaged saddles. And yesterday, the corral gate left open and the horses loose. I also had to consider the fake snake in Sally's saddlebags and the conversation Sally had overheard. Someone was behind all this, and I was determined to find out who.

Conversation at breakfast was almost nonexistent. Apparently, Abby and Sally had similar thoughts on their mind.

"I'll grab Four and Jake from the barn," I said as we finished eating. "Abby, meet me in my office. Sal, you find Peter or Gabe and work with them until this meeting is done." I rose from the table.

"Now hold on," Abby said. "Sally should be in that meeting as well. Jake has already accused her of damaging the saddles. If you're going to talk about her, then she should be there."

"I agree," I said, "but I don't think Jake would. I want to hear his opinion, and he might hold back on what he really wants to say if Sally is in the room. Are you all right with that, Sally?"

She looked at me, then at Abby. "I agree, my presence might influence Jake's input. Seems I don't really have a choice."

"You're right. I'm not giving you a choice. I'm sorry. Seems to me someone is doing their best to discourage or scare you and chase you back to Kansas City before your four weeks are completed." I shook my head and sat back down.

"Chase me away? More like kill me," Sally grumbled.

"I don't want to believe it's Leslie, but she's made her position quite clear. She's complained and grumbled constantly," I said.

"But what can she hope to accomplish with her complaining?" Abby asked.

"Probably to change my mind about contesting the will. I really don't know myself. I only know that she's become selfish, snobbish, and greedy. Let's get this meeting over with, shall we? And keep my suspicions about Leslie to yourselves." I rose and headed to the barn. I found Jake and Four in the office, discussing the day's tasks.

"Good morning," I said as I entered the office.

"Good morning," they echoed.

"What's up, Pop? You look upset about something," Four said.

"I am. The gate to the corral was left open yesterday. Abby, Sally, and I had to round up ten horses when we got home from town. I guess everybody was too busy doing their chores to notice horses prancing around the driveway. I'm calling a meeting in my office right now." I turned and headed back to the house, Four and Jake following.

We all got settled in our chairs and I began. "After yesterday's mishap, I've come to the conclusion that none of what's happened here since Sally arrived has been an accident."

"Are you saying you think that shooting was intentional as well?" Four asked.

"Yes, that's exactly what I'm saying. And I'm going to say what I've been trying to avoid. Someone here at the ranch is behind it." The fact that Sally had overheard a suspicious conversation during the roundup cemented the fact that someone at the ranch was behind all that had been happening.

"That's absurd," Abby exclaimed. "Why would any of our people—"

"Because someone doesn't want Sally to complete her requisite four weeks," I finished the sentence for her.

"But how do any of those things affect her being here?" Jake said.

"Come on, Jake, you can't be that dense. Those shots might have been intended for her. And that rattlesnake didn't just magically find its way under her jacket. It was planted there," I insisted.

"Pop, why would anyone be so blatant? I mean, wouldn't it be better to just discourage her enough to make her say no to the inheritance and leave?" Four asked.

"I'd say nearly getting shot and getting bit by a rattler would accomplish that—for any normal female. But Sally isn't your normal female. She's an ex-Marine. She served in the Middle East. The woman has grit and bulldog determination," I explained. "Whoever is behind all this forgot that or didn't account for it at all."

"Who says it isn't Sally causing these problems here at the ranch?" Jake asked.

"Why?" Four said. "What would that accomplish for her?"

"I don't know. Women don't think like men. And you just said, she ain't normal. Maybe she's gone a bit crazy like a lot of soldiers do after they get out of the service. You know, PSD or whatever they call it."

"PTSD, post traumatic stress disorder," Abby said. "She's been out of the Marines for at least fifteen years. I think that would have shown up before now."

"Maybe it has and she didn't tell us. Why would she? It could put things at risk," Jake countered.

"Put things at risk? PTSD or not, it wouldn't affect her inheritance," I said. "She told me the day we came home from the roundup. I found her staring at her saddlebags on the bed. She was struggling to open them, convinced there was another rattler waiting to strike."

"What'd she say? That she does have PTSD?" Abby asked.

"That she's never been diagnosed with it. But she had a panic attack while I checked and emptied her bags. Said she'd had a few run-ins with venomous creatures in the Middle East. She didn't deny she was panicked."

"I rest my case," Jake boasted. "She ain't in her right mind. Besides, she was nothing but snooty to me the whole time we were movin' the cattle."

"That's the first I've heard that. Why haven't you said something before now?" I asked, but Jake's poor English only came out when he was angry. What did he have to be angry about where Sally was concerned?

"Being snooty didn't affect her performance. I figured it was just personality differences."

"Four, how'd she behave toward you?"

"Fine, Pop. She might have mentioned Jake's tobacco habit. That spit can be disgusting."

"Maybe so, but that's no reason to act rude," Jake protested.

"Wait a minute," Abby interjected, "she told me you tried to come on to her."

"I never did any such thing!" Jake said, jumping from his chair.

"Enough!" I commanded. "Everybody just calm down."

Jake took a deep breath and sat back down. Abby crossed her arms. Four shifted in his chair. Clearly, emotions ran high and opinions differed.

"So what do you want us to do, Pop?"

"Keep alert. Watch everybody and report anything suspicious to me and only me. This stays between us."

"What about Michael, and Peter and Gabe? They've been working with Sal the most," Four asked.

"Especially not them. It'll affect how they act around Sally and she'll sense it." I looked around at each of them, their faces troubled. "I can see none of you are happy about this. I'm not either. Tomorrow's Sunday. Sally will be starting her last week. I think it's time to take her into town to the magazine. I'm certain there are plenty of aspects about magazine publishing that are similar to book publishing. She'd probably enjoy a tour. Make that Monday, Abby. For now, you two finish out the day with Gabe and Pete."

Abby nodded and rose from her chair.

"Everybody back to work."

They each left by way of the french doors and headed to the barn.

I had my suspicions about who was behind all this, but how could I prove it? What had Sheriff Daniels found out? Time to update him on the recent mishaps.

But first a conversation with Sally was in order. I headed to the barn. I spotted her in the corral, surrounded by foals. As she jogged around the corral, the foals followed her like the Pied Piper. She seemed more at home with the horses than with people. Guess I couldn't blame her for that, knowing that her father had abused her. Then I remembered she said too many people had betrayed her. Maybe it was time to ask her about that. I approached the fence.

"Hey, Sally." I called to get her attention.

"Hi, Chase." She walked toward me, the foals following.

"The boys weren't kidding when they said you had a way with the horses. Do they always follow you like this?"

"Yeah, they do." She smiled and wrapped her arms around the closest two.

"I hate to break up the fun, but let's take a ride."

She shrugged. "Okay, I won't refuse a chance to escape to the wide open range." She climbed the fence and jumped down. We walked to the barn and saddled our horses.

"Gabe, Sally and I are going for ride. See you in about an hour."

"No problem, Pop. See you guys later," Gabe said and waved goodbye.

"Can we let the horses have their head for a bit?" Sally asked as we cleared the last outbuilding. She had learned some ranching lingo.

"Don't see why not."

"Hyah." Sally urged Sandy on and soon Sandy was in a full gallop. I hung back a little and watched as Sally leaned back in the saddle, her arms outstretched, head back. If she'd had long hair, it would be flying out behind her in silky brown waves. No matter, the day's warm breeze tousled the sleeves of her shirt instead. Being out here on the open prairie, on the back of a horse, transformed her. The bitterness that had been so obvious the first day I met her disappeared. She let down her guard, that ever present guard. Something learned while in the Marine Corps or a self-protection coping mechanism learned as a child?

I urged my horse into a gallop and caught up with her. We let the horses run until they slowed down on their own. Sally let out a whoop and Sandy neighed in answer. Amazing. The two had truly bonded. How would Sandy react when Sally returned to Kansas City?

How would I react? We had enjoyed many sunsets together, despite her imposed silence during our evening sunset rides. I watched her as she mucked out stalls, as she and Abby interacted. Sally belonged here. Obviously, somehow, Pop had come to the same conclusion.

"A penny for your thoughts?" I said as the horses slowed to a walk.

She shrugged in the way that I had come to recognize was a habit for her and looked over at me. "Just reveling in the freedom. Relishing the warm breeze on my face, the scents of the prairie. I'm really going to miss this."

"I expect we'll all miss you, too."

"Not everybody. Somebody doesn't want me here. What'd'ya find out during the meeting?"

"Not much. But Abby mentioned something I wish you'd told me. Did Jake really come on to you?"

She scoffed. "I know I'm not prettiest filly in the barn, but you say that like I'm the ugliest pig in the pen." Her cynicism returned.

"I didn't mean that at all. You have a bad habit of misconstruing my words. Jake denied the accusation. I want to hear your side."

"Jake was being a typical man. Made innuendos, looked at me like he was stripping me naked. Leslie noticed his looks. She confronted me about it."

"So she did give you that split lip, didn't she. You should've told me."

"Why? Daddy's little girl wraps you around her little finger whenever she wants."

"If that were the case, I wouldn't have sent her home five days after the roundup began. And just what do you mean by 'being a typical man'?"

She scoffed again, louder this time, and gave me a sarcastic look. "You're a man. Figure it out."

"Typical men don't make innuendos or strip a woman of her clothes with their eyes."

"I can count on one hand the men who haven't approached me in that way. So yes, typical."

"You toss out generalizations about men like corn to the chickens. There are plenty of honorable, decent men in this world. You are the most cynical person I've ever met!"

She abruptly reined up Sandy, Sandy jerking her head in protest and prancing in a circle. Sally stared at me for several seconds. I tried to read the emotion in her eyes but failed. What thoughts were rampaging through her mind? Finally, I broke the tense silence.

"You told me about your father's abuse. But you said 'too many people' had betrayed you. Who else did? Someone close? Must have been for your bitterness to be so deep."

"I think it's time to head back to the ranch." She turned Sandy and began to head back.

"Oh no you don't." I reached out and grabbed Sandy's bridle by the bit to stop her. "We're not going another step until you tell me."

"Guess we'll be here quite a while. Did you bring some chow?"

Her words struck me as funny and I burst out laughing. "You've got grit, Sally Clark, but a stubborn streak as solid and wide and high as the Rocky Mountains. Don't you think it's time to let go of that bitterness and forgive the people who've hurt you?"

My words struck a chord. She thrust her hands onto her hips, leaned forward in the saddle, and glared at me.

"How dare you. You know nothing of my life or the battles I've fought."

I released my hold on Sandy and sat up. "Unless you tell me, I can only imagine. But God knows. He's been there, right beside you, in the midst of those hurts."

"Then why didn't He do something to stop them?" she yelled.

"Only God can answer that. But one thing I can say. God gave mankind freewill, and He won't overrule a person's choice. A parent hurts right along with his child but isn't always able to prevent that hurt. God loves you. Don't doubt that. Jesus died for you. He wants to heal those wounds in your heart."

"Just forget it. I'm tired of fighting. Tired of trying to prove my worth. Tired of getting hurt every time I open up my heart. Let's just end this conversation right now."

"No. God brought you to this family for a reason. …Wait a minute!" I paused as realization dawned. "Prove yourself? We never asked that of you."

"Really?" she said, sarcasm dripping from her lips. "From the moment we met in Kansas City, you've watched and judged me every waking moment."

"I've done no such thing," I protested.

"Do you think I didn't notice the way you sized me up that evening at supper? I felt like a cow to be culled then, and I still feel that way."

"I was merely noting the differences between you and Abby."

She harrumphed at my words. "You go on telling yourself that lie if it makes you feel better."

I sat there, contemplating her words. Then I remembered the Lord telling me Sally felt like a cow to be culled. I felt the conviction of Holy Spirit at the truth of her words. "You're right. I apologize for making you feel that way. It certainly wasn't my intention."

As soon as I spoke the apology, Holy Spirit impressed me with His response for Sally. "Sally, maybe you don't realize it, but you're working to prove yourself to God as well. That's what living under the Old Testament law demands. Christ's death on the cross fulfilled those demands. We're saved by God's grace, not because we've proved ourselves worthy."

She jumped down off Sandy and walked several steps away. My experience with women told me that at this point I'd better keep my mouth shut.

She took a deep breath and released it slowly, several times, then turned to face me. "I guess life has made me more cynical than I realized. I have been working to prove myself to God. And what's worse, I expect Him to let me down like most of the men in my life have. Is it any wonder I have never experienced His love. I've never opened up my heart to let it in."

I saw a tear trickle down her left cheek and her shoulders jerk as she silently cried. I dismounted and walked over to her.

"You don't need to prove yourself to God. He loves you just as you are, Sally. And He'll never leave you or forsake you." And with that she gently stepped into my waiting arms. I hugged her as I had hugged Abby so many times over the years. I hoped she accepted it as the brotherly hug it was.

I allowed her to cry as long as she needed. Moments later, her tears spent, she stepped out of my hug. I tried to imagine the years of hurt those tears represented, but I wouldn't ask her. I pulled a handkerchief from my pocket and handed it to her. She accepted it with a wan smile, wiped her eyes and nose, and handed it back.

"Thank you. Can we continue our ride?"

"Most definitely. And I want to reiterate, you do not need to prove yourself to me or anyone else at this ranch. Abby, Four, and Jake have been told I suspect someone tried to kill you. That someone here at the ranch is behind all these little accidents. I've asked them to keep that to themselves. The fewer who know the better, as far as I'm concerned. I'm going to apprise the sheriff of the recent mishaps and find out if he's discovered anything new."

We mounted our horses and headed north, the horses in a gentle walk, and a comfortable, though brief, silence between us. I regretted the moment when we had to turn around and head home.

"All that sounds workable, Chase. Only one week left for me. The killer might be getting desperate."

A knowing look passed between us.

# Chapter 26

## Sally

But the LORD will not let the wicked succeed or let the godly
be condemned when they are put on trial. Psalms 37:33

My ride with Chase that day kept me awake nearly all night. His calm response to my tears amazed me. Most men would be telling me to stop crying. But he just held me like a father would a hurt child—or a big brother would as he comforted his sister.

The moment he said I was trying to prove myself to God, I realized they confirmed what I'd heard from God. I reached over and turned on the light, then grabbed my Bible. "Holy Spirit, lead me to a verse that will speak to my heart," I whispered out. I sat silently for a moment, waiting for His answer.

*Ephesians 1.*

Ephesians, of course! Paul's epistle that speaks about our relationship with Christ more than any other book in the Bible. Verses 1 through 14 spoke to me on so many levels. I understood them in a way I never had before. But verses 4 and 5 set my spirit on fire.

"Even before he made the world, God loved us and chose us in Christ to be holy and without fault in his eyes. God decided in advance to adopt us into his own family by bringing us to himself through Jesus

Christ. This is what he wanted to do, and it gave him great pleasure."

He knew me and loved me before He even made the world! It was His "great pleasure" to adopt me. This revelation brought fresh tears. I pulled my journal from the drawer and spent the wee hours of the morning journaling and talking to God.

When I woke later that morning, I felt the warmth of God's love permeating my spirit.

Instead of shame and dishonor, you will enjoy a double share of honor. You will possess a double portion of prosperity in your land, and everlasting joy will be yours.

That promise from Isaiah 61:7 cemented itself in my spirit. I no longer doubted. This *would* come to pass in my life. I didn't know how God was going to do it, but I knew He would.

Sunday passed without event and when Monday morning arrived, I rose with God's love still radiating in my heart.

Abby gave me a tour at the magazine and then put me to work. I thought spending time at the magazine would be fun, but at every turn, Leslie shot cruel words or angry looks at me. I put to good use the skills I had learned in ignoring my step-dad's verbal abuse.

Once I learned how much my calm perturbed Leslie, I used it against her. I smiled as she yelled at me. I whistled a happy tune while I worked. I know it was wrong of me, but the more I thought about her hypocrisy, the angrier I grew. Tension began to build in my stomach, and my teeth ached from grinding them so hard each night. At least no one could take a pot shot at me while I was at the office.

As Thursday dawned, I took solace in the fact that my four weeks was nearly done.

"Aunt Abby, the money from the petty cash box has been depleted. Do you want me to go to the bank for more?" Emily said from the doorway of Abby's office. Abby and I looked up from what we were doing.

"Depleted? I checked it barely an hour ago, and the usual $1000 was there."

"Well, it isn't now."

"I saw Sally acting rather suspiciously with the cash box about an hour ago," Leslie said, coming up behind Emily.

"Suspiciously? I was simply putting it back like Abby asked me to," I told Leslie.

"Leslie!" Abby rose from her chair. "Thanks to your bickering words toward Sally all week, everyone in the office is on pins and needles. These insinuations end now. Sally did not take that money, and I don't want to hear one more word of accusation."

"If she didn't take it, then she won't mind us checking her desk and purse." Leslie stared me down, daring me to defend myself.

"I said that's enough of your insinuations. Emily, have you called the police?"

"No. It never occurred to me that someone might have taken the money. I just thought it had been used for one thing and another like it always is."

"Well, best call the police."

I looked over at Abby. "I didn't take it, Abby. How could I? The box is locked."

"Sally, I don't for one minute believe you took that money."

All work halted and everyone was sequestered in a conference room.

When the police arrived, Abby ushered the two men into her office. The rest of us waited in the conference room. A few minutes later, one officer came to the conference room and one by one took someone into Abby's office to question. The other officer began a search for the money. Most of us stood at the conference room window, watching as the officer made his search.

Only an hour or so had passed since Abby had counted that money and Emily discovered it missing. Someone in the office had to be responsible.

"Miss Reynolds!" the officer searching called. He stood at my desk, my opened purse in his hands, staring into it. Abby joined him. His call alerted us all, and everyone but Leslie and me now stood staring out at the action unfolding.

Leslie stood in the corner of the conference room, her arms crossed, staring at me, a triumphant smirk on her face.

"Is this the money?" the officer asked Abby as he pulled a wad of bills out of my purse.

By the time the group recovered from the surprise and turned to look at me, Leslie's smirk had vanished. Without a doubt, she had planted that money in my purse. But how was I to prove it?

Abby called Chase to come help sort through things. Now he, Abby, the two police officers, and I stood in Abby's office. The other employees had returned to their tasks for the day. Abby closed the blinds to her office window. No one could peer in or out.

"Officer, please explain the situation," Chase said.

"We got a call of a suspected theft. I questioned each employee individually, and my partner, with Miss Reynolds' approval, began a search of the office. Miss Reynolds was adamant the money couldn't have been removed from the office. Only an hour had passed since the cash box had last been opened and no one had come or gone during that hour. Miss Clark was the last person to have the box in her possession. We found the missing money in her purse."

"Thank you," Chase said, nodding his head as he spoke. "May I speak with Miss Clark and my sister privately for a moment?"

"Yes, sir," the sergeant said. He and his partner left the room. Certainly not the action I'd have taken as an MP, leaving the primary suspect alone.

Chase sighed deeply a couple of times and rubbed the back of his neck. "Who discovered the money was missing?"

"Emily," Abby answered.

He opened the door and called Emily in, then closed the door behind her.

"Emily, was there any particular reason you got into the petty cash today?" he asked her.

"The copy paper we ordered hasn't arrived and we've run out. I was headed to the store to buy more to tide us over."

"Did you notice anyone else with the cash box?"

"No, but Leslie said she noticed Sally putting it back."

"Okay, hon. Thanks." He ushered her out and turned to me. "We've had nothing but trouble since you came here."

"Now wait a minute!" I said.

"Chase, Sally did not steal that money, and she's not responsible for the vandalism that's occurred at the ranch either."

"Why would I do any of that? Do you honestly think I'm stupid enough to steal that money and then stuff it into my purse where it could easily be found?" I stared at the pile of hundred-dollar bills sitting on Abby's desk. I shook my head.

But Chase was right, it had been one thing after another. First, my saddle coming loose and dumping me to the ground. Then a dead steer and the stampede. A snake bite and the planted fake snake. Damaged saddles. Horses let loose. And now theft.

"I didn't say—"

"I should have realized the moment I met you and you touted your Christian heritage that it was all a facade. Like I said then, those who insist on stating it are the worst offenders. I'll pack my bags and be gone. You can keep your precious inheritance. I don't want it." I got my purse from Abby's desk and headed for the door.

"Not so fast," Chase said, grabbing my right forearm. His vice-like grip sent a lightning bolt of pain through my snake bite. I fought the urge to punch him. "You're going to face the police for this."

"Chase!" Abby stepped forward, placing her hand on his shoulder. "Don't be ridiculous. Sally did not do this, and I refuse to let you or anyone else railroad her."

He released his hold on me and stared at Abby for a moment, then turned to stare at me. I stood tall, shoulders back, head held high. My warrior spirit raged within me. My heart pounded. Was this the war

Michael had prophesied about?

Chase stood in front of me, but I saw my father and remembered his abusive tirades and his constant claims of "you're not my daughter." After our ride last Saturday, I thought Chase had, at the very least, accepted me as his sister. Now he stood accusing me of theft. I'd been a fool to think I'd fit into this family. I didn't fit anywhere.

"You and your precious inheritance aren't worth having. Longstanding Christian heritage. Live by the Golden Rule. From the moment I arrived I've been met with nothing but trouble. One incident after another made to look like accidents. Those accidents were deliberate attempts to get rid of me. I am innocent. I stand justified and righteous in Christ." I pulled my head back at that, astonished at the words that had come so calmly out of my own mouth.

Chase blinked several times. Maybe my words surprised him as much as they did me.

"You can keep your money. I want nothing to do with this family." I turned again to the leave the room.

"Sally, stop," Abby pleaded. "Don't do this. Chase will see sense, eventually."

I looked at Chase and gave him a moment to respond to Abby's claim. He didn't.

"You two are more stubborn than a bull moose at the peak of rutting season," Abby said.

"Only the Holy Spirit can knock any sense into that stubborn head of hers," Chase said.

I jerked open the door and stomped toward the exit.

"Officers, stop her! I want her arrested for theft," Chase hollered.

# Chapter 27

## Chase

So don't go to war without wise guidance; victory
depends on having many advisers. Proverbs 24:6

I watched as the officers handcuffed Sally.

"We'll need you to come to the station and file charges," the sergeant said.

"I'll be there soon," I told them. I watched briefly as they led Sally out, then turned to Abby. "Let's take this argument back into your office." I turned and headed that way. If Abby chose not to follow, I'd consider the argument over.

"This is not an argument," she said as we entered. She closed the door behind us.

"Why do you believe she's innocent? We know she was arrested for theft three times—"

"As a teenager! She served this country proudly for fifteen years. She did an exemplary job on the roundup from what Michael tells me. Why are you so quick to believe she's behind all this vandalism, because that's really all it is?"

"Shooting a steer is not vandalism. Stealing a thousand dollars is not vandalism. And I don't think the police would see it that way either. Look," I sighed, "I don't think she took the money, but no one gave me a chance to say so."

"Oh yes we did. We both waited for you to respond to my comment about you coming to your senses."

"And at that point in the conversation, my words would have fallen on deaf ears." I dropped down into a chair. "I sure wish Pop had told us about Sally the moment he decided to change his will."

"Well, he didn't, so live with it," Abby grumbled.

"Abby, I'm sorry." I stood and hugged her. "Sally and I had a long talk during our ride last Saturday. Men have repeatedly hurt her. Her wounds and bitterness misconstrue every word she hears me speak." I released my hug and smiled at her.

"Several people have access to the petty cash. Just because Sally was the last one seen holding it doesn't mean she did it," Abby said.

"No, but don't you find it odd the trouble at the ranch stopped the same week you two are in town and then trouble starts here at the office?"

"If someone's trying to discredit Sally, that pattern makes sense."

"Exactly. The attempts to get Sally to leave early have failed, so now someone is trying to frame her for this theft. I imagine that would certainly keep her from getting the inheritance," I said. "It's time I told you the whole story. Sit down."

"That sounds ominous," she said, taking her seat.

"Sort of. The day I shook out Sally's saddlebags, we found a fake snake. Someone distinctly was attempting to scare her. But…after her panic attack subsided, she told me about a few other things. Primarily a conversation she overheard that enforces the possibility that someone is not just trying to discredit her but to kill her."

"What! Why?" Abby jerked forward in her chair.

"Isn't it obvious? If she's dead, she can't inherit anything. The sheriff is investigating but hasn't found any evidence that points to anyone in particular. We have to get to the bottom of whoever is doing this. Having Sally arrested seemed like the only way to keep her here and for her not to forfeit Pop's inheritance. I'll explain as much to the sheriff."

"I'm coming with you."

"That works." I grabbed my Stetson from Abby's desk, and we headed to the sheriff's department.

My gut churned as I drove. Pop's voice rang loud in my head, *Treat others the way you want to be treated.*

"Let's pray before we talk with the sheriff," Abby said.

"By all means."

"Holy Spirit, if there's some other way to resolve this, show us how. Give us wisdom and insight," Abby prayed.

I hated doing this to Sally. She opened her heart to me and now here I was having her arrested. "Lord, protect Sally's heart. Don't let this situation make her shut down or be an excuse to let bitterness consume her."

Doubts about Leslie, the shooting, the snake bite, the vandalism at the ranch pricked my conscious daily. More and more I'd come to believe Leslie was behind those events, though the authorities had found no evidence to prove the shooting or the rattler were anything but accidents. Leslie hadn't been at the ranch for several days when they found the damaged saddles. But the stolen cash was from the magazine's office. Were Leslie and Jake in on this subterfuge together?

As Abby and I arrived at the sheriff's department, I cringed at the thought of Sally spending time in the Cascade County jail. I wondered what Sheriff Daniels would say if I asked if I could bail her out as soon as they were done filing charges.

I parked the car and turned off the engine. For a moment, I watched deputies come and go through the front doors of the station.

"Abby, you go on in. I'm gonna call Karl. I'll be in a minute."

Abby got out and made her way to the door. I took a deep breath, let it out slowly, then dialed Karl's number.

"Karl, let me warn you about what's coming. I've had Sally arrested for theft."

"You can't be serious! What is she supposed to have stolen?"

"The thousand dollars we keep for petty cash at the magazine," I told Karl.

"What proof do you have?"

"We found the money in her purse. Is that proof enough?"

"Only if she was the only one with access to the cash and to her purse. I can't imagine her doing something like that. Are you sure?"

"No, I don't believe she did it, but it was the only legitimate reason I had to stop her from going back to Kansas City."

"Going back? But she's got to complete her time at the ranch. Does she realize she's forfeiting everything by quitting?" Karl asked. He sounded dumbfounded.

"Yes, she knows. Said she didn't want it."

"Do I dare ask what precipitated this decision?"

"She thought I was accusing her of the theft and recent vandalism at the ranch."

"You didn't? And now you've had her arrested. What burr got under your saddle today?"

"Abby asked pretty much the same question, only with different words. I don't believe Sally's done any of these things, but we've got to figure out who has."

"What do the police have to say?"

"I'm outside the sheriff's department right now. I have to go in to press charges. I'm going in as soon as we hang up."

"I'll meet you there."

When Karl arrived, he, Abby, and I made our way to Sheriff Daniels' office, and I explained all that had happened as well as my suspicions about Leslie.

"Let me get this straight, Chase. You're saying you suspect your own daughter of framing Miss Clark?" Sheriff Daniels said.

"Yes. I don't want to believe it. But it's the only thing that makes sense. Let me lay out the events again."

"No, I think I got 'em. Your dad's will named Sally Clark as part owner in the ranch and magazine. He cut Leslie out of any profits but gave her $200K. And she's been het up since. Then once Sally showed up on the scene, all kinds of things started happening. But how could

Leslie be responsible for shooting that steer or putting a rattlesnake under Miss Clark's jacket?"

"You're right about that. Maybe those were just accidents, but—"

"Deputy Lone Wolf did a thorough investigation and found nothing to say otherwise," Sheriff Daniels said. "With what you've told me previously, I am inclined to believe they were intentional. But our additional investigation found nothing to prove otherwise. I agree the vandalism at the ranch and the theft have malicious intent behind them."

"Wait a minute. I'm missing something here," Karl said. "What previous conversation has Chase had with you, Sheriff?"

"He and Miss Clark came in shortly after getting back from the roundup. Miss Clark overheard a conversation that pointed to an intent to kill her."

"Kill her! Chase, why haven't you told me this?" Karl asked.

"I don't know, Karl. I've had too many other things on my mind, like keeping an eye on Sally." I sat there shaking my head for a moment, then turned to the sheriff. "During the discussion of how the money got into Sally's purse—planted, no doubt—she lost her temper. She declined the inheritance and said she'd return to Kansas City today. I didn't want her to do either. Having your officers arrest her seemed like the only way to stop those things from happening."

"Sounds like everyone was acting in the heat of the moment," Sheriff Daniels said.

"Yeah, you're right about that. It's only been about six weeks since Pop died. One thing after another has thrown us for a loop. Add grief on top of that and none of us is thinking too clearly," I said.

"That's not an excuse, Sheriff, just an explanation," Karl added. Now he was shaking his head. I could almost see the cogs gyrating in his mind over all these developments.

"Maybe you'd better not formally arrest her, but can you hold her for twenty-four hours or something until we can unravel this mess?" I asked.

"As I see it, she is a suspect. You found the money in her purse.

That's enough for us to hold her. But, Chase, I don't know that we can determine the real culprit in twenty-four hours."

"Yeah, I know, Terry. I'm praying God will reveal who's behind all this. Can I see Sally before we leave. I'd like to explain things to her."

"Sergeant Wilkins is busy processing her now. I'll ask if she wants to talk to you." He rose and left the office. I drummed my fingers on the chair while we waited for him to return.

"Sorry, Chase," the sheriff said as he reentered the room, "she doesn't want to see you."

"Okay. I'm not really surprised. Karl, is there anything in Pop's will to cover a mess like this?" I asked out of frustration.

"Actually, yes. If I'd been apprised of what was going on, I might have been able to end all this before it got started."

# Chapter 28

## Sally

Surely He shall deliver you from the snare of the fowler
And from the perilous pestilence. Psalms 91:3 NKJV

Once the deputy finished booking me, I asked for my one phone call. He allowed me my cell phone long enough to make the call. I searched my contacts and punched Jen's number.

"Sally! How are you?" Jen squealed with joy as she answered.

"I've been arrested. Ask John if he knows any good criminal attorneys in Montana, and get me some help asap, please."

"Why are they arresting you? John, come here!" The glee in Jen's voice died a quick death. "I'm putting you on speaker, Sally."

"What do you need, hon?" I heard John say. He must have been in another room. He certainly never called me hon.

"It's Sally on the phone. She says she's been arrested. I've got her on speaker."

"Arrested? Sally, what happened?"

"Too much to explain right now, John. I'm at the Cascade County Sheriff's Department in Great Falls. They said they're holding me on suspicion of theft. Looks like I'll be spending some time in jail or until I get bailed out. See what you can do, will you, please, John?"

"Of course," he said.

I clicked off the call, handed my cell phone to the sergeant, and he led me to the cells. They put me in a holding cell with several other women.

"What are you in for, honey? You look too respectable for us lot."

"I've been arrested for theft."

"Yeah? What'd ya steal?"

"Nothing. They suspect I stole a thousand dollars."

"That's nothing but petty theft. You shouldn't be in here. Who says you stole it?" the girl asked. She looked to be in her early twenties. Her turquoise T-shirt and blue jeans were threadbare, and she looked in need of a bath. I guessed she was homeless. Did she know what she was talking about saying $1000 constituted petty theft?

"Chase Reynolds."

"Ooooo," chorused the three women.

"He's got lots of pull in this town. And an impeccable reputation," the young girl said. "They probably put you here cuz he said so."

"Exactly. He was talking with the sheriff as I was being booked." I claimed a top bunk among the several beds and climbed up. I closed my eyes, focused on the Lord, and began quoting Bible verses to myself. "I know the Lord is always with me. I will not be shaken, for He is right beside me. No weapon formed against me shall prosper. I am more than a conqueror. I will fear no evil."

God, why has this happened? The noise of the other women in the cell kept me from hearing God's answer. They were busy talking about me.

That's what you get for giving in to discontent, Sally, I admonished myself. I turned my back to the women and tried to sleep away the rest of the day.

⌒〜⌒

Breakfast arrived around 8:00. A simple meal of scrambled eggs, toast, and water. I talked with the other ladies in the cell, until one by one, a policeman arrived and took them away. To court, I assume, or to be released. None returned, and by 4:00 that afternoon, I sat alone in the cell with the realization that it was Friday and exactly four weeks since I had come to Montana.

"God, is this is how You prove Yourself to me? Your Word says, 'Instead of shame and honor, you will enjoy a double share of honor.' You've told me and I believe it, but this sure is an odd way to deliver on that promise," I prayed out loud. Why not? No one was around to hear me. The jingle of keys warned me someone was coming.

"Okay, Miss Clark," said a policeman as he unlocked the jail cell door, "your lawyer's here." He held the door open as I walked through, then he turned and led me to an interrogation room.

"John!" I rushed over and briefly embraced him. "What are you doing here?"

"I'm your lawyer. I wasn't going to sit in KC while you were here in Great Falls facing a felony charge."

"Well, I appreciate it. I figured you'd find someone local to help. What have you found out?"

"I spoke with Sheriff Daniels a few minutes ago. They were only holding you on suspicion and could only hold you twenty-four hours. But you'll have to stay in Great Falls while they investigate the theft. He said something about some vandalism as well. But hey, let's get out of here first, then you can tell me exactly what's been going on."

He took my arm, we retrieved my phone and purse, and left the police station. John had rented a car and he drove us to a hotel. "Let's get you a room. I'll see if there's one available next to mine. Why don't you give Jen a call and let her know you're okay while I get things arranged?"

He went to the reception desk, and I walked over to a lounge area of the lobby. I pulled out my phone and called Jen.

"Oh, Sally, are you okay? I trust John was able to get you out of jail?"

"Yeah, I'm with him now. He's getting me a room at a hotel here in Great Falls. I can't leave town."

"A night in jail. That must have been awful."

"I've been in worse places. I'll explain everything to John. I'm sure he'll update you yet tonight on when to expect him home."

"What does this do to you getting that inheritance?"

"I already told the guy he can keep his precious inheritance. I can't be rid of this family fast enough. But…"

"But what?" Jen said.

"I don't want to lose contact with Abby. She's my twin sister."

"Twin sister?"

"Yeah, remember me telling you about seeing her picture on the wall? I don't know if we're biological twins, but it sure looks that way."

"Well, I never liked that stipulation that you had to spend four weeks there."

"Like they say, if it looks too good to be true, it probably is. I can't believe I fell for all this. I bet they had every bit of this planned. Discredit me, discourage me every step of the way so I'd just turn down the inheritance and walk away."

"I can't believe that. Although I suppose that's cheaper than contesting the will in court."

"For sure. Listen, John's standing here with a key to my room. Talk to him while I freshen up." I traded my phone for the key in John's hand. "I'll meet you in the restaurant. Give me fifteen minutes to clean up a bit. I'll need you to go out to the ranch to collect my stuff. I never want to see Chase Reynolds again."

I felt much better after a shower, even though I had to put back on the same grungy clothes. Not that I needed to wash off any grime, but the hot water rushing over me rejuvenated me. I went down to the hotel restaurant. John was still chatting with Jen as I approached the table and took a seat across from him.

"Sally's here now, so I'll connect later. Have Paul review the O'Toole case. I may need him to step in for me. Thanks, Kelly," he said and hung up, then handed me my phone.

"I thought you were still talking with Jen."

"Checking in with the office. When I left, I wasn't certain how long

I'd be up here. Are you hungry?"

"Yes, lunch was meager." I perused the menu and decided on chicken strips. Would I ever want beef again? This whole experience had left a bad taste in my mouth for cattle ranchers. A waitress appeared and took our order, and I settled back into the chair. "Was I wrong to accept this inheritance? When you have to earn it, how can it be called an inheritance?"

"Yes, people can be very particular about what they pass on and how." John leaned forward over the table, his arms resting on the edge. "Tell me everything. Start with the day you arrived."

"From the git-go, it went wrong. The daughter Leslie was supposed to meet me at the airport. She didn't. I rented a car and drove to the ranch. They were in the midst of a barbecue. A lot of the people were quite nice, but there were those who were rude as well. You'd think I'd stolen the whole ranch out from under them." I explained further and John jotted down notes as I related the tale and we ate.

"She slapped you?" he asked, when I told him about the second night of the roundup.

"Yeah. Split my lip open."

"You could charge her with assault."

"That's not my way, besides she could probably charge me."

"Did you slap her back?"

"No, but a few seconds later she grabbed my arm as I was walking away, and I maneuvered her wrist into a jujitsu hold. I applied enough pressure to make my point. Self-defense as far as I'm concerned." I shrugged. "The woman has been nothing but spiteful and rude to me, but I'm not going to stoop to her level by pressing charges."

"Okay. I know there's got to be a lot more. You aren't one to give up, but, Sally, there's defeat written all over your face."

I sat and considered his comment. John was right; I hadn't made it this far in life by giving up. But this battle had touched a place deep within my soul. Chase's words *there are plenty of honorable, decent men in the world* had reverberated in my mind every waking moment as I sat in that jail cell. I'd spent time considering whether I was bitter and unforgiving like Chase said. I realized I was. People had wounded me more times than I could count. This was one more.

And one too many. I wanted to go home, hibernate for the winter, and, come the new year, regroup.

"Because that's how I feel." I took a deep breath and continued. "I thought Chase and I had begun to understand each other. Sometimes I even thought he might be attracted to me—yeah, right—and then he accuses me of theft without the benefit of 'innocent until proven guilty.'"

"What happened to get you to that point?"

I told him about the steer getting shot, my rattlesnake bite, the fake snake in my saddlebags, and the vandalism that had occurred at the ranch. He took lots of notes.

"Wow, someone has been very busy. What have the police been able to find out about any of this?"

"From what they tell me the rattlesnake was an accident. Could have happened to anyone, but they don't know who was behind the shooting. Here's the kicker, John. I overheard a conversation that convinces me someone is trying to kill me."

John's grip on his pen slipped a bit. "Kill you? Surely not. What did you hear and where?"

"It was the night of the stampede. What heard was 'I told you, if she's dead, she can't inherit anything.' Whoever he was talking to tried to protest, but he got cut off with 'No buts. You'll be richly rewarded.'"

"Did you report this to the police?"

"Yes, I told Chase first, then we both went to the sheriff's office. As far as I know, they chocked the shooting up to a tourist out hunting. They get a lot of out-of-state hunters," I said by way of explanation.

"That might be so. If it had been just the one shot, I'd agree. But you said it was two and the shots were spaced apart. If a hunter had been shooting at a deer or a bear and missed, the second shot would have come quickly after the first."

This caught my interest and I sat up in my chair. "You're right. I hadn't thought about that."

"Sounds like they didn't either," John replied. He looked at his watch. "I've got a lot of investigating to do. I'm going to go back to the sheriff's and find out about each of these incidents."

"Before you go, one of the ladies in the lock-up said $1000 isn't a felony, just a misdemeanor."

"Okay. Felonies and misdemeanors do vary from state to state. I'll check on it," he said, nodding his head and making another note. "I'd like to talk the Reynolds family. But…maybe I should start with their lawyer. He seems reasonable and level-headed." John stood and put his notepad into his briefcase.

"Can you wait? I've got a question."

He sat back down.

"I feel they breached the conditions of the will. In fact, I could argue they broke it the first day I arrived. I'd like to try to get some kind of settlement."

"After hearing all that's happened, I agree."

# Chapter 29

## Chase

It is not right to acquit the guilty or deny
justice to the innocent. Proverbs 18:5

Three days had passed since the police released Sally. It was time
to get an update from Sheriff Daniels. I drove to his office.

"Chase, there are way too many fingerprints on the cash
to make any determination whether Sally ever handled it. And the
fingerprints on Miss Clark's purse are too smudged to determine if
anyone but her handled it," Sheriff Daniels said.

"Did you ask everybody at the office if they saw anyone near Sally's
desk?"

"Detective Hanson handled things. He's always very thorough. Only
Leslie claims seeing Miss Clark with the cash box."

"That speaks volumes," I said, rubbing my fingers through my hair.
"Leslie is really the only one with a motive to get rid of Sally. None of my
other kids, nor Abby, stand to gain anything with Sally out of the picture."

"That's got to be tough, Chase. Your own daughter. But if she is
behind any of this, then she has an accomplice."

"Jake is certainly an obvious choice. What makes you believe that?"

"Because she doesn't live at the ranch. Her presence there would be
noticed, wouldn't it? How often does she come to the ranch, and could

she come and go without anyone noticing?"

"Great questions. And you're right, she doesn't come that often. She rarely goes to the barn. If she plans a ride, she has Jake bridle and saddle her horse. What did Hanson find out about the incidents at the ranch?"

"None of them were ever reported. Any evidence got tainted between the time they occurred and when you told me about them. Hanson questioned Four and several other men. Where the damaged saddles are concerned, a ranch hand named Toby says he went into the tack room right after Sally left it. So either he's lying or Sally is."

"Wait a minute. Four told me each incident had been reported, but you have no record of it?"

"No. Our people would have been out there the day it happened otherwise. And my men are excellent at keeping up the required paperwork. It's not here."

"That is suspicious. I'll talk to Four and find out who is supposed to have reported things to the police." I stood and paced the office. "Maybe Leslie enlisted Toby's help in this scheme."

"I'll brief Hanson on all this. He'll want to question everyone again."

"How can we force the culprit out into the open?"

"Forcing someone's hand can get dangerous. Whoever it is might decide to make another attempt at killing Miss Clark," Sheriff Daniels said.

"Exactly. Can we create a trap?"

"Don't even think about it. Let Detective Hanson continue to investigate." Sheriff Daniels rose from his chair and extended his hand. "I'll let you know what we find out. In the meantime, don't take matters into your own hands, and if you get any ideas, pass them by me first. All right, Chase?"

"Agreed, but reluctantly." We shook hands and I left for Karl's office.

"Chase, what a mess we have, eh?" Karl said as his secretary ushered me into his office.

"And what mess is that?" I asked. I heard Karl harrumph as I poured myself a glass of water and took a seat.

"You can't be serious," Karl said. "The theft, the vandalism, Sally being held for theft. I've had her lawyer in here several times and he has a good case against you."

"What?" I exclaimed. "What have I done?"

"Not you specifically, but against the terms of the will."

"I don't follow, but first tell me why you wanted to see me."

"The will. This whole mess. Sally was to actively participate in the ranch's daily activities. Has she done that?"

"Yes, but remember, she told me she's no longer interested in receiving the inheritance," I said.

"But you said you don't want her to give it up. Her lawyer is claiming the Reynolds family broke the terms through deliberate attempts to force her to leave early. At this point, there's no proof an attempt has been made on her life, but the conversation she overheard gives credence to that possibility." Karl pulled a thick file folder from his in-basket, opened it, and prepared to take notes. "Her lawyer is asking for a large cash settlement."

I chewed this over for a moment. "It's not like Pop gave us guidance on any of this. Buffalo chips, he didn't even tell us about changing his will and naming Sally as a beneficiary."

"True." Karl nodded. "I fully believe he intended to but circumstances got in the way. When he and I discussed this change, he believed the family would accept Sally as readily as he did. On top of that, he had confidence you all would apply the Golden Rule, just as he had for most of his life."

"Karl, we have applied the Golden Rule, except for Leslie."

Karl raised his eyebrows at me.

"Alright, I was rude at first, but we got past that. None of us foresaw all this trouble. It's not like we set out to make things intentionally hard."

"That's where Sally's lawyer disagrees." Karl paused, tapping his index fingers together as he thought. "Chase, be honest with yourself.

In all your years of ranching have you ever experienced these kinds of troubles and so much of it at one time?"

Karl had me there. Hard times were common enough, but it was usually the weather or disease spreading through the cattle, feed prices going through the roof. Natural disasters and economic problems. Never a shooting, vandalism, or theft.

"Your silence tells me you agree. What has the sheriff determined?"

"Nothing as of yet. I'm not sure they'll ever have any conclusive evidence." I sat forward and looked Karl in the eye. "I just found out this morning from Sheriff Daniels that none of the vandalism at the ranch was ever reported. You know my kids almost as well as I do. Would any of them do such things?"

"Six months ago, I would have said no. Now, I have my suspicions."

"Six months? What's happened in the last six months?" I returned to the sideboard and poured myself some coffee this time. "Can I pour you a cup?"

"No, thank you. Let's push on. Six months ago your father came to me to request the change in his will. Of course, I questioned him why."

"Obviously his answer was adequate or his stubbornness prevailed." I smiled, thinking about Pop's stubbornness. It had served him well as a rancher, but as a father it sometimes got in the way.

"He told me about Leslie."

"Go on. Be honest, even if it hurts."

"He had noticed changes in her behavior, her attitude, even in her words. He said he struggled with it. I believe his exact words were 'She's become a spoiled snob.'"

"I've noticed those same things. Especially the day you read the will." I shook my head. "I can't imagine what's influenced that, if anything."

"Your dad wasn't sure either. We spoke extensively. You know I was his sounding board after my father died?"

"Yes. Pop had several people he sought counsel from. So I take it you both got peace from Lord about the change in the will?"

"Yes." Karl nodded as he spoke. "It was the deciding factor. Of course, the day I read the will I didn't want to say that outright to the whole family. As far as I'm concerned, at that moment, all Leslie needed to know was that I had asked your father to reconsider."

"I agree. But that doesn't bring us any closer to a decision about things, does it? I mean, how does any of that answer Sally's lawyer's claims?"

"I think it speaks very clearly to those claims. Sally was to participate in the daily routine of the ranch. You were to determine where her heart was with the Lord. Very straightforward, until someone began an attempt to discourage or discredit her. Leslie's behavior had changed enough to prompt a change in the will. To me that means that everything that's happened could very well be her attempt to thwart things in her own way since your dad said not to contest." He flipped open the file folder on his desk and turned to the back. Stapled to the back was a small manila envelope. He pulled it loose from the folder and shook the contents into his hand. It was a thumb drive that he held out to me. "I think this will help clarify things…at least I hope it will."

I grabbed it from Karl's palm. "What's on here and why will it help?"

"It's a video from your dad, but I haven't viewed it. He gave it to me with the instruction to view it only if there were problems. I think it's time."

# Chapter 30

## Sally

Show me the right path, O Lord; point out the
road for me to follow. Psalms 25:4

Three days sequestered in my hotel room thinking, thinking, thinking. Enough! I wished I could saddle Sandy and take a long ride by myself, but that wasn't going to happen. At least Abby had been nice enough to pack my things at the ranch and bring them to my hotel the day the police released me.

"Sally, please think about this. Chase doesn't want you to give up the inheritance and neither do I. He never for a moment thought you stole that money. He just didn't know how to keep you from leaving except to have you arrested."

"Where I'm concerned, he seems to put his foot in his mouth a lot."

"He's told me you tend to misconstrue everything he says." She put up her hands as if in surrender. "And before you say anything in defense, you're probably both guilty of misunderstanding each other."

"Eh, maybe. Listen, I'm really tired. Sleeping on the ground was more comfortable than that jail cell bed. I think it's probably better all-around if we don't talk or see each other while the police investigate this." I saw my words wounded Abby, but I needed some distance from the family for a few days.

Now it was Monday; those few days had passed. And I was no closer to wiping the dust of this place off my feet.

My cell phone jingled. I pulled it from my pants pocket and looked at the caller ID: Berkeley Snyder. Ugh! No doubt calling to entice me back to work. I answered it only to have the pleasure of refusing his dramatic pleas. Everything Berkeley Snyder did he did with drama.

"No, I'm not coming back to work for you," I said quite calmly.

"What kind of greeting is that? You have no idea why I'm calling," he huffed.

"Well, isn't that why you're calling? Why else?"

"Okay, yes, that's why I'm calling, but there's no need to be rude," he said.

"That's true. I apologize. But I still don't want to come back to work for you."

"Please hear me out. Your departure surprised me. I thought you were happy working here."

"I was, until you came bringing erotica and micro-managing everything." Why not be honest? What could he do? Fire me?

"I sat down with Jen last week and had an enlightening conversation. She opened up and told me about how discontent you both are. She was bold enough to tell me her opinion about the erotica and that it was undermining the good name of Pendrake Publishing."

Wow, Jen, good for you! "And what did you do with all that honesty?"

"I mulled it over. I'm not the idiot you think I am."

That statement pulled the rug out from under me. I dropped down onto the bed. "Did you come to any decisions?"

"Of course I did. That's why I'm calling. Jen also told me you two are considering starting your own publishing company, so here's my proposal. If you come back, we'll drop the erotica and form a new imprint that handles only Christian fiction and nonfiction, and you and Jen will be in charge of the department."

"That's tempting, Berkeley, very tempting. But you said if I come back. Does that mean things stay the same if I don't accept your offer?"

"That's right."

"I need to think about it and talk to Jen. How long do I have? I'm not sure how much longer I'll be here in Montana." I wasn't about to tell him I'd given up the inheritance; besides he didn't know the immensity of the inheritance he was negotiating against. I wanted and needed the upper hand in this situation.

"I'll give you forty-eight hours to decide, but that doesn't mean you have to be back here in that time. As long as I have your decision, then I can move forward with the details or not. Agreed?"

"Agreed. Forty-eight hours."

# Chapter 31

## Chase

My child, listen when your father corrects you. Proverbs 1:8

I pushed the flash drive into the USB port on the television and told my kids to find a seat.

"Let me first say I love you each. Remember that as you listen to this video. It's from Poppie, with the instructions that we were to view it if there were problems concerning Sally. I'm sure you'll all agree, that's where we are." I took a seat and pushed play on the remote.

"That you are listening to this video is a disappointment," Pop began. "That means there's been trouble accepting my decision to will a portion of the ranch and magazine to Miss Clark. Perhaps I was expecting too much bringing a total stranger into the family.

"Where do I start? ...Guess I'd better start with Abby's adoption. Whether Abby and Sally are twins, I don't know. I only know that when your grandmother and I decided to adopt a little girl, the orphanage didn't tell us Abby had a twin. Maybe they didn't know either. Maybe the family gave up only one of the twins because they couldn't afford to support both girls. I don't know. If I had, I'd have adopted both.

"When I first met Sally while vacationing in Paris, I was convinced she is Abby's twin. Not just because they looked alike, but because every time she spoke I thought it was Abby. In my heart, I adopted

Sally, true blood to Abby or not. The moment we returned to the States, I had Karl do some investigating with the orphanage where we adopted Abby, but he was unable to find any records."

I paused the video. Some of it was a repeat from Pop's video to me and Abby, but it was all new to the kids. "Anyone have any comments or questions?" No one spoke up. "As far as I'm concerned, that makes Sally a part of this family. No matter what the investigation into all the trouble proves." I turned my attention back to the television and started the video. Having viewed the video at Karl's office, I kept my eyes on Leslie to see how she would react to what was coming.

"Leslie, I know this decision had to be an enormous surprise and disappointment," Pop said.

"You can say that again, Poppie," Leslie interjected.

Several of the kids shushed her in unison.

"While several items influenced this decision, the primary ones were the leading of the Lord and the changed behavior I have noted in you over the past year."

That tidbit seemed to prick her attention.

"I don't know what caused the change, and I may not have noticed it if I saw you every day. But I only saw you when you came to the ranch. And when you did, each time I saw a woman who was becoming a snob, someone concerned with her status in society and bent on accruing wealth. It broke my heart. I tried a couple of times to talk to you about it, but you always put me off. Which in turn, drove me farther down the road to this change. Have you read the letter I wrote you? I wonder..." Pop paused in his presentation, giving me a chance to further observe Leslie.

Her cheeks flushed bright pink and tears welled in her eyes. Did she realize the truth in Pop's words?

"I've spoken too long, but again, I want you each to know how much I love you. I pray you will find it in your hearts to accept Sally into the family as an adopted daughter-in-heart.

"I'll see you on the other side." And the video ended.

Silence ruled the room. An uncomfortable silence, punctuated with sniffles.

Who would be the first to speak?

"Mr. Kandell," Four said, finally breaking the long silence. "Why couldn't we have seen this the first day? It would have made things so much easier."

"I agree, Four, but I had to abide by your grandfather's wishes. He stated it was to be viewed only if there was trouble that couldn't be resolved."

"Accusing Sally of theft certainly qualifies for that," Gabe commented.

"Leslie, does this answer your doubts and questions?" I asked.

She looked at me, her tears now trickling down her cheeks. She opened her mouth as if to speak, closed it again, and raced out of the room, sobbing.

"Leslie," I yelled after her.

"Let her go," Abby said. "I'll check on her later."

"I've been fine with Sally since the day we met," Gabe proclaimed. "I've worked with her more than any of you. I don't think for one minute she stole that money or that she's behind any of the vandalism. I think all this is someone's pathetically stupid attempt to discourage her and force her to leave before her four weeks were done."

"Agreed," Michael and Peter chimed.

"What about the rest of you? Have you seen or heard any talk among the ranch hands that points to who might be behind all the trouble?" I asked. Everyone either said no or shook their head. "Then we'll have to rely on the sheriff to find out."

"Can we get back to work?" Four asked.

I needed to find out from Four about who was supposed to have reported the vandalism, but I wanted that to be private. I'd catch up with Four later. "Fine with me," I said. Gabe, Peter, Michael, and Four rose and left the room. That left Emily, Abby, Karl, and me. I pulled the thumb drive from the television and handed it to Karl. "Any questions, comments?" I said to the remaining group.

"This confirms what I've sensed from the Holy Spirit," Abby said. She looked a bit tearful. Maybe seeing Pop renewed her grief at his loss. "I believe Sally is my biological twin. A DNA test would be conclusive, but I don't need one, and I don't want one."

"Emily, how about you? What do you think of this?" I asked her. She had been quiet throughout, nothing unusual for her. She'd always been my quiet child.

"I've been thinking about how Leslie must feel. I've tried to talk to her about Poppie's decision, but she refused. I didn't realize it, but after hearing Poppie say it, I have to admit, he's right about her behavior. I have noticed things a time or two. I just didn't know how to approach her or if I even should."

"I'd say Poppie got through to her. And it's not like she got totally cut out of the will. Two hundred thousand dollars is nothing to sneeze at," I said. "Abby, how best and how much of this do we communicate to Sally?"

"She deserves to know exactly what Pop said about her and about the adoption. I think she has a right to see the video up to the part where Pop addresses Leslie. Maybe only Leslie should have viewed that portion, but that's a moot point now."

"Karl and I viewed the video the day he told me about it. I know it was hard for Leslie, but I felt it was important that everyone know why Pop made the choice he did," I said.

"After seeing this, I understand why Pop stipulated Sally spend four weeks here. She's completed the four weeks, and trouble or not, I think she should still get the inheritance," Abby said.

"Good point, Abby. Karl, what say you?"

"Frankly, after hearing what your dad had to say about adopting Sally, I agree with Abby. But the will is a legal document and must be executed as such," Karl said. "However, we ran into things no one could have anticipated."

"I don't know about any of you, but Pop reached beyond the grave to reprimand me. I owe Sally yet another apology," I said. "Seems I've been doing that a lot."

"Don't be so hard on yourself, Pop," Emily said. "This has been a tough situation for all of us." She rose from her chair. "I'm going home. Matt and I are supposed to go look at wedding rings. I'll see you tomorrow, Aunt Abby." She leaned down and gave Abby a kiss goodbye on the cheek.

"See you tomorrow, darlin'." Abby smiled her goodbye and got up. "I'll go check on Leslie, if I can find her."

"Abby, wait a minute. I've got one last question." I kissed Emily goodbye and waited for her to leave the room.

"Do you need me to leave," Karl asked.

"No, you need to hear this, too. In light of everything that's happened and what Pop had to say, I think it's time to tell Sally the inheritance is hers. Abby?"

She looked at me as a smile slowly spread across her face. "I agree." She turned to Karl. "Any problems with that?"

"There could be. She certainly can't inherit if she's found guilty of all this trouble. In the meantime, she's requested a cash settlement instead. I haven't had an opportunity to review the brief her lawyer gave me earlier today, but I think if we all sit down and explain things, she'd be fine with the original plan. She did complete the four weeks, albeit some of it in jail. I'll call her lawyer as soon as I get back to the office and arrange a meeting. I think it would be good for you two to be there, to offer an olive branch, as it were."

"I agree," I said.

"Me too," Abby said.

The room emptied, leaving an emptiness in my heart as well. Why had I been so up and down in my behavior toward Sally? More than once I had wanted to hug her good morning as she bounded into the dining room each morning, full of energy and excited to face the day. I thought it was simply that I was responding to her like I would Abby. But now I realized that desire to hug her contained more than brotherly love. Lightning striking me couldn't have surprised me more.

As I made my way out to the barn, I mulled over this realization. I'd not known Sally long enough to be in love with her. But was romantic love budding? I remembered Sally saying that one moment I was rude and the next seductive. I shook my head at that thought, just as I had when she said it.

What kind of relationship could we have now? I'd done a bang-up job at burning bridges when I accused her of theft and had her held. I pulled in a deep breath and let it out slowly. Lord, how do I fix this mess? I can't. I need Your intervention.

When I got to the barn, I went straight to the office. Four and Jake were both there.

"Four, let's saddle a couple of horses and ride out and check the fencing on the west range."

"Checked that yesterday. Winter prep is well underway."

"Well, saddle up anyway. I want to satisfy myself."

Four looked at me, a bit of question in his eyes as if I didn't trust his abilities. I turned to Jake. "Double check the AI list and make sure we've got things ready for the vet when he comes tomorrow."

"Sure thing. I got it," Jake said as Four and I headed out of the office and to the stalls.

"What gives, Pop?" Four said as soon as we were out of Jake's earshot. "Are you suddenly not trusting my work?"

"Not at all, son. I needed an excuse to get you away privately so we can talk."

"What happened to 'I need to talk to you?'"

"Wanted to keep Jake satisfied." I wrapped my arm around Four's shoulders and gave him a fatherly squeeze. "I'll tell you all about it when only cattle and crickets can hear us."

We each saddled a horse and loped west. Once we were half a mile from the ranch, I reined my horse to a walk. Four did the same and came along side me.

"Okay, Pop, out with it. What it is you don't want anyone else to hear?"

"Have you noticed anything different about Jake? You see him every day so maybe you haven't. But Poppie noticed changes in Leslie, and I can't help thinking that her changes could affect Jake."

"Now that you mention it, I have noticed that he comes in angry a good deal of the time. I haven't pressed him about it. I figured maybe he and Leslie had been arguing or something."

"How long has that been going on?"

"Several months. But it's not every day."

"I witnessed an argument between them during the roundup. He got physical in a way he shouldn't have. I didn't hear everything that was said, but the gist was that Jake had a roving eye," I said.

"Did you confront him?"

"No. I did ask Leslie if everything was all right. She said it was fine, nothing she couldn't handle. On another tack, Sheriff Daniels told me yesterday none of the vandalism had been reported?"

"Not reported? My understanding was that Jake did. Mike, Pete, and I were out checking fences every day that week. We didn't hear about any of it until we came back in for the day. Gabe filled me in and that he'd told Jake to report it." A look of realization crossed Four's face as though a thought had dawned. "Surely Jake isn't the one behind all this."

"I'm not sure myself, but it's why I didn't want to risk him hearing anything. Based on what Sheriff Daniels told me, I don't think it's likely they'll find the real culprit. Any evidence there might have been was long gone by the time Detective Hanson was sent out to investigate. I've noticed several conspiratorial powwows between Jake and Leslie. It—"

"Pop, you can't believe Leslie is behind any of this!"

"I don't want to, but like I said, I don't like what I've witnessed between her and Jake. She's done nothing but complain since the day Karl read the will."

"You're right about that. That morning she blurted out that Sal was a thief and the daughter of a killer," Four shook his head, "it shocked me."

"That reminds me. She also said she wasn't going to allow 'that Clark woman' to steal her inheritance. I...I...It breaks my heart, but I've come to the conclusion that she and Jake are in this together."

After my ride with Four, I went back to the office. Abby had returned to town, and apparently so had Leslie. I wasn't able to ascertain whether

Abby had talked with Leslie or not. I grabbed the phone and called Abby.

"Chase, what can I do for you?" Abby answered.

"Did you have a chance to talk to Leslie?"

"No, I didn't. When I went looking for her, Rita mentioned Leslie had stormed out of the house in tears. I'll give her some time to calm down and process things, then give her a call."

I heard a doorbell ring.

"Chase, someone's my door. Hang on a minute."

"Will do." A text message from Leslie arrived while I waited.

*Please meet me at Aunt Abby's.*

"Chase, Leslie's here. She wants to talk to us."

"I just got her text. I'll be right over."

"She says Sally needs to be here, too," Abby said before I hung up.

"That sounds foreboding. I guess you'd better call her. I think she'll listen to you."

"And I think it would be better coming from you," Abby insisted.

# Chapter 32
## Chase

People with integrity walk safely, but those who follow
crooked paths will slip and fall. Proverbs 10:9

I dialed Sally's cell phone and waited.

"What do you want?" Sally grouched in answer.

So she had my number in her phone. I had rather hoped she wouldn't know it was me calling.

"Hello to you, too."

"I suppose you have more accusations."

"Would you shut up and listen?" I took a deep breath and tried to calm down. What button did Sally push that prompted me to be rude so often? "I'm headed to Abby's. Apparently Leslie is there and wants to talk to us, including you."

"So I can be blindsided yet again? Forget it. I told you the other day I didn't want your money. I'm out of jail, but I can't leave town, otherwise I'd have left this place by now. And tell Leslie to take a flying leap." And she hung up.

That went well. I could only imagine her hurt. Lord, this is such a mess. Only You can fix it. I headed to Abby's.

"Chase, where's Sally?" Abby asked as she met me at her front door. "I thought she'd ride with you."

"She refused to come." I leaned down to give Abby a quick kiss on the cheek to soften my harsh tone. "I'm sorry. I'm taking my frustration out on you. I'd have had better results negotiating with a grizzly."

"Leslie's in the living room. Let's see what she has to say."

Leslie stood from her chair as Abby and I entered the room.

"Daddy, I'm so glad you're here. Is Sally coming?"

"No, she refused. Can you blame her?" I asked.

"No, I guess not." Leslie hung her head and took a few deep breaths, then looked up. "This needs said and said now.

"After seeing Poppie's video, I realized how true his words about me were. I've spent the last several hours examining myself. I finally read Poppie's letter, too, the one Mr. Kandell gave me when he read the will. Then I prayed. ...Pray. I haven't done that in quite some time."

We all stood there, looking back and forth between ourselves.

"I planted that money in Sally's purse," Leslie blurted. "I'm so sorry. I'm so sorry." She began to cry softly. Abby and I stood rooted to the floor. Leslie wiped at her tears. "Please forgive me."

Was this a drama queen or a broken woman standing before me? I felt the prompting of the Holy Spirit telling me her apology was sincere and heartfelt.

Abby rushed over and hugged Leslie. "Of course, I forgive you." Abby looked over at me, her eyebrows raised.

"Are you sincere about this or trying to manipulate the situation like you often do?" I asked.

"Daddy, how could you say such a thing?"

I looked at her come askance.

"I...I guess you're right. I do manipulate, but no more. I'm serious about this, and I truly wanted to say this first to Miss Clark."

"Let's take a seat." I took the closest chair. Abby hadn't yet relinquished her hold on Leslie; they sat together on the couch. "Are you saying you're also responsible for the vandalism at the ranch?"

"No, Daddy. All I did was take the petty cash and put it in Sally's purse."

"Did you suggest to Jake that he commit that vandalism?" I said.

"No, of course not! Besides, Jake would never do anything like that."

"But several times I've seen the two of you conspiring. What was that all about?"

"Just me complaining about the situation. All Jake ever did was try to calm me down. He said Sally was an okay lady. But…" Leslie paused, poised to go on, but then didn't. Jake's opinion about Sally didn't jive with what he'd told me.

"But what?" Abby asked.

Leslie took another deep breath. "I saw how he looked at her, and I didn't like it. It's not the first time I've caught him looking lustfully at another woman. His behavior only served to fuel my anger toward Sally."

"Do you have any idea who might be behind the vandalism?" Abby asked.

"No. I'm rarely at the ranch, so I have no idea."

"Okay, sweetheart. I'm proud of you for coming forward. I want you to know, Abby and I have already decided to move forward with giving Sally the inheritance."

"That's fine, Daddy. But thank you for telling me."

A puff of air would have knocked me over. Her calm response convinced me of her changed attitude and sincerity.

"Why don't you head on home? You look wrung out." I gave her a kiss on the top of her head. She smiled up at me, then hugged Abby, and walked to the door. Abby and I listened to Leslie's high heels clipping against the hard wood floor of the foyer. With the click of the front door, I turned toward Abby.

"Let me call Sheriff Daniels about this, and then I think we need to head over to Sally's hotel. If either of us called, she'd just ignore the call."

"She's that mad at you?"

"She's that mad. Embittered probably says it better," I said with a sigh.

# Chapter 33

## Sally

Oh, give me back my joy again; you have broken
me—now let me rejoice. Psalms 51:8

The phone call from Chase stunned me. The rock that had settled in my stomach the day he had me arrested grew bigger. He must be insane to think I'd face off with Leslie, Abby, and him standing in one corner and me in the other all by my lonesome.

I decided to call Jen. She could advise me. Besides I needed to talk to her about Berkeley's job proposal.

"Hello. Pendrake Publishing."

"Hey, Jen. Sorry to bother you at work, but I needed to hear a voice of reason."

"Oh, Sally. Is it that bad? John told me he got you out of jail. He's supposed to be meeting with that other lawyer today or tomorrow. What's going on?"

"I asked John to try and get me a cash settlement. But that's not why I called. Berkeley called about the new job offer for us. I wanted to get your take on it. Is he sincere?"

"I think so."

"Jen, you mentioned wanting to quit Pendrake. How interested are you in starting our own publishing business?"

"Very! John and I have talked about it several times while you've been gone. I think he likes the idea more than I do. Hey, we'd have all the free legal help we need."

"At first with this inheritance and all, I tossed around the idea of buying Pendrake, but I don't want to come back to KC. Would you and John be willing to move or can we make it work long distance and handle everything online?"

"I've been in KC for so long, I can't imagine anywhere else. But it might be fun to move."

"You're just humoring me. It's hard moving. You have to find a new home, new friends, a new church, a new everything. What did Berkeley offer you? I mean, did he say anything more than cutting the erotica and starting a Christian imprint? Did he talk salary?"

"No, he didn't mention salary. What he did say was that it was all contingent on you coming back. He must feel he couldn't do Christian books without your leadership," Jen explained.

"Did you ask him about you heading up the imprint without me?"

"No. I sensed he wanted only you."

"So, if I don't come back, what will you do if we don't start our own company?"

Jen was silent for several moments, and the rock in my stomach got heavier still.

"I've tossed around the idea of quitting. I haven't given it too much thought. Listen, you do what God leads you to do. Don't make a decision to come back just because of me."

"Jen, you're my friend. I don't want to leave you to the wolves." I heard a knock at the door. "I have to give Berkeley a decision by tomorrow. There's someone at the door. I'll try to call later so we can talk more. Bye for now." I hung up and walked to the door of my hotel room. I figured it was John, but I opened the door to find Chase and Abby.

I stuck my head out the door and looked both ways down the hallway. "No Leslie? No police?" I asked, looking at each of them.

"At ease, Marine. We're waving a white flag here," Chase said. I looked for his flag, but his hands were empty.

"Don't start, you two. Can we come in? We've got great news," Abby said.

I stared at Chase. He stared back.

"I guess you can come in." I turned and walked back into the room. I took a seat on the bed and let Abby and Chase take the only two chairs in the room.

"Leslie confessed to planting the money in your purse," Chase said. "She had hoped to apologize to you."

"I've known all along Leslie planted the money," I said.

"What do you mean you've known all along? How?" Chase asked.

"The police had us all in the conference room while they searched the office. The minute they called Abby over to my desk, I kept my eye on Leslie. The smirk on her face as the police pulled the money out of my purse said it all. So what did she hope to gain with her confession to you two?"

"Strangely enough, nothing," Chase said. Apparently he expected Leslie's manipulations as much as I did.

"So why the confession?"

"A video and a letter from her grandfather explaining why he didn't give her what he gave the other kids," Abby said.

"Do you think she was sincere about wanting to apologize?" I asked.

"Yes, we do," Chase answered for Abby. "When we told her we were giving you the inheritance, she didn't bat an eye. Said she was fine with that."

"She's an excellent actress. Probably missed her calling," I said. I got up from bed and walked to the window. I had a nice view of Great Falls. I only wished I could enjoy it. "Wait a minute." I whirled around to face them. "Did I hear you right? You're giving me the inheritance?" They were giving me the inheritance? And Leslie agreed? My brain was screaming, it's a trap, it's a trap!

"Yes, we are, even though you said you don't want it," Abby said. "And we made that decision before Leslie ever confessed."

"Sally," Chase rose from his chair and walked over to me. I stepped away as he approached. He sighed and stopped where he stood. "None of us ever believed you took that money. But you never let me get the words out. I'm sorry. In the heat of the moment, having you arrested was my hair-brained idea to keep you here long enough to sort it all out and grant you the inheritance. ...You don't appear too excited about this decision."

"I'm just wondering what kind of ambush you're setting up," I told him. I stood in my most aggressive posture and stared at him like I was sighting in on the enemy with my rifle. He stared back.

"You know, your cynicism probably served you well as a Marine on the battlefield, but in family relationships it's a real killjoy. You need to trust people more," Chase said.

"Trust is earned. You know that full well," I spat at him.

"True. But if all you ever expect is a stab in the back, that's all you'll ever get. As a man thinks in his heart so is he, according to Proverbs 23:7." Chase moved away but didn't sit back down.

I stepped back, took a deep breath, and tried to relax.

"Sally," Abby said, approaching me. She put her hands on my shoulders. "This isn't a trap. Your mind is screaming it so loudly, I can almost hear it audibly. Forgive those who've hurt you. Open the door to your heart and let us in; let God in."

"But someone has been trying to kill me."

"That might be true, but I can tell you with confidence, it hasn't been me or Chase."

I checked out of my hotel room and returned to the ranch with Chase, in the good graces of the Reynolds family once again.

"Is it true you've decided to give Sally the inheritance?" Michael said through his mouth full of food as Chase and I entered the dining room.

"Whoa, son, where'd you hear that?"

"From Jake. He left here about an hour ago. Apparently Leslie called saying as much and sobbing uncontrollably. He rushed out like his house was on fire."

"I thought she got those tears out at Abby's, but yes, we decided to grant the inheritance pending the investigation on the theft. With Leslie's confession everything can move forward. Leslie said she was fine with that. Did Jake say anything else?" Chase said.

"No, just that Leslie was in a bad state."

"That's understandable."

"What do you mean, Leslie's confession?" Michael asked.

"A few hours ago she confessed to planting the money in Sally's purse. I'll inform the rest of the family in the morning at breakfast." Chase went to the sideboard and filled a plate with two pork chops, a baked potato, and some green beans.

Michael sat astonished for a moment. "Was Leslie behind the vandalism, too?"

"She says no." Chase sat down next to Michael. I filled a plate and sat across the table from them.

"We meet with Karl tomorrow morning at nine," Chase explained.

"Do the police have any idea about who committed the vandalism?"

"Not that they've told me," Chase said. "I think it's a moot point."

"Why do you say that?" I asked. "Don't you want to know who's behind it? Besides, more than likely whoever is behind the vandalism is also the one trying to kill me. Announcing that you're giving me the inheritance will probably push whomever into the corner and force his hand."

"I hadn't thought of that. Maybe the sheriff can put a guard on you," Chase said.

"Hold on a minute," Michael said, a dumbfounded look on his face. "Someone's trying to kill Sally?"

"Yes, it appears that way," Chase said before I could answer. "Now about that bodyguard."

"I don't need a guard. I just need a handgun I can carry with me. Got a spare .357 magnum lying around? I had to leave mine at home."

Chase smiled at my words, but I was serious.

"I'm not joking, Chase. I need to be able to protect myself. Give me a revolver or a pistol."

"What good is a revolver when the would-be killer uses a rifle?" Chase asked. "Can't shoot what you can't see."

# Chapter 34

## Sally

Show me your unfailing love in wonderful ways.
By your mighty power you rescue those who seek
refuge from their enemies. Psalms 17:7

The next morning I awoke a nervous bundle. How strange, but comfortable, to be back at the Reynolds' ranch. I grabbed my Bible from the bedside table and opened it to Psalms. As I flipped the pages to the psalm for the day, my eye caught a verse I had highlighted many moons ago.

"Show me your unfailing love in wonderful ways." How many times had I prayed that verse, asking God to show me His love? Too many. But my icy heart wouldn't let His love enter in. Abby's love had begun to melt that ice.

I checked the weather app on my phone for the temperature: 36 degrees. No matter, I needed a run to dissipate my nervous energy, so I dressed warm and headed out. I meditated that bit of Psalm 17 all through my run. "Heavenly Father, my heart yearns desperately for Your love, but I'm afraid. Afraid You'll reject me like so many others have. I'm so tired of being hurt by those who say they love me, and recent accusations only serve to prove my point."

*Perfect love casts out all fear. If you are afraid, it is for fear of punishment, and this shows you do not fully understand My perfect love.*

*I love you with an everlasting, unfailing, unchanging love. I would not have sent My Son otherwise. His sacrifice was the ultimate act of love.*

Those words stopped me in my tracks. Never had I heard so clearly from God. I stood quietly, letting His message soak deeply into my spirit. Despite the cold air, a warmth began to permeate me, rising from within me and spreading outward. I recognized the warmth as the Holy Spirit infusing me with God's love. I was as positive of it as I was that my heart was still beating. I reveled in the moment, not wanting it to end.

"Father, thank you. Help me to never forget this moment or how it felt when Your love washed through me." I stood there a few moments longer and watched a blood-orange sun crest the horizon as though God was sending me His kiss.

When I went in for breakfast, Chase, Michael, Four, Peter, and Gabe were all there. None were eating, only drinking coffee. Was I about to be ambushed again?

"Why the crowd? Wouldn't you prefer to have breakfast with your family, guys?"

"Pop called a meeting," Four explained. "Jake called to say he wouldn't be here. Something about Leslie being sick and needing to stay home with her."

I poured a cup of coffee and sat down, looking questioningly at Chase. He leaned forward.

"Leslie confessed yesterday to taking the petty cash from the office," Chase said.

There was a general murmur around the table. "No way," Gabe said. "Why would she do something like that?"

"She didn't say why and we didn't ask. I assumed it was because she wanted to keep Sally from getting the inheritance," Chase said.

"Sal, you don't seemed surprised to hear this. Did you already know?" Peter asked.

"Yes, Chase told me yesterday."

"She said Pop's video and his letter convinced her. She seemed a very broken woman," Chase said.

"We all saw the video, Sal," Peter said. "Poppie was pretty straightforward about his reasons for putting you into the will. Leslie ran—"

"That's between Leslie and God, Peter. It's enough that Leslie's confessed. I want you all to know Abby and I are moving forward today with settling the details of granting Sally the inheritance."

"That's terrific, Pop. I'm glad," Gabe said. "Sal, you make a wonderful addition to the family. What are your plans?"

"Thank you, Gabe, but I haven't made any decisions yet. My old boss wants me back and has agreed to make me head of a new department in the business." I looked over at Chase but couldn't read his expression.

"Your old boss wants you back? What does that mean?" Chase asked.

"Just what I said. He wants me back."

"But that implies that you left. You said you had time off."

I looked around the table. Everyone was staring at me, waiting for an answer. I had forgotten I hadn't told Chase I quit. I couldn't very well sit there and lie about it when I'd been constantly accusing him of hypocrisy. I set my coffee cup on the table and leaned forward.

"My boss wouldn't give me the time off, so I quit. I apologize for lying, but I didn't want that to affect things."

"Wow, you jumped into the deep end coming here," Gabe said. "Kind of scary, but I'm glad you did."

"Not so scary. I had a Plan B in place if all this didn't work out. I was on the verge of quitting the job anyway. This situation merely precipitated my decision." I looked at Chase. His face held the hint of a smile, certainly not what I expected. This topic made me uncomfortable, and I needed to shift things in another direction. "Can we eat now? I'm hungry."

"I think we should celebrate," Four said. "How about Michael picks a steer to slaughter and we have another barbecue? The weather will turn soon, and we won't be able to picnic again until spring."

"Sounds like a great idea. Make it happen," Chase said. "Additionally, Michael, Gabe, and Pete, you three are going to take shifts in guarding Sally. Michael can work up a schedule."

"Guarding Sally? Why?" Peter asked.

Chase explained the situation, including the conversation I'd overheard during the roundup.

"Look, guys, I've tried to talk your dad into giving me a revolver to carry, but he says that won't do me any good. This killer made the first attempt with a rifle. He'll probably rely on the same method, especially now that the inheritance is a done deal," I told them. "God protected me while I was in the Corps. He'll continue to do so. He's given me promises about this inheritance, and His promises never fail."

We all rose from the table to fill our plates with breakfast. Before I took one step away from the table, Four, Peter, Michael, and Gabe inundated me with hugs and encouraging words to stay in Great Falls. What a wonderful way for God to punctuate His message of unfailing love.

As soon as we were done eating, Chase and I headed for town and our meeting with our lawyers. How would all this pan out? I realized I still needed to call Berkeley and let him know my decision about his job offer. In my heart of hearts, I hoped to be able to buy Pendrake Publishing with the profits I'd get from the Reynolds' estate.

According to God, I would receive double the honor and divide the land as an inheritance. What did that really mean, and how was God going to bring it all about?

I prayed in the Spirit the whole way to town.

# Chapter 35

## Sally

*I cry out to God Most High, to God who will
fulfill his purpose for me. Psalms 57:2*

Abby and John were waiting when we arrived at Mr. Kandell's office. I introduced John to Chase, and Mr. Kandell's secretary ushered us all into the office. She asked if we'd like coffee, tea, or water, and offered us a plate of warm cinnamon rolls. I turned them down. A stomachful of butterflies was already competing with my earlier breakfast, why add more?

"Hang on to your seat," I whispered to John as we all took seats around Mr. Kandell's desk.

"Sally, you're going to love it," John said, smiling from ear to ear. Had Mr. Kandell already informed him of Chase and Abby's decision?

"If everybody's settled, let's get started," Mr. Kandell said. He looked at each of us in turn and then proceeded. "Mr. Maxwell and I have spent some time hammering out details—"

"Karl, what's there to hammer out? I told you to move ahead with the inheritance as Pop wanted it," Chase said. He looked over at John as if to ask what's up. "Did Karl not tell you about that development?"

"He did. But we've spent time putting things into writing, examining Mr. Reynolds' video, and determining there aren't any surprise expectations," John explained to Chase. Then he turned back to Mr. Kandell. "Sir," he said with a nod of his head.

"What about the video? I thought it was for Leslie," I said.

"That's a good place to start, Karl," Chase said.

Karl turned his monitor around so I could see it. The face of a man I assumed to be Chase's father covered the screen.

As I watched, the butterflies multiplied. The orphanage never said anything about a twin, and I realized we'd never know for sure without a DNA test. I pushed my thoughts aside and tried to focus as the video continued.

"In my heart, I adopted Sally, true blood to Abby or not." At that point, Mr. Kandell stopped the video.

"The next portion is directed to Leslie, but there's a bit more you need to hear." Mr. Kandell fidgeted with his mouse for a moment or two, then clicked play again.

"I pray you will find it in your hearts to accept Sally into the family as an adopted daughter-in-heart." There the video ended.

"I wish I'd seen this when it all began," I said.

"We all said pretty much the same thing," Abby said. "For some reason, Pop thought differently."

Again God had shown me His love. A tear escaped my left eye and trickled down my cheek. I brushed it away. Everyone was staring at me, and my butterflies refused to stop fluttering.

"The inheritance as stated will be executed today and all funds as yet not paid out will be paid. That means Leslie will get her $200,000—"

"Hang on a minute there, Karl," Chase said. "Given Leslie's behavior we need to revisit whether or not she gets that money."

"Hmm." Karl sat quietly for a moment as he mulled over Chase's words. "I'll have to examine the will again. I'm not sure you have that choice. Right now, we're here to discuss Sally's inheritance; we can certainly talk about Leslie at a later date.

"Sally, direct deposits will be set up with your bank to receive the profit payouts when they occur, the first of which will be from the magazine at the beginning of October. Abby's accountant can tell you the amount.

Additionally, given Abby's and Chase's approval, an additional $150,000 will be paid out as remuneration for the troubles you've suffered these past several weeks." Karl looked first at Chase, then at Abby.

My cheeks flamed and my whole body grew hot. How could they say no with me sitting here? I stood. "I'll leave while you discuss that stipulation. John, this should have been presented to them without me here. How can you put them in such a difficult position?"

"It's not a difficult position for me. I agree. It's only money, Sally. Family is more important," Abby said. Her answer made sense, but Chase?

"Abby's right. Family is more important. Sit down and let Karl continue," Chase said authoritatively.

"There is no expectation for you to stay in Montana. You're free to do as you please. Are there any questions?"

No one spoke.

Then Chase leaned forward in his chair and looked over at me. "Sally, I hope you'll consider staying. To be a part of the family and of the ranch."

"No. If I stayed, I'd always be looking over my shoulder wondering if that was the day I'd end up six feet under."

Friday morning as I came down for breakfast, I found the dining room abuzz with conversation and packed with the whole Reynolds clan, including Leslie and Jake, and all the wives and grandchildren. Linda was the first to greet me with a hug.

"Sally, I'm so glad this ordeal is over. I'm sure you are too," Linda said.

"Definitely. I'll miss you all, and Montana."

"I hope you'll consider coming back for Thanksgiving. You're part of the family now," Abby said.

"I'm not sure I'll be able to get away. My friend and I want to start our own publishing company. I expect that will keep me occupied."

We all filled our plates and took our seats around the table.

"I've asked Chase to have his pilot file a flight plan to Kansas City for some time tomorrow afternoon."

"So soon?" Emily protested.

"'Fraid so," I said.

"Today is yours, Sally. Do whatever you'd like," Chase said, then turned his attention to the biscuits and gravy on his plate.

"I'd like to take a short ride on Sandy and then work with Gabe and Pete like I have been. I'm going to miss those horses!"

Leslie chose that moment to stand and tink her glass for everyone's attention.

"I don't want to put a damper on things, but I would like to apologize to you, Miss Clark, and all the rest of you. I…I tried to frame Sally for theft because I wanted what Poppie had given her. Totally not a good thing. Poppie was right in saying what he did about me, but I want to encourage you all that I've repented and want to make things right again." She gave a smile and sat back down.

"Thank you, Leslie. I insist we never mention it again," I told her. "It's forgiven."

Jake reached his arm around her and gave her a gentle squeeze and an encouraging smile. His face looked strained, like he was forcing that smile.

Once we finished breakfast, we all went about our daily business. Moms drove the kids off to school and each of Chase's sons walked out to the barn to begin their usual routine. I headed for Sandy's stall. On my way, I swallowed a butterfly leftover from yesterday.

# Chapter 36

## Sally

God says, "At the time I have planned, I will bring
justice against the wicked." Psalms 75:2

Sally, are you sure you want to do this?" Chase asked me as I
bridled Sandy. He grabbed her saddle and lifted it effortlessly
onto her back. "I can't talk you into staying?"

"No, I think leaving is the right thing. I'm going to miss this place,
but I need a rest from all the happenings of the last several weeks. Right
now, I could use the solitude before I start the day's work. I'd like one
last ride. Is that not okay with you?" I wanted the pleasure of one more
ride to carry me home.

"Of course it's fine. I just don't want you to get lost."

"I won't get lost. I'll be somewhere in Montana." My joke flew over
his head or he ignored it. "I'll be fine. If I'm not back by lunch time,
send Gabe out in the helicopter. I'll head northwest and stay along the
fence line." I lifted my left foot into the stirrup and mounted. Sandy
skittered around a bit, forcing Chase to step back to avoid her. No
doubt, she was excited to get out on the open prairie herself.

"Here," Chase said, holding out a can to me. "Take this can of bear
spray. And let me get you a rifle, too."

I took the can and shoved it into my jacket pocket. "I'll be fine. And you can forget the rifle. I need solitude; so, no guard. Go about your business. God will protect me."

He opened the stall gate and led Sandy out of the barn where I nudged her into a lope.

As I left the bustle of the ranch behind me, my spirit soared. Amazing how in a five short weeks I had gone from being bothered by city noise to being bothered by ranch noise. This morning I craved nature's music—the buzz of bugs, the screech of a bird, maybe even the low of a cow.

Leslie's apology was still sinking in. The inheritance was mine and an extra $150,000 to boot. All that was left was for the sheriff to discover who had perpetrated the vandalism. Whether someone really was trying to kill me, it didn't matter. Without knowing who had caused all the problems, I couldn't stay in Great Falls and be at peace. Right now I needed the barrenness of the prairie to hear God's voice as I sought direction for the next step.

I rode a couple miles northwest of the ranch like I said I would and then reined up Sandy. I leaned over and rubbed her neck.

"This feels good, doesn't it, girl? I'm going to miss you when I leave here. Are you going to miss me?"

She pawed the ground. Was that a yes or a no?

To the east, the mid-morning sun cast a golden glow on the Bear Paw Mountains. An earthy scent-filled cool breeze caressed my cheeks, announcing fall's arrival. I continued northwest and began to pray.

"Father, thank You for bringing resolution to all this. Thank you for helping me open the door of my heart to Your unfailing love. You are so wonderful, so amazing. Thank You that I've been cleared of the theft. Help us find the vandal and would-be killer. As always, I need your guidance—"

The sound of approaching hooves interrupted my prayer. I looked behind me and watched as horse and rider galloped toward me. It was Jake.

"Sally," he called out as he neared me. He reined his horse to a stop so closely I could have reached out and grabbed him.

"Hey, Jake. What's up?" I noticed he had a pistol strapped to his hip as well as a rifle in a leather scabbard attached to the saddle. "Are you expecting bears or something? What's with the pistol and rifle?"

"A rifle won't do me any good if a bear gets a hold of me." He smiled, but I noticed a wild, almost maniacal glint in his eye.

"But don't the bears pretty much stick to the forested areas?"

"Not always," he said. "Anyways, I came to get rid of one particular bear."

One particular bear? A sense of foreboding settled in my stomach. Stomach acid killed what remained of yesterday's butterflies, and my stomach began to churn like it did when I was in the Middle East, preparing for a day's excursion into a new city. We never knew what might meet us and when. IEDs, suicide bombers, snipers. I shook my head to clear my thoughts and focused back on the moment at hand.

"A particular bear? How do you tell one from another?"

"I know you're not that stupid," he scoffed. "I can't let you take what belongs to me."

"I'm not taking anything from you."

"Leslie's my wife. What's hers is mine."

"She might disagree with you on that. Besides, how do you plan to kill me and get away with it? You got away with trying to shoot me once because you missed and everybody thought it was a wild shot from a hunter. But if I turn up shot today, you're certain to get caught." I had to keep him talking while I prayed for the Lord to provide an escape plan.

"Yeah, you're right about that. Should never have relied on Toby to do the shooting. I thought that rattler would do the job. You're tough to kill."

*I have given my angels charge over you.*

"That's because God's angels are protecting me." I slipped my hand into my jacket pocket, glad for the bear spray Chase had insisted I bring. I felt for the safety valve and released it. Would the spray affectively incapacitate Jake?

"Where are those angels now?" He started laughing and I grabbed the opportunity. I jerked the can from my pocket and sprayed his face.

"Aaahhhh!"

I tried to spur Sandy into a gallop, but in even Jake's pained condition, he had the presence of mind to lunge for me. We both toppled to the ground. Jake rose to his knees, his hands frantically attempting to wipe the spray from his eyes. I rolled away from him and stood.

"Sandy," I called.

"Oh no you don't. You're not getting away this time." Jake stood, pulling his pistol from his holster, and lurched toward me.

Sandy must have sensed the danger. She neighed and reared, and the next thing I knew she had knocked Jake to the ground. I jumped into the saddle and she galloped straight for the ranch. After a bit, I looked back to see if Jake was in pursuit. I couldn't see him, but I urged Sandy to run faster. How far was I from the ranch?

*Remember, I have given my angels charge over you.*

Thank you, Lord.

I strained my eyes to see the ranch ahead. Nothing.

I heard a shot ring out, but I just kept riding. Soon the barn and house came into view. I spotted Gabe and Peter at the corral with the foals.

"Gabe, Pete, help!" I yelled as I pulled Sandy to a stop near the fence.

"Sal, what happened?" Gabe said, rushing to the fence and jumping over.

"Jake. He just tried to kill me."

"Pete, get Pop!" Gabe commanded. Pete took off toward the barn. "Sal, let me help you down."

"I sprayed him with this so I could get away." I held out the spray, still clutched in my hand. Gabe took the can from my hand and tossed it to the ground, then helped me dismount.

"Jake, of all people. Why would he do this?"

"Because he wanted that inheritance to go to Leslie." I worked to slow my breathing.

"Sally!" Chase called. He and Pete were running toward us.

"I'm fine. But I'm not so sure about Jake. He wanted to kill me, but I used that bear spray on him, Chase." I turned back and looked for Jake.

How could he be dumb enough to show his face now?

"Pete, call the sheriff," Chase said. "He tried to kill you?"

"Yes, plain as day said he planned to kill me. He admitted it all. That Toby was the one who shot the steer in an attempt to shoot me, that he planted the rattler. …Chase, I think he's gone mad. He had this wild look in his eyes. With that bear spray, his eyes must look like raw meat now."

"Gabe, find Four, and you two take the Jeep and go find him. Take your rifles and be alert."

Gabe rushed off. By now other ranch hands had begun to gather around us.

"Are you sure you're all right?" Chase asked. "You've got some blood here and there."

"Probably just some scrapes. After I sprayed him, he lunged for me and knocked me to the ground."

"All the same, let's go into the house and get you cleaned up. Back to work everybody. Sally's gonna be okay." Chase led me toward the house. "I never should have let you take that ride. My gut kept telling me Jake might be behind all this."

"But gut feelings don't stand up in a court of law. Did you have anything but suspicions? Did you tell the sheriff?"

"Yes, I told the sheriff. You know what this means, right?"

"No, what's that?" I asked.

"You won't have to look over your shoulder anymore."

# Chapter 37

## Sally

But as for me, I will always proclaim what God has done.
Psalms 75:9a

Spirits ran high that night as we gathered around the fire pit where a side of beef roasted on the spit. Only Leslie was absent, understandable given that her husband had tried to kill me.

Gabe and Four had found Jake sitting in the dirt, laughing. He laughed all the way back to the ranch and kept mumbling something about Toby. The sheriff's deputies had carted him off to the psychiatric ward for evaluation and dragged Toby to the station. He spent the afternoon singing a cop-a-plea tune that would make any prosecutor happy. From the sounds of it, Jake could face a long prison sentence if he was found competent to stand trial.

"Sal, has all this changed your plans? Will you consider staying in Great Falls after all?" Gabe asked. "Please stay. You have a way with the horses."

"Gabe, in all honesty, I'm not sure what I'm going to do. Like I mentioned before, my friend and I want to start a publishing company. But I'll admit, I don't want to stay in Kansas City. Montana has cast her spell on me."

Abby stepped closer and put her arm around my shoulders. "I hope we've cast our spell on you, too. Why don't you buy that company you were working for and move it here to Great Falls?"

"I suppose that's an option. But I'm not sure my friends want to leave KC." I shrugged. "I can't make a firm decision until I know whether the owner will sell. I have to consider the people who work for the firm as well. They'd be out of a job if they didn't want to move with the company."

"Sounds to me like you'll make an excellent boss," Chase said. "We'll send the plane down to get you whenever you want to come visit. And you'd better mark off Thanksgiving and Christmas right now. We expect you here to celebrate with us, period. No excuses about work to do."

A bit of fat dripped into the cook fire, causing it to spit and flare. Scents of barbecue and hickory wafted through the air, leaving their taste on my tongue. As I searched the depth of Chase's eyes, they reflected the fire's glow and its warmth. What an enigma he had been throughout this ordeal. Rude one minute, friendly the next. Why was that?

Cook approached the roasting beef and tested it for doneness, then promptly announced, "Let's eat!"

"Sally, we already missed the sunset, but it's a full moon tonight. Will you join me down at the corral to watch it rise?" Chase asked.

"Okay. I guess that side of beef isn't going anywhere."

We walked in silence to the corral. The night had grown chilly already, but Chase's body heat warmed my face. We took a seat on the fence and gazed to the east, searching for any evidence of a rising moon.

"Gabe is right; you have a way with the horses. If the publishing company thing falls through, you've got a job here working for me."

I laughed at that.

"Is that such a bad idea," he asked.

"I don't know anything about horses."

"Doesn't matter. They like you, and you'll learn. ...Sally?"

I looked over at him, waiting for him to finish his sentence.

"I've been...chaotic in my interactions with you. I know that. You arrived on the scene immediately after Pop's death and on the fifth anniversary of my wife's death. Tumultuous describes my state of mind and emotions for the last several weeks." He paused, staring deeply into my eyes. "I know you might find this difficult to believe, but I've begun to love you. Not as a sister. As a woman. Please think hard about staying in Great Falls."

No one had ever said those words to me. My mind reeled; my heart raced.

"I don't know, Chase. Maybe." But he'd just given me the best reason of all to return.

# Will being stranded by a blizzard reawaken Sally's numb heart?

Find out in *Discovering Her Inheritance,*
book 2 of this series.

When a blizzard traps Sally Clark in a small country church with her twin sister and three strangers, long-buried family secrets churn to the surface, exposing the anger and unforgiveness she's carried for so long. As four days pass in isolation, the church works its own miracles—on Sally and the strangers around her.

But the surprises don't stop there. A haunting nightmare, the relentless storm, and a dying letter from Sally's father all collide to lead her toward a new chapter in her life.

Discover the power of faith and unexpected miracles in Book 2 of the Her Inheritance trilogy. Follow Sally as she uncovers her true inheritance. Buy now and continue the journey!

# About Debra

Debra L. Butterfield dreamed of being writer since she was a pre-teen. Fulfillment of that dream began when she was forty-five years old and Focus on the Family hired her as a junior copywriter. In 2006, she stepped into the world of freelance writer.

She is the author of *Unshakable Faith* Bible study and *Unshakable Faith Leaders Guide, Abba's Answers, Abba's Promise, Carried by Grace, Mystery on Maple Hill* (a short story ebook) and *7 Cheat Sheets to Cut Editing Costs.* She has contributed stories to numerous anthologies, magazines, and blogs.

Debra is a US Marine Corps veteran, enjoys the outdoors and, oddly enough, likes the smell of skunks. (Her kids always tell her take a deep breath whenever they smell one.) Like most writers, she loves to read, usually not one book at a time either. She has lived as far west as Hawaii and as far east as Germany and lots of places in between. Now living in Missouri, Debra has three adult children and two grandchildren.

Discover more at DebraLButterfield.com.

# Acknowledgments

Thank you to Pam Taylor, Pamella Bowen, Steven Hightower, Heather Hart, and Susan Sanchez for their help in titling this book. It was fun working together!

To my brother Mark, thank you for your witty sayings, of which ended up in the book.

# Did you enjoy
# Claiming Her Inheritance?

## You'll LOVE the next book
## in the Her Inheritance Series!

Her Inheritance
Book 2

*Discovering*
*Her*
*Inheritance*

Discovering Her Inheritance

Butterfield

DEBRA L. BUTTERFIELD

Available in bookstores and from online retailers.

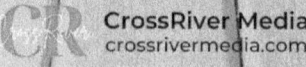

# Discover more great books at CrossRiverMedia.com

## ANTS ACROSS THE PAGE

Set in the 1960s, Ants Across the Page follows eleven-year-old Luke, a motherless, undiagnosed dyslexic boy, as he hatches a plan to spruce up his grease-stained father and win the heart of "the Sarge." Through Luke's eyes, this heartwarming story shows that whether you're a kid whose letters dance on the page or a man awkwardly chasing love, there's always hope. Filled with laugh-out-loud moments and heartfelt tears, this tale will charm you from start to finish.

## LOVE FINAL SUNRISE

Ruth Jessup, a New Yorker, and Joshua Stutzman, an Amish man, couldn't be more different—yet their lives collide as they face a psychopath and the chaos of the New World Order. Struggling with amnesia, Ruth awakens in a world of buggies and lanterns, far removed from modern life. As the biblical seven-year tribulation unfolds, an unexpected bond grows between them. Can Joshua's Amish ways help them endure the next three-and-a-half years without taking the mark of the beast?

## SURVIVING CARMELITA

Josie was driving. Her foot on the pedal, her hands on the wheel. Her fault. Sweet Carmelita will never see her fifth birthday. Overwhelmed by guilt and unable to function, Josie flees to Key West, seeking refuge with her cousin. But her journey is guided by an unseen hand, leading her to unexpected encounters—a trailer park pastor, a battered horse, a pregnant teen, and a mysterious beachcomber. Together, they might just show Josie the way to unimaginable hope and redemption.

# Bold faith starts here.

DIVINE DETOUR — WOOD

UNBEATEN — LINDSEY BELL

ABBA'S HEART — CLYMER

ABBA'S ANSWERS — BUTTERFIELD

ABBA'S LESSONS — LAKE

SURVIVING CARMELITA — MIURA

OBEDIENT UNTO DEATH — EYERLY

FORTUNES OF DEATH — EYERLY

ROOTS REDEEMED — SELLARS

# If you enjoyed this book, will you consider sharing it with others?

- Please mention the book on Facebook, Instagram, Pinterest, or another social media site.

- Recommend this book to your small group, book club, and workplace.

- Head over to Facebook.com/CrossRiverMedia, 'Like' the page and post a comment as to what you enjoyed the most.

- Pick up a copy for someone you know who would be challenged or encouraged by this message.

- Write a review on your favorite ebook platform.

- To learn about our latest releases subscribe to our newsletter at CrossRiverMedia.com.

www.ingramcontent.com/pod-product-compliance
Lightning Source LLC
Chambersburg PA
CBHW060913250626
47159CB00008B/2985